BOOKS BY E.M. SMITH

The Agent Juliet series
Broken Bones

BOOKS BY TIM MCBAIN & L.T. VARGUS

Casting Shadows Everywhere
The Awake in the Dark series
The Scattered and the Dead series
The Clowns
The Violet Darger series

WHAT LIES

BENEATH

WHAT LIES BENEATH

A VICTOR LOSHAK NOVEL

E.M. SMITH
L.T. VARGUS & TIM MCBAIN

WHAT LIES
BENEATH

PROLOGUE

Waiting.

Waiting for the witness to leave.

The shadow ducks in the bushes, nestles to the point of invisibility among the manicured landscaping, hidden away from the greenish pole lights lining the cul-de-sac. He sidles close to the McMansion, his body practically hugging the brick siding, limbs splayed against the façade like a starfish.

Still. Motionless. Waiting.

Insects chirp in the distance. Crickets. Cicadas. Swarms of buzzing mosquitoes snuffling around for blood to suck. Their voices overlap and warble out endless sounds, rising and falling and filling up the emptiness.

It almost makes him laugh for some reason, all that racket. Life is everywhere, he thinks. Thrashing and mindless as ever.

He listens for anything beyond the bug sounds. The thump of footsteps. A closing door. Any sign of movement inside the house.

Nothing.

Sweat bleeds down the sides of his forehead, stinging where it touches the corner of his left eye. His fingers twitch, wanting only to swipe the wet away.

But no. No.

Let it burn.

After what feels like a long time, the shadow lifts its

1

head, peeks through a pane of glass. Pinpoint eyes watch the scene within. Eyes squinted to wrinkled slits. Eyes full of smoldering anger.

A pair of middle-aged men sit in what looks like the formal dining room, decorated like some upper-class suburban cliché. Marble floors. Vaulted ceilings. Tall, thin vases with dried up weeds sticking out of them sitting in the corners.

Tumblers of scotch sweat on the table before them, a bottle with a black label resting between them. The closer man, the homeowner, reaches for the bottle, grips the stopper with his pudgy fist to remove it, tips the glass to top up his drink, puts it back.

Looking beyond the table, he can see the empty spot in the drink cart where the bottle should be — a gap there like a missing tooth.

The homeowner sits with his back mostly to the window, face hidden away. Concealed.

That's OK. The shadow knows what he looks like from the picture. He studies the guest instead.

Suede patches swath his elbows. Messy hair juts out from both sides of his head, the tangles sculpted into something so asymmetrical it almost looks like weird shapes forming as two cloud formations collide. Little round Harry Potter glasses perched on his pointy nose.

The professor type is not on the list, whoever he is. He'll live.

The other? Not so much.

The shadow drifts down the side of the house to the next window, retracting deeper into the shrubbery, into prickly, waxy leaves dappled with the green glow from the pole lights. The air grows dank as he enters the thickest brush. Heavy. Almost feels like it's wetting the skin everywhere it touches.

Again, the dark figure lifts his head to look through the window. This angle gives him a better look at the homeowner's jowly profile.

Soft and porcine. Chubbier than the professor. Weak chin with its double underneath. Dark hair that's thinning on top and curling a little at the sides and back. He dresses like one of those slick-looking businessmen who perpetually have wet hair, but that image doesn't ring true somehow. Not all the way. There's something missing, some kind of savvy or intelligence the homeowner doesn't have. Nothing behind the eyes of this one, the shadow thinks. Like there's not a person in there, not anything souled at all.

He's smiling now. Dimples taking shape in the jowls and emphasizing his tucked-back chin. Skin pulling taut in a way that makes the soft flesh ripple. When the homeowner smiles, he looks just like he does in the picture the shadow has studied.

Good. Perfect.

Hatred thrums in the shadow's neck. Blood beating hot and fast, its pulse quaking against the walls of muscle there. For a second, he wants nothing more than to smash out the window, climb inside, and drag that wet, balding, pig-faced man out into the darkness. Wants it so bad that it makes him dizzy.

The dark figure slumps against the bricks again. Closes his eyes. Tries to staunch the aggression mounting in his skull and find the cold, logical intention he came here with.

It's hard when you get this close.

He breathes.

Waits.

There can be no witnesses. None but the insects.

He opens his eyes. Stares at the grid of mortar, gray veins running between the bricks.

Focus on the task at hand. Focus on the target.

His mind obliges. Runs through the info he has as though reading a dossier.

The jowly homeowner is one Neil Griffin. A business owner. A political wannabe. A member of boards and councils and charitable organizations too numerous to list. A member of the Moose Lodge, even, as ridiculous as that seems in this day and age.

A company man, a community man, a public servant.

But that all ended today. Neil's name got called. His number was up.

So the fuck be it.

The shadow can picture the end. Looks forward to it.

He closes his eyes again.

Sees the wound. The open place from which this pig-faced man's life spills out on the floor of his tacky house. Watches the red crawl over the marble, his life a spreading puddle as it vacates his being.

The whooshing creak of a door opening startles the shadow out of his thoughts. He stands up straighter, a rush of electricity running through his limbs, sharpening his senses.

He listens for it.

And there it is, a car door closing.

The professor's shiny blue Land Rover eases down the

long driveway and disappears around the bend. Soon it'll pull onto the street, be let out of the little gated community by some half-assed rent-a-cop in a little glass tower.

Too bad for Neil Griffin that the gates couldn't keep the shadow out, huh?

The dark figure stands, moves toward the back door. His heart thumps in his ears, but that's OK. It's just adrenaline this time. The cool, logical mindset is back.

Neil's name got called, and now the shadow is here to collect.

He draws the 9mm from the holster inside his jacket.

The wait is over.

Guess who's coming to your house tonight.

CHAPTER 1

Special Agent Victor Loshak slipped off his sunglasses and blinked a few times, then rubbed his eyes lightly. Very, very lightly in the case of the right one. The damn thing was swollen and tender. He looked and felt like he'd lost a fight with a doorknob. Hence the sunglasses on an otherwise moderately lit flight.

With a groan, Loshak slipped the shades back on, closed his eyes, and rested his head against the seat. He could've kicked back without bothering anyone — the window seat was empty and there was nothing but aisle to his left — but he didn't want to fall asleep just to be nudged awake in a minute or two. Still, he was glad for the moment alone. Relieved, honestly.

It was almost funny. Not that long ago, he'd been alone all the time. Lonely even. Guess that was just proof you should be careful what you wished for.

He glanced at the empty seat next to him, knowing it wouldn't be that way for much longer, and then he tipped his head back to gaze up at the plane's ceiling. Fought the urge to grind a knuckle or maybe the heel of his hand into that itch emanating from his right eyelid. He blinked a few times as though that might help. It didn't.

Now they were headed for Kansas City to investigate a rash of murders that seemed to spill over both sides of the state line. Though homicide cases that crossed state lines were always given federal jurisdiction, Loshak would be playing his usual role of profiler and consultant for the local task force.

The victims in this case seemed unrelated at best, a mishmash of random targets. A wealthy businessman-slash-philanthropist was the latest. Neil Griffin, killed in his home in one of those gated communities with the pretentious nature names that sounded like rest homes. Flowing Oaks, Shady Pines, stuff like that.

Two bullets shattered Griffin's skull, entering the back of the head at point-blank range. Quick. Efficient. Execution style.

The victim's body had then been posed after death. Staged. Laid out face up just next to the smear of blood where he'd originally fallen. A single glove lay over the face, positioned to cover the right eye. The left eye remained open, staring up at nothing.

Beyond the staging and prop — the brown cloth glove seemingly didn't belong to the victim — no evidence had been left at the scene. No prints. No signs of forced entry. Nothing.

The other victims included a city councilman, the owner of a car dealership, and the defensive coordinator of a Division II college football team. So far, no personal or business connections had turned up among any of the deceased.

The other crime scenes had been similar to that of Griffin's. All victims killed in their homes, three of the four in a matching execution style. The football coach served as the odd man out in that capacity — taking a bullet in the forehead rather than the back of the skull, as if perhaps he'd wheeled on his attacker a beat too late.

The manner of execution and lack of evidence made the killings seem like professional hits — perhaps suggesting organized crime or mafia involvement — but from what Loshak could tell, these victims were squeaky clean rich folk. No records beyond speeding tickets. College educations and silver spoons all around. No discernible ties to the criminal underworld.

And that damn glove matched at every scene, too, of course. The matching piece of brown cloth handwear laid over half of each corpse's face, always blocking out one eye. The media had loved that grim little detail, plastering it in the headlines and leading with it on the bulk of the evening news broadcasts.

Loshak rolled his head on his neck, trying to loosen it up. In cases like this, there was always a missing piece, some scrap of information that made sense of all these disparate parts that didn't seem to fit together. Figuring out what the hell that might be? That was the hard part.

Profiling was a game of incomplete information, like poker. The entire game revolved around not knowing what cards the other players at your table had and knowing that they didn't know what cards you had. You bet blind.

In chess, everyone could see the board and each and every piece on it. It was all strategy. Each decision, each move proceeded based on a computation of known information. The best players' brains worked like computers, processing logical predictions about where the game would go based on the board laid out in front of them.

But poker players had to make intuitive leaps at every stage of the game. They had to trust their guts, pick their spots to bluff or fold based on instinct, based on feel. The best of the best could often read exactly what cards the other players had. An uncanny accuracy based on almost no evidence.

Feet shuffling in the aisle behind Loshak drew him out of the depths of game theory. He'd almost drifted off there.

He opened his eyes just in time to see the back of a lavender polo shirt and jeans trying to climb over to the window seat without jostling him.

Loshak sat up and tucked his feet back under his seat, trying to make his long legs magically shorter. It was a losing battle.

The reporter, Jevon Spinks, tripped and shoved his way through the tangle, then dropped into the seat beside him, perching his long arms on the armrests. His left knee bumped against Loshak's right, so he shifted in his seat until his thighs slanted from the corner of his seat toward the bulkhead of the plane. A pair of diagonal lines.

"Man," Spinks said, shaking his head as if getting to his seat had exhausted him. "Two guys our size just aren't meant to sit next to each other on flights."

CHAPTER 2

"Hey, I thought of a name for the book," Spinks said.

Loshak glanced his way. Slight quirks at the corners of the reporter's mouth gave away the smile he was trying to hide.

"Alright, let's hear it."

Spinks spread his hands out in front of him as if framing a glowing marquee.

"*Shaknado: The Victor Loshak Story.*"

And there it was. The smile bloomed as Spinks struggled not to laugh, spreading to touch every corner of the reporter's face.

Loshak pursed his lips and pretended to consider it.

"You don't think a *Sharknado* reference will be dated by the time the thing actually comes out?"

"Well, yeah." Spinks' smile faded, and his hands dropped back into his lap. "I mean, obviously. It kinda ruins the joke if you take it seriously."

"It's my life story. I figure I should be the one to take it seriously, maybe. But don't worry. You'll find a title for the thing. My life is a joke, right? A cruel one. This kind of thing writes itself."

Spinks smiled again. Clapped Loshak on the shoulder.

"See? That's what I like about you, partner," he said, giving him a shake. "Your positive attitude."

Loshak leaned back in his seat. Stared at the ceiling again. Tried not to think about the pain in his eye, which was impossible.

Next to him, Spinks pulled out a little green notebook and jotted something in it like a pulp novel private eye. Except when he did it, Spinks chuckled to himself.

He'd been doing that ever since he signed the deal to write a book about Loshak. Pulling out the notebook. Jotting something. Chuckling to himself.

Every time the notebook made an appearance, Loshak wanted to ask the reporter what he'd just written, the impulse flailing about and screeching in his skull, but so far he hadn't followed through on the urge. It was like that therapy-couch paranoia people got when they said something off-hand and their psychologist said, "Interesting…" and hurried to scribble it down.

At this point, Loshak had to grit his teeth to keep his mouth from asking. It had become some kind of purity test to see how long he could avoid the temptation, a matter of pride or something.

When he really thought about it, Loshak couldn't imagine a book about him being interesting. Then again, Spinks was a good writer. If anybody could salvage the thing, it would be him. And the Bureau was over the moon about the prospects of a high profile biography, thinking it would yield a lot of positive PR. The kind of thing that would make the public believers again and rocket the cadet enrollment rates off the charts. Maybe even help some of the insider factions make their case for federal funding — the full-on bureaucratic wet dream.

Something akin to *The Silence of the Lambs*, which was still on the Academy's curriculum. In the years after the movie had come out, the number of women applying to the FBI had shot through the roof. They showed it at least twice a year to cadets as an example of what good publicity could do.

It'd been a while since that kind of good publicity had come the Bureau's way, and they were ready to do anything necessary to help get it flowing again. Even going so far as to grant Spinks a consultant ID. The reporter now had the same clearance level as a rookie. And even though that was barely any clearance at all, Spinks was ecstatic. He'd even started calling Loshak "partner" every now and then in this joking tone that was clearly meant to sound like sarcasm but didn't quite make it.

The Bureau was happy. Spinks was happy.

Loshak wasn't sure what he was.

Whenever he heard Spinks jokingly-but-not-jokingly say "partner," Loshak thought of Darger. How the FBI dream had gone sideways for her. Last he'd heard, she'd been consulting on the Kathryn Porter case, still on leave. At least she wasn't giving up on profiling. Not yet, anyway. He found himself thinking all sorts of fatherly things at that point. Stuff like, *If she could just stick with it…* and *She's got so much talent and raw grit…*

His stupid eye prickled.

Loshak slid his sunglasses off. He had to force himself not to rub it. Instead, he dabbed his finger just at the edge of the puffy eyelid. It didn't help at all, but it felt like he was doing something, at least.

"Yikes," Spinks said, leaning back toward the window as if to get a better angle on the eye. "Nice shiner. Finally decide to take up cage fighting?"

"Nah, it's nothing. I got something in it the other day, a

piece of dirt or something, and I did exactly what all the medical texts say you're supposed to do — I rubbed at it frantically and messed with my eyelid until it got worse."

When Spinks laughed, making that hissing, airy sound, Loshak had a hard time not smiling.

"For real?" the reporter asked.

"Yeah, but it's getting better. I think whatever was in it is gone, at least. Now it just stings when I blink. And when I don't blink."

Spinks laughed again and grabbed for his Dick Tracy notebook.

"And sometimes when I look at things, it's like I can't see them quite right. They're not blurry or doubled or anything like that. Just off somehow. Distorted. I guess it makes it hard to tell what I'm really seeing."

Loshak slipped his shades back on.

"Real pain in the ass."

CHAPTER 3

"Is the Bureau really that tight with money?" Spinks asked. "Or are you just one of those embarrassed types who doesn't like to go for the new, flashy cars?"

The reporter had been making jokes about the age of the sedan since they walked away from the rental kiosk with the keys.

"There's nothing wrong with this car." Loshak tapped the steering wheel with his thumb.

The GPS indicated that they needed to get off at the next exit. Loshak flipped on his blinker.

In spite of being one of only three cars on that particular stretch of I-435, the shiny suburban just behind him in the right lane sped up rather than let him over. Loshak hit the brakes so they would pass and get out of the way, but the SUV took the ramp ahead of him and Spinks. Assholes.

"No, there's nothing wrong with this car," Spinks said in the voice he used when setting up a joke. "I loved it when Scully and Mulder were driving around in it. I'm pretty sure it was brand new back then."

"This thing is three years old."

"I'll believe that when I see the title."

Deciding to give ignoring Spinks a shot, Loshak followed the curve of the horseshoe, then turned onto a smaller four-lane. A small brown sign indicated that the Corporate Woods was their next left.

14

"Pretty oxymoronic," he mumbled.

"What is?"

Loshak gestured at the sign.

"Huh." The reporter leaned back in his seat and tugged at his chin. "Well, gotta project that green image nowadays or everybody'll figure out that you're a soulless corporation."

They passed orderly subdivisions and brightly colored postmodern apartment complexes broken up by stretches of trees here and prairie there.

Statues dotted street corners.

Young urban professional types were out walking dogs, jogging, and pushing strollers.

Though Loshak had known they were headed into one of Kansas City's wealthiest suburbs, it was still baffling to see the security that money bought. He'd seen the numbers. Kansas City laid claim to the second highest rate of murders per year in the country — second only to St. Louis — and likewise found itself in the top three for violent crimes.

Every single one of these pedestrians rushing past faced a fifty percent chance of becoming a victim of violent crime at some point this year just because of where they lived. If they knew the statistics, would they still be pushing their babies down the street in brand new jogging strollers?

His right eye prickled and he swiped at it with his thumb, aggravating it more.

Loshak guided the car through the moderate traffic, past a shopping center of upscale outlets and restaurants, then a museum built out of faux rusted steel and sparkling glass in unnaturally bright magentas, golds, and blues before turning into a stretch of prairieland lined with gated communities.

Thick sound-baffling concrete walls decorated with reliefs of blowing leaves and abstract shapes surrounded the neighborhoods so the people inside wouldn't have to listen to the constant traffic. More of that purchased security and peace of mind. Block out the noise. Forget that there's a city full of cars, people, exhaust fumes, violence, and death creeping outside the walls.

Loshak pulled the rental into the line of cars at the gates of Prairiefire Estates. The community looked as if it had been built to match the museum they'd passed, its faux rust-covered gates dotted with angular plates of blue, magenta, and gold glass. The line to get in was six cars deep with more piling up behind them.

One by one, however, a security guard in a navy blue jacket turned them away.

"Gawkers?" Spinks wondered aloud. "Or maybe press?"

Loshak shrugged. A big white Navigator two cars in front of them pulled forward, turned around, and drove away. Before it left, he caught sight of a magnetic ad on the side for Sheila Proper Realty.

"Oh, duh!" Spinks popped himself in the forehead with the heel of his hand. "Realtors."

"Uh-huh. Realtors. And that's obvious because?"

"We're on the Kansas side of the border," Spinks said. "Realtors here don't have to disclose if a murder went down on a property."

"OK, but a nice place like this, the murder will be all over the news. 'Quiet community rocked by violent homicide.' People will recognize the location."

Spinks shook his head.

"You don't get it. The housing market in Kansas City is insane. Friend of mine did a piece on it a while back. When the rest of the housing market in the US crashed, KC's skyrocketed. Realtors showing eight to ten houses a day. People calling to look at a house, but by the time they get across town, it's already under contract. Folks offering way over asking just to get a shot. Now contractors are moving in by the dozen, turning the prairie and swampland into spec properties, and still they can barely keep up with demand. You mark my words, these realtors are all trying to get in so they can get the contract on Griffin's house. A vacancy in a fancy community like this? It's prime real estate." The reporter stopped suddenly and chuckled to himself. "Literally."

Loshak nodded slowly. "They'll make a killing on it."

The hiss of Spinks' laughter filled the car as he reached for his little pad and pen. Loshak gazed out the window, avoiding the obvious question. As simple as it might be to assume Spinks had written down his cliché joke, it was more likely that Spinks had caught a glimmer of something more telling.

Loshak had read two of the reporter's books and a few of his articles. Face-to-face the guy might seem like a barrel of laughs, but his writing revealed a sharp eye for the flaws of human nature. Maybe a little too sharp. Loshak wasn't sure he wanted to know what that eye saw when it was directed at him.

The car ahead of them, another expensive SUV with a well-dressed woman in the driver's seat, pulled away from the gates and merged into traffic without looking. Their turn with the security guard had come.

Loshak eased the rental to a stop in front of the magenta and blue glass security booth and rolled down his window. The guard frowned at them.

"Can I help you folks?" he asked, putting both hands on the car door and leaning down until he was nearly face-to-face with Loshak.

The number of cops per year shot in the face on routine traffic stops because they did that very thing flashed through Loshak's mind. He forced a smile and showed the guard his badge.

"We're here to investigate the Griffin crime scene. I'm Special Agent Loshak with the FBI, and this is—"

"Wait a minute, I have something for this."

Spinks was flipping open the little black wallet the Bureau had given him along with his special clearance. He held out his laminated Consultant badge long enough to make sure the security guard got a good look at it.

"I'm his partner. Special Consultant Jevon Spinks."

The security guard glanced from Loshak to Spinks as if he was pretty sure one of them was joking, but couldn't figure out which one it was. He opened his mouth.

Spinks raised one finger in a silent, *Wait for it.*

"Esquire," he finished.

That did it. The guard chuckled and shook his head.

"Y'all can go on back," he said. "I'll buzz you in. You're gonna hang a right, then straight ahead until you get to one-sixty-eight on your right side. Numbers are on the curb."

"Thanks," Loshak said.

"Thank you, agent. Believe me, everybody around

here'll sleep a lot better knowing the FBI's after this guy."

The security guard gave the car door a double-slap, then headed back to the booth and leaned inside. The rusty, glass-lined gates rolled open, and with his free hand, he waved Loshak on. Loshak returned the gesture and eased off the brakes.

"Weird."

"What is?" Spinks looked up from trying to fit his credentials wallet back into his jeans.

"Usually the locals are leery of feds." Loshak craned his neck to watch the house numbers on the curb go by. "Especially this far west. I mean, we're what? Half an hour from Jesse James' hometown? Folks who idolize outlaws tend not to trust anybody with ties to the government."

The reporter's dark brows scrunched together.

"Could be an outlier," he said, shrugging. "The one pro-Big Brother guy in the state."

Loshak answered with a noncommittal grunt. They slid on down the street. There was more open space in here than he'd been expecting. Each house sat on a few acres of land, McMansions on their little piece of country estate. Some of them had trees. One had a pond.

"There it is," Loshak said and eased the car into 168's cedar-lined driveway.

The house was nearly identical to the mansions on either side of it, riverstone-colored brick, neutral toned trim, huge custom-shaped windows with strategic shrubbery planted just outside. The lawn was cut uniformly short in that checkered pattern of professional landscaping companies, and every tree was decorated with neat skirts of mulch surrounded by fist-sized white rocks.

The only difference here was the fluttering strips of yellow crime scene tape crossed over the door.

Loshak parked in front of the three-car garage and shut the engine off. Beside him, Spinks had gone uncharacteristically silent, his eyes locked on the front door, unblinking.

A human being had been murdered inside. Wasted. Snuffed out.

Neil Griffin had lived here. Called this his home. Not all that long ago, really. A single second changed everything. Two little syllables from the barrel of a gun. A cold, execution-style death he never saw coming. Thinking about that was enough to make anybody sober up.

They climbed out without speaking and headed up the sidewalk.

As they approached the front door, a knot formed in Loshak's gut, and the short hairs stood up on the back of his neck. Something about this place felt very, very wrong.

For a moment, the memory of his partner Darger being attacked at a crime scene by that sniper in Georgia flashed through his head. He shivered and glanced over his shoulder.

"Did the Overland Park PD give you a code for this?" Spinks asked.

Trance broken, Loshak turned around to find the reporter holding up an electronic lockbox hanging from the doorknob.

"Yeah," he said, fumbling in his pocket and pulling out the scrap of paper he'd written it on. "Four-seven-four-four."

Spinks entered the digits. The keypad flashed, then with

a beep, the box sprang open. The reporter swished his long fingers around inside and came out with a brass key.

A cawing screech behind them made Loshak jump. A trio of crows flapped noisily away from one of the Griffins' driveway trees.

"Got it," Spinks said, oblivious.

The front door creaked open. He gestured for Loshak to precede him inside.

Loshak went, feeling stupid for getting spooked. Almost as soon as he crossed the threshold, that feeling of being watched by an unseen horror faded. Cloudy gray light filtered through the big windows, showing him twin staircases, one on either side of the room, and a central fountain. It wasn't on. The silence filling the house harbored the same strange, almost religious hush he'd experienced in nearly every crime scene he'd been in. Something sacred lingered in these spaces. The words, *the halls of the dead*, came to him though he didn't know from where.

They made their way through the rooms on the first floor one at a time, from the grandiose foyer to a sunken den with an enormous flatscreen TV and a ridiculous number of speakers, to a dining room with a table long enough to seat a football team.

Finally, they came to the scene of the crime, another living room sort of space, but lined with couches and chairs and end tables. A wet bar stood in one corner.

And just below it, a huge puddle of blood on the white carpet, still drying.

Loshak checked the crime scene photos, the images of Neil Griffin's body lying on all that red that had leaked from the back of his head, the death-pale hands folded on his chest, that dark glove laid out flat on the face, covering his right eye.

An empty tumbler and a bottle of Lagavulin 16 rested on the bar, another empty tumbler on the floor by his body.

According to the report, the crime scene techs had found the fingerprints of an English teacher from a local private school, Jack Willamette, on the first tumbler and the scotch bottle, but nothing had come of two extensive interviews.

Loshak had read through the transcripts, both contained in the file, and both as sterile as an operating room because they'd been conducted through Willamette's lawyer. In the second one, the English teacher had claimed the lawyer was there to make sure the detectives stuck to the laws and to keep them from violating any of his rights. On paper, it sounded like something a liberal arts professor would say whether he was involved or not, but Loshak would have to watch the tapes from the interviews — actually see the guy's body language and hear his tone of voice — to gain any further insight.

While he was thinking about it, he made a note in the margin to ask the OPPD for access to the tapes. Then he flipped the file closed and turned back to the blood stain.

No swipes or trails at the edges, so the killer had left him where he fell. Maybe just pushed him onto his back. The spreading blood would have hidden any smaller disturbances like that. Maybe the killer had even known that when positioning Griffin.

Blinking his irritated eye, Loshak turned away from the

stain to inspect the pictures and plaques littering the walls. Membership acknowledgments to local organizations. Letters of thanks for large donations to notable charities. The photos showed Neil Griffin shaking hands or playing golf with what must have been prominent members of the community. One featured a few dozen men in suits surrounding a banner for the local Moose Lodge. Willamette would be in there somewhere. Loshak recognized Griffin and a state senator he'd seen on the news not that long ago, but nobody else.

He jotted down another quick note in the file — *check identities in photos on crime scene walls.* The local detectives were probably already on it, but it didn't hurt to make sure.

"Yeesh," Spinks said from the far corner of the room. He was leaning down in front of a glass case, studying its contents.

Loshak crossed over to him and peered into the case. It was a butterfly collection. Butterflies and moths of every size, shape, and color combination were pinned to black velvet and labeled in painstakingly neat handwriting. Brilliant blue morphos, a huge green and yellow lunar moth the size of Loshak's hand, and the orange, white, and black death's head moths with their infamous skull.

"Dead bugs in a murder room," Spinks said, a slightly defensive tone in his voice, as if to excuse his disgusted reaction. "It's kinda morbid, don't you think?"

Loshak shrugged.

"Everybody's got to have a hobby."

"Yeah, but a guy who gets posed after being shot execution-style? With a damn glove covering one eye?"

The reporter drew out each word as if he were leading up to something that should be obvious to Loshak.

"Covering one eye? You know what that symbolizes, right? The all-seeing eye? That's some Illuminati shit. Now throw in the display of a million of the most iconic and symbolic bugs in the world and tell me you're not tripping even a little."

"Wait a minute…" Loshak tucked the file under his arm and cocked his head at Spinks in disbelief. "Illuminati?"

He tried and failed to keep the disappointment out of his voice.

"You're not one of those conspiracy theory nuts, are you?"

Spinks put both hands up as if to back him off.

"Look, man. You do investigative journalism long enough, you see some shit. Let's just say my mind is open to all the possibilities. Wide open."

"Right."

"I'm telling you," Spinks said. "There's crap going on out there that you wouldn't believe."

"I guess not," Loshak said, leading the way back out into the hall.

The next door on their left was a bathroom. Marble floors, granite countertops, gilt-edged mirrors. The door on their right was an office with an enormous wood desk, featuring a humidor full of cigars and an engraved gold pen set from the Moose Lodge. Straight ahead was a laundry and mudroom leading out onto a patio with a full set of furniture, a huge brick barbecue pit, and an outdoor entertainment center with another massive flatscreen and set of speakers. Loshak wondered if they bothered lugging all that inside when it rained or snowed. Nightmarish.

They headed back toward the foyer, both of them falling quiet as if obeying the religious hush of the house.

On their way past the kitchen, a rotten stench curled its way inside Loshak's sinuses. He grunted involuntarily.

Beside him, Spinks grimaced. "Stinks like death."

All at once, every synapse in Loshak's brain seemed to fire. That rotting stink, like bloated roadkill. The posed body. That feeling of horror lurking just out of sight. Maybe there was something going on here after all. Some dark evil hiding under this tacky nouveau riche veil. Something the instinctive, primitive part of his mind was trying to tell him.

Loshak eased open the swinging kitchen door and flipped on the light. More granite. Copper apron-front farmhouse sink. Rustic hickory cabinets with crown molding. One of those fridges with see-through doors and constant backlight, showing off every food and drink inside.

Spinks followed him in, the back of his hand pressed to his nostrils to block the smell out. It was a strangely feminine gesture on the reporter.

Brain still screaming out a warning, Loshak moved to the sink. Opened the cabinet underneath. Cleaning supplies. He tried the one to the left. It rolled out on a slide, a huge, deep drawer containing the trash can.

A swarm of fruit flies circled up from it, along with a fresh blast of that rotten stink.

Sitting on top of the rest of the garbage was a pair of bloody Styrofoam trays from a meat department. With the tip of his pen, he flipped up the edge of the label. Ground beef.

Loshak closed his eyes and exhaled. Felt his shoulders drop a few inches as the tension seeped out of his body.

It was nothing crazy or horrific. Just the smell of old garbage. He'd gotten worked up over nothing.

"Eighty-twenty," Spinks read the label over his shoulder. "Hard evidence that our vic was not a health freak, then."

Loshak kneed the sliding trash can back under the cabinets.

"Let's go."

CHAPTER 4

After a call to the Overland Park Police Department, Loshak plugged the address of the Stony Brook Inn into the GPS. Spinks offered to do the same into his phone so they wouldn't have to keep waiting for the route to load, but Loshak rejected this with a dismissive wave of the hand.

According to the OPPD, Griffin's wife Pam was staying at the Stony Brook while her house was being processed as a crime scene. They'd made arrangements to meet her there.

As they exited the gated community and crossed the wealthy suburb, Loshak wondered whether the widow would want to go back to the house. Could she sleep another night there? Live there? He'd seen relations of victims do it — return to live in the home where their loved one had been killed. Personally, he couldn't wrap his head around it. He'd hardly been able to stand the house after his daughter died, and Shelly hadn't even passed there. How could someone take showers, sleep, make breakfast — hell, do any of the normal life things they'd done before — in the house where their spouse had been murdered? How could a place where the other half of your life had been stomped out ever feel like a home again?

The Stony Brook Inn had been built to look like a huge timber frame log cabin, with rustic posts and a wraparound porch populated by wooden rockers. Sculpted evergreen bushes sprouted beneath the windows, and a pair of tall cedars flanked it on either side. It was as if the builders had created their own little forest biome in the midst of all the modern aggregate stone chain hotels.

Loshak and Spinks flashed their badges in the lobby, and the desk clerk gave them directions to the elevators which were also outfitted with split log siding. Almost no metal visible anywhere.

"That's how you know it's expensive," Spinks commented as the elevator car rose, pointing at one gnarled, bumpy board. "They've got enough money to make it look like they just slapped whole trees up everywhere and called it a day. I got Lisa a live-edge topped coffee table for our anniversary the year she remodeled the house."

He raised his hand and rubbed his thumb and fingers together.

"That was some ridiculous coin — and basically all they're doing is scraping the bark off and putting a finish on it. Half the work, ten times the money."

"Some people like that sort of thing," Loshak said with a shrug. "Having something that looks natural around."

The elevator stopped, and Loshak stepped out into a hall with thick maroon carpet and plank walls. The doors were all the color of the cedars outside.

"Yeah, nature, except without all those pesky animals and leaves," Spinks said, following close behind. "Just add an entertainment center, an espresso machine, and climate control you can run from your phone."

Loshak halted in front of suite 314 and checked the number he'd written down.

"Wait."

Spinks' fist hovered over the door, ready to knock.

"It's 312," Loshak said, scooting down one door. "This one."

"Awkward encounter averted," Spinks said as he relocated and knocked on the correct door.

They waited. Either someone was moving around in there and talking or the television was on, but no one came to the door.

Loshak leaned in and pounded a little harder than Spinks had.

After a few seconds, he thought he saw the light change behind the peephole. He flipped open his badge and held it up to the little fisheye glass.

"Mrs. Griffin? It's Agent Loshak with the FBI. Detective Pressler said he was going to call ahead and let you know we were coming."

The handle turned with a metallic *clunk,* and the door opened. A stocky middle-aged woman with teased hair, a thick layer of makeup, and a multitude of rings smiled pleasantly up at them. She looked confused.

"Mrs. Griffin?"

"Yes?"

Loshak decided it would be best to try again, in case she hadn't gotten any of his introduction through the door.

"A detective with the OPPD said he was going to call. I'm—"

"Oh. Of course, yes, the FBI agents." She stepped back from the door. "Please come in."

As they entered, Loshak noticed Spinks didn't bother correcting the woman's assumption that he was an agent, too.

"Can I get you boys anything?" she asked, shutting the door and following them into the suite's sitting/dining room. She went straight to the minibar and opened it. "We have Sprites, Cokes, some nuts…"

Loshak glanced at Spinks. She sounded like a soccer mom trying to feed the team after the big game.

"Thank you, Mrs. Griffin. We're fine."

"I just wish I had some coffee cake here." She closed the fridge, shaking her head. "I make my own. Neil always loved my coffee cake. Maybe a little too much. The sugar wasn't good for him…"

For a second, her face spasmed, kind of crunching inward like she might burst into tears. But she shook her head again, and it was gone, replaced by that slightly befuddled smile.

"Mrs. Griffin—"

"Oh, please, call me Pam," she said as if she hadn't heard him use her last name at least three times now. "And have a seat. Anywhere is fine."

"Thanks."

Loshak pulled out one of the chairs from the two-person table and sat while Spinks eased himself onto the arm of the overstuffed leather sofa.

"Are you sure there isn't anything I can get for you?" she asked, tugging at the cuff of her sweater. She eyed the coffee machine on the counter. "I could fix you boys a cup of coffee. There isn't any coffee cake to go with it, but…"

"No, thank you."

The repetition made Loshak wonder whether Pam was suffering from a dissociative fugue state. That happened sometimes with the spouses of victims, mentally tuning in and out, remembering some things and completely skipping over others. Half the time, most of them said, none of it felt real, like they were living some strange dream or having an out-of-body experience. Memories came back to them later, and they said it felt as if everything had been happening while they were on autopilot. Drifting, drifting.

Pam gave her head another shake, then shrugged and slipped into the seat across from him.

"Well, if you're sure…"

"I'm sorry to have to go through all this with you again," Loshak said, hoping that getting down to business would help her focus. "But I need to ask you a few questions about your husband's murder. Where were you the night Neil was killed?"

"I went to bed early," she said. "I've never been a stay-up-all-nighter like Neil."

"Did you hear anything?'

"Oh, heavens no. I take sleeping pills." She touched the center of the table lightly, her rings clicking against the wood. "It's hard for me to shut down at night; my mind just keeps sawing away. Without my meds, I wouldn't sleep at all. But I can't hear a thing once I'm out."

At the mention of pills, Loshak checked her pupils. They seemed a little wide, but not anything unusual for the room's designer soft lighting. Maybe her mental distance was coming from an antidepressant or Xanax. Benzos seemed to have that effect on people.

"Were you the one who found him?"

She nodded.

"The body was in the cocktail room. I… I don't

remember calling 911, but the EMTs showed up, and their number is in my phone, so I must have. I do remember showing the paramedics where the body was, leading them into the cocktail room," she said, then paused to blink several times in quick succession. "We call it that because we always have our little get-togethers in there. Neil calls them our boozehound parties."

"The detectives on the case have confirmed that a Jack Willamette was over that night," Loshak said, steering her back toward the relevant details. "Did Neil tell you he was having someone over?"

"Oh." Pam stared at Loshak, surprised. "I don't remember. But he did just get in a new scotch, so that wouldn't be strange. He's always looking for new, better brands and then calling his buddies over to try them. He says you can taste the price difference. Something about it being smoky or peaty. Like peat moss or whatever, I guess. It all sounds pretty gross to me, but…"

Loshak tried to tread carefully with his next question, knowing it held the potential to sound as if he were accusing the victim of wrongdoing or infidelity.

"Did Neil usually have friends over after you'd gone to bed?"

Unperturbed, Pam waved that away, her rings clinking.

"Oh, he knows I don't care for that silly boy stuff he and his friends get up to. Besides, I'm always up and out of the house fairly early. We're both so busy."

Loshak let her go on. Did she realize she was speaking of a dead person in the present tense or did it seem, in her current fugue, as if Neil were still alive?

"I mean, Neil alone has his hand in so many pies I can

hardly keep track of them. Charities, nonprofits, the Lodge… anything that helps the community, he wants to be a part of. Sometimes I swear he does something every day of the week, running in and out of the house like it has a revolving door."

When she finally ran herself out, Loshak asked, "Were there any acquaintances Neil was having trouble with? Maybe an argument within one of the organizations or someone who didn't care for the charity work he was doing?"

"No, no. Neil is everyone's friend. People love him. You know he's on the board of Kansas City for Environmental Protection and Preservation — that environmental charity? And of course the local big businesses just hate KCEPP, they were always butting heads. Until they sent Neil in. Within a week, he had half the local offices just eating out of his hand. He's—"

Her face spasmed again, but a series of blinks brought it back under control. She touched the corner of her eye as if to make sure nothing had escaped.

"He *was* just that sort of guy. Every organization he was a part of knew when you want to make a friend out of an enemy, you send Neil."

Spinks leaned forward on the arm of the sofa.

"Do you think maybe that was why you two never had any kids, Pam?" the reporter asked softly. "Because Neil was always so busy helping out elsewhere?"

Loshak shifted uncomfortably in his seat. It wasn't a case-related question, and even though Spinks had asked it in a gentle tone of voice, the childlessness was a potential sore spot if the couple had been infertile or one wanted kids and the other didn't.

But across the table, Pam didn't seem fazed by Spinks' sudden digression. She swiped a puff of hair off her forehead.

"I always figured we would have kids somewhere along the way." She shrugged. "It just never happened. Maybe you're right. Maybe all the clubs and boards and community improvement projects took the place of children. Maybe they were his kids. But he really believed that people need to open up their eyes and see that throwing money at a problem isn't enough. You've got to get in there, use your talents, your expertise to make a tangible difference. To him, it's not just a duty, but an honor to try to make the world a better place."

With another tug, she pulled the sleeves of her sweater down again, then wrapped her arms around herself as if she was cold.

"I can't imagine who would want to do... do... *that* to him," she said more quietly. "From what I heard about the other men — the other victims — they weren't hurting anyone, either. Is this sicko just going around killing every good man he can find?"

CHAPTER 5

It was late afternoon when Loshak and Spinks left the Stony Brook Inn, not quite late enough for people to be getting off work, and still early enough that a visit to another of the victims' widows wouldn't be considered rude.

After another quick call to make sure they weren't stepping on any toes, they drove across Kansas City to Independence, a more modest satellite of the megacity, this time on the Missouri side of the border.

Loshak parked in front of the home of their oddball victim, Mike Dent, and shut the car off. The engine pinged a couple of times as it wound down, and then the silence rushed in to replace it.

Right away, the quiet brought back a little tremor in the hollow of Loshak's chest — a vibration that echoed that feeling of intense dread he'd experienced just before he peered into Neil Griffin's garbage can and found its contents utterly mundane. Funny how life tended to work out that way so often. It got you all scared, filled your head with dark visions, snaked its icy fingers around your heart and gave it a good squeeze, and then it wound up making a fool of you two seconds later. Made you feel small. Old. Insignificant. Made you feel like the universe was laughing at you. Spinks should put something like *that* in his book.

Loshak let his hands slide off the steering wheel, but he didn't move to exit the vehicle. Not yet. Instead, he craned his neck to look up at the property through the driver's side window.

The Dent place was an old two-story Victorian in the process of an exterior remodel. The lower level had been re-sided in a dark redwood with a deep green trim, but the siding trailed off like an interrupted thought just above the front porch. Faded pastel paints in clashing colors — a signature look of the Painted Lady houses, now grimy with pollution and age — peeled from the fish scale siding that covered the second story.

In spite of the unfinished renovations, the Dents' home was attractive. It had good bones. That was a phrase Loshak had picked up from some house flipping show he'd had on for noise during one of his countless hotel stays. But unlike the homage to money and status that had been the Griffin McMansion, this old house had character. History. The whole neighborhood seemed as if it could've been around a hundred years ago, Victorians and Colonials lining the street. Maybe even longer, considering Independence had been a jumping off place for pioneers headed West. The Dents' Victorian looked to be par for the course, most of the other houses mirroring that shiny, updated look of a neighborhood not quite impoverished enough for gentrification and not quite rich enough for new construction.

The lower lid of Loshak's aching eye twitched, aggravating the sensation of being scratched in the cornea. He fought the urge to rub it and turned to find Spinks jotting something in his Dick Tracy notebook.

When Spinks finally glanced up, he grinned.

"Are you winking at me, Agent?"

"Funny. Ready for this?"

Spinks squinted up at the house and slapped the little notepad against his palm a couple times.

"Do you think Pam Griffin offered the EMTs coffee cake when she led them to the body?"

"What?"

"Not like I'm making fun of her," the reporter said. "But that motherliness seemed like a major part of her coping mechanism. Offering us coffee cake repeatedly. I wonder if she's like that when she's not grieving for her dead husband, or if his death brought it out. Kind of why I asked her about the kids. She seems like the type of lady who would want a whole minivan full."

"Maybe."

Unable to ignore the scratching in his eye any longer, Loshak compromised and pressed his fingertips to the spot just below it while he considered Spinks' theory.

"She did ultimately attribute not having kids to Neil. Agreeing that maybe his clubs and community projects took the place of actual children."

"I wonder if she resented him for that a little," Spinks said. "Maybe not even in a way she noticed consciously, but always going to bed without him and being up and out early every morning, not wanting to be a part of hanging out with his friends, not caring about who he brought over every night, taking sleeping pills…"

The reporter rested the notepad against his chin.

"Doesn't it all seem weirdly disconnected for a marriage?"

Loshak sensed something different in Spinks' voice now, a pensive tone he wasn't used to hearing from the boisterous reporter. Thinking back, he realized Spinks hadn't said much on the drive over. Not even a fresh crack about the rental car.

"I wondered if she wasn't suffering from dissociative fugues caused by losing her husband," Loshak said, shrugging. "But maybe she's just like that all the time. A space cadet."

Spinks was back to slapping that notepad on his palm again.

"Yeah, maybe." He didn't sound convinced. "But what if there was something in their marriage she blamed him for, and what if that thing was not having kids? Like they were fine once, then they sort of fell apart the longer they went without the kids she always dreamed of?"

Spinks fell silent, still looking up at the house, but Loshak waited him out.

"After Davin died, things changed between me and Lisa," the reporter said. "Not all at once, you know, but like a little bit at a time, I started to realize we weren't what we used to be. There was this space between us. Well, *space* isn't the right word. More like a cooling down. I still love her, you know, and she still loves me… I'm pretty sure she does, anyway… But now we're more like close friends than soulmates."

Spinks let out an uncomfortable laugh, but the accompanying smile disappeared almost before the sound ended.

"As cliché as it sounds, it's like a fire went out. There's no heat there, and I don't really know how to get back to what we were. Maybe you can't after something like that. Maybe in ten more years, we'll be like the Griffins," he said with a sigh. "Just two people living in the same house. Roommates."

Loshak shifted in his seat. Spinks was looking for the answer to whether his wife resented him for the car wreck that killed their son in the few details they had about the marriage of a murder victim. The analytical side of his brain said that was a waste of time, that the two situations couldn't reliably inform one another, but he knew that wasn't the answer Spinks was looking for.

The problem was, it was entirely possible that Lisa — either consciously or unconsciously—did resent her husband. He'd been the driver, and even though the guy operating the other car had been drunk, emotions didn't always care about facts like who was actually to blame. Without talking to Lisa in person, there was no way for Loshak to make a reliable intuitive leap, and even then, who could really tell what was going on inside anybody else's head? He'd been around Jan for a full two months after their daughter Shelly passed and still the divorce papers had been a shock.

Before Loshak could formulate a response, however, Spinks slapped the notepad against his palm one more time.

"Anyway," Spinks said as if that were a segue. The good-natured smirk Loshak was accustomed to seeing on his friend's face reappeared, and Spinks tucked the notepad into his pocket. "Widow number two. Let's go see what Mrs. Dent can tell us. Maybe she'll have some coffee cake on hand."

CHAPTER 6

Despite her husband having been killed over two months prior, Tricia Dent looked the part of a grieving widow much more than Pam Griffin had. Reddened eyelids. Makeup that couldn't quite hide the dark circles underneath. The eyes themselves were dry, but there was a weariness there.

She hovered in the doorway, hesitating, blinking as she took in the sight of Spinks and Loshak on her doorstep. Then she shook hands with both of them and invited them inside.

Loshak had hoped Mrs. Dent would be more lucid than the Griffin woman, given that she'd had some time to come to terms with her husband's death. But after getting that first look at her, he wasn't sure that would be the case.

The Dent living room was furnished in dark, tasteful tones that matched the new siding on the house. A vase of large, blue flowers, fluffy prairie grass, and spiny-looking sticks sat on a wall table under a family photo, the kind people had taken by a second cousin or the child of a friend who suddenly decided they were professional photographers.

Loshak paused to study the portrait. Two boys and two girls all in or around their teens, a much happier looking Mrs. Dent, and a tall guy with broad shoulders and unruly copper hair stood together on a wooden bridge in a generic rural setting.

"I sent them out. The kids, that is," Mrs. Dent said, her gaze following Loshak's to the frame. "I've been trying to get things back to normal around here. Or as close to normal as I can."

She stared at the photo for a few seconds before swiveling to face Loshak.

"I hope that's OK. That the kids aren't here, I mean. You don't need to talk to them, do you?"

"No, I don't think that'll be necessary," Loshak said with a reassuring smile.

Pictures of football teams covered the rest of the walls. Team photos, most with a school name and year underneath. In the corner stood a glass-front trophy case, populated by golden plastic footballs on top of sparkling pillars.

If the man's file hadn't specified that Mike Dent was a defensive coordinator for a local Division II football team, the explosion of memorabilia in the living room would have given it away.

Mrs. Dent went immediately to a brocade-covered easy chair by the window, the imprint of a large body worn into the fabric. Another picture frame sat nearby on a glass-topped end table. She brushed the gilt frame with her fingers as she curled up in the seat, adjusting the frame so it angled toward her.

Loshak only caught a brief glimpse of the photograph before she'd moved it, but he was pretty sure it was a headshot of Mike Dent.

"Please, make yourselves comfortable," Mrs. Dent said, indicating the couch. "Though I have to say, I'm not sure what else I can tell you. I've already been over it a hundred times with the police."

"I'll be asking a lot of the same old questions, I'm afraid," Loshak said. "Why don't you start out telling us a little about how your husband spent his time. His work, hobbies, that kind of thing."

A weak smile appeared on Mrs. Dent's lips.

"That's easy. Football, football, and football."

"He coached over at Central Missouri?"

"He was their defensive coordinator, yes."

"And how long had he been there?"

"Six years at Central. He started out as an unpaid grad assistant at Mizzou. That's where we both went to school. And where we met," she said, eyes drifting to the portrait of her husband on the table. "After that, we were all over the place. Made a lot of stops across the Midwest for a year or two at a time. Moving from school to school as Mike worked his way up the ladder. I guess I should say that I made stops. Mike was always on the move. Always out on the road recruiting. At least, that's how it felt those first few years."

The fingers of her left hand bunched and unbunched as she spoke, squeezing something. A tissue, Loshak thought. She was mashing it into a tight little ball.

"People think football coaches only work from September to New Year's, but it's not that way at all. Recruiting is 365 days a year. In-home visits with prospects, sometimes as far away as Hawaii. Watching film to scout talent. We're talking high school freshmen and sophomores. Calling. Texting. Writing letters. It never ends."

Spinks spoke up, scratching his chin inquisitively.

"The University of Central Missouri. That's out in Warrensburg, if I'm not mistaken." At a nod from the widow, he continued. "That's a bit of a scoot, isn't it? Has to be at least an hour commute."

Loshak and Spinks had planned this part of the interview on the drive. Loshak found it curious that Mike Dent had chosen to work a little over an hour away from his family and wanted to explore that angle without arousing any defensiveness from Mrs. Dent. So he opened up the interview and had Spinks slide in the question about the distance almost as an afterthought.

With the way Spinks had snuck in the question about the Griffins not having children in the last interview, Loshak figured he'd use the reporter's knack for broaching the more difficult topics to his advantage.

But just now, Loshak was wondering if Spinks hadn't been a little too smooth with his, *if I'm not mistaken.* Loshak's eyes wandered over to the widow, who luckily seemed to have bought the overly casual delivery.

"An hour is about right. Two hours there and back a day. So a lot of times it just made sense for him to stay there. Especially on late nights."

His mind was whirring now, but Loshak didn't so much as twitch at Mrs. Dent's answer.

"Did he have a place in Warrensburg? A favorite motel? Or an apartment?"

Mrs. Dent's eyebrows rose.

"Gosh no. We wouldn't have been able to afford that. We barely managed the mortgage on this place."

"Where'd he stay, then?"

"You're going to laugh, but he slept in his office. Went

43

out and bought cheap twin mattress from IKEA and kept it propped up against the back wall when he wasn't using it. He called it his DIY Murphy Bed."

The corners of her mouth twitched.

"I'm probably making him out to sound like some kind of crazy workaholic, but it wasn't like that. I mean, he worked. Hard. Gave everything he had. Because he believed in it. It was his passion. That was one of the things that attracted me to him. We were both barely twenty when we met, an age where I don't think most people know what they want out of life. Half my friends switched majors at least twice. But not Mike. He knew his goals as clear as day. He wanted to coach. And he was willing to work his ass off to get it."

The widow's hand started kneading the tissue again, working it into something smaller, more compact.

"The first real coaching job he got — this was right after we got married — he told me, 'My salary is $5000.' I thought he meant monthly, but that was for the whole year."

Her head shook back and forth as if she still couldn't believe it.

"The school didn't have real housing for us, so they gave us this junky little trailer out in the middle of nowhere. It was awful. No one had lived there in months, so the grass around the place was up to my waist, and the whole thing was just overrun with rodents. Everyone just referred to it as 'The Shack.' Even us. But looking back, I wouldn't change any of it. We were grateful for it in a way, because looking back, it showed how far we'd come. Showed how if you believe in yourself and you work hard,

44

you can do anything. Mike always said that. To his players. To his kids. To me. Sometimes I feel like he willed it to be true for all of us."

Mrs. Dent paused and put the fist still wadded around the tissue to her mouth. She cleared her throat and pushed herself out of the chair.

"Would you excuse me for a moment?"

"Of course."

A few moments after she disappeared through a doorway off to the left, they heard the babble of running water. At first, Loshak thought she was getting herself a drink. Maybe her throat had gone dry from all the talking. But the water ran and ran for some time. Longer than it took to fill a glass.

Spinks leaned a little closer and broke the stillness of the living room with a whisper.

"Germaphobe."

"What?"

"You know. One of those obsessive-compulsive types. She had to shake our hands and everything. Probably couldn't wait to wash up."

Loshak raised an eyebrow, not sure if Spinks actually believed in this little theory or whether he was trying to fill the void. There were a lot of people out there like that. Couldn't stand the silent moments in life. It made them restless. Agitated. And so they filled the empty spaces with idle chatter.

Spinks was better at it than most. Usually people didn't have much to say. They weren't observant or self-aware enough to have genuinely interesting ideas or entertaining anecdotes, so they just blathered on about sports and celebrity gossip.

A creaking floorboard announced Mrs. Dent's return. Loshak noticed her hands were empty. The little tissue-ball was gone.

"Sorry about that," she said, settling back into the chair. "If I got us off-track before, I apologize."

Loshak rested his hands on his knees.

"No, ma'am. You were doing just fine."

"Shall we continue, then?"

At a nod, Loshak fired off his next question.

"How did your husband seem before his death? Any changes in mood or shifts to his routine?"

Mrs. Dent stared at her husband's photograph as she spoke, like she was talking to it instead of Loshak.

"He was a little amped about the game against Western. Missouri Western. There's a bit of rivalry there. He was basically camped out for most of that week, breaking down film and working on scheme stuff. I think he stayed over in Warrensburg three nights in a row. But that wasn't unusual. Not during the season. Like I said, when he wasn't on the road, Mike basically lived in the football offices half the time."

"How'd that turn out?" Loshak asked.

"Pardon?"

"The game against Western."

"Oh," she said, frowning deeply. "We lost. 31-28. Missed a damned field goal that would have tied things up with four minutes left. Mike was livid. Gave Todd Flickinger a piece of his mind after the game."

"Todd Flickinger?"

"Special Teams coach."

Loshak leaned forward.

"And this would have been the day before your husband was murdered?"

"Yes, but—" She sat up straight in the chair. "Oh, you don't think that had anything to do with…"

She shook her head, not finishing the thought.

"It wasn't like that. Not at all. Things get heated sometimes, sure. All the guys Mike worked with are competitive. But that's what makes it so they can do the job. So maybe Mike goes off on someone during a game or after a loss. It's never personal. They all know that. Lots of things get said in the heat of battle, but it's forgotten by the time Monday rolls around."

Settling back against the worn leather, Mrs. Dent tilted her head to one side.

"In some ways, football was therapy for him. He never raised his voice at the kids or at me. He was a different person on the field than he was off. He was calmer at home. I think it was because he got it all out in the games. In practice. It was good for him. An outlet."

She folded her hands in her lap and looked at Loshak squarely.

"So I guess what I'm trying to say is Mike didn't have enemies. His life revolved around us and the team. There wasn't time for anything else. Football was all he knew. He couldn't tell you anything about current events or pop culture. Certainly wasn't entangled in any local politics or anything like that. If it didn't have to do with stopping an air raid offense, he didn't have time for it."

With a dry chuckle, she added, "I think the last time we went to the movies, it was to see one of the Matrix sequels.

47

Not great."

She tried to laugh again, but her voice caught. There was a box of tissues on the table in front of Loshak, and he passed one over to her.

"Thank you."

Dabbing at her eyes, she angled her face toward the framed photo of her husband.

"I'm sorry. I was just thinking about how we'd been planning a big family vacation. The first one in… I don't know how long. The kids and I would go visit my parents in San Diego every year or so, but Mike always had to work. This year it was supposed to be different. The plan was that I would finish up the house by Spring, get it on the market, and then all six of us would fly out to Hawaii for a week. The big island."

"You're doing the renovation work yourself?" Loshak asked.

She tore her eyes from her husband's photograph to examine her surroundings, gesturing with a wave of her hand.

"Mike's thing was football. Mine is houses. Fixer-uppers. I started doing it when we were moving around all the time. Mike would get a job, and I'd scout around for a cheap house to flip. And while he was off at school or recruiting, I'd fix the place up. Then we'd sell it for a small profit once it was time to move on again."

Craning his neck, Loshak made a show of studying the crown molding and paneled walls.

"It's a beautiful house."

"Thank you," Mrs. Dent said. "It's my proudest project to date. And the most ambitious. It's not finished, of course. I thought Mike would have a heart attack when he saw it the first time. It was in rough shape. But he only smiled and said he couldn't wait to see what I did with it. He never doubted me."

"Sounds like that went both ways," Loshak said.

With her eyes closed, the widow sighed.

"Central Missouri is still relatively small-time, but I think he would have gotten a shot at an FBS school before long. Maybe even a Power Five team. His defense led the conference in total yardage three years in a row. Points per game improved every year under his watch. He'd made some connections at coaching conferences, too. He was about to get his shot. What he'd wanted all along."

Again, she got to her feet and excused herself.

"I'll be back in just a moment."

But this time, the running water wasn't loud enough to cover the sound of her sobs.

Loshak combed his fingers through his hair and eyed Spinks.

"I think we've done enough damage here. Let's move out."

CHAPTER 7

A weariness settled over Loshak as they trod down the front steps of the Dent house. Tricia Dent had delivered that sense of loss, grief, anguish that accompanied most every homicide case. Here was the hurt, the wound that would never heal, the pain everlasting.

Law enforcement officers inevitably grew callous to the violence, to the morbidity, to the senselessness of murder. The dead bodies slowly but surely lost their ability to shock or disturb. Police numbed themselves to these things.

But the families left behind? The victims who lived and suffered on and on? Those could still twist the blade in a cop's heart. Not always, but sometimes.

Tricia Dent trying to cover the sounds of her weeping by running water in the kitchen sink had done the job. Turned the knife. Gotten to Loshak pretty good.

As they headed back down the walk, Spinks shook his head

"I don't know, man."

"About what?" Loshak asked.

"I get that all violence is senseless and all of that, but something about these murders seems to go beyond that. Why is this guy making such a spectacle of killing squeaky clean types?"

The reporter gestured over his shoulder toward the Dents' house.

"Does he just look around until he finds the most

normal, nicest family in the neighborhood, then go apeshit?" Spinks looked over at Loshak, anxiety puckering his brow. "I mean, what the hell is going on here? Another chaotic type like Zakarian?"

"I doubt it."

Loshak frowned down at the sidewalk. Zakarian's targets had been opportunistic, people who left their doors unlocked, their windows cracked. The Kansas City targets had been chosen with purpose.

"The execution-style killings, the posed corpses... This is a highly organized person. They're acting with a purpose, trying to accomplish a tangible goal. We just don't know what that goal is yet. There's a missing piece out there, a reason that will make sense out of this."

Spinks squinted at him.

"Doesn't it make you anxious, though, the way none of this remotely adds up? Like, what if we never find that piece, and we don't catch this guy?"

Darger's frustrated scowl flashed across his neurons.

"It isn't your job to catch this guy," Loshak said. "You're here to write a book."

"Whoa." Spinks stopped in his tracks, putting both hands up as if Loshak were holding a gun on him. "The hostility out here just jumped up to eleven. Something bothering you, partner?"

"That's not how I meant it."

Loshak turned back to the reporter, resisting the urge to rub at his irritated eye.

"Thinking about it like that, like everything depends on us or on you figuring this out, you're one step away from blaming yourself for the killer's actions. It stops you from thinking objectively about the facts, and it's a quick way to burn out."

"OK, that's fine," Spinks said, falling back into his long strides. "I just need some warning if you're gonna go all cliché lone wolf movie cop on me and start a falling out right before the big, final fight."

Loshak huffed a laugh. "I'll let you know."

"So, riddle me this: they're in the middle of remodeling this house to sell, and they were looking for a nice, big house in a ritzier neighborhood. In one of the earlier interviews in the file she said they bought cars for the two oldest kids. They're sending all four to college. I know the big time coaches are multi-millionaires and all, but just how much does a Division II assistant coach make annually that they could afford all that?"

"There's a good chance he had an employee benefit that would allow the kids to go his university for free," Loshak pointed out.

"True, but that's not what she told the police," Spinks said, waving around his index finger. "She stressed how much they had to scrimp and save back when they got the first kid his junker. Suddenly they're able to afford all the rest of this, plus a retirement fund? Doesn't that smell a little fishy to you?"

Loshak nodded.

"As a university employee, Dent was technically working for the state. His salary is public record."

He flipped open the file and scribbled a note in the margin: *Pull university contract for Dent.*

"We can check whether there were any significant changes to his contract over the last year that might explain—"

"What's that?" Spinks asked.

Loshak glanced up to find the reporter pointing at a folded piece of notebook paper pinned under the driver's side wiper of the rental.

"Huh." Loshak lifted the wiper an inch, removed the paper, then let the blade fall back in place.

The edge of the page was ragged, the tear so haphazard that it split the would-be rectangle down to an uneven taper. It'd been folded over so the thin end covered a string of jagged black marker. Loshak unfolded it.

The scrawl of blank ink stood out bold from the white paper. All caps. Something aggressive expressed itself in the tilt and points of the spiky letters.

DON'T TRUST THE LOCALS.

CHAPTER 8

A prickle of cold crept down the nape of Loshak's neck. Icy fingers brushing him there ever so softly. Was this shock? Fear? Confusion? A mixture of all three, he thought.

He swiveled his head. Scanned the area. He didn't see any movement in the yards or on the street. No shades falling back into place in dark windows or cars burning rubber to get away.

He could feel the hair on the back of his neck all pricked up, the flesh crawling a little as he rotated his head. It was probably just a reaction to the note, but he couldn't shake the paranoid feeling that he was being watched even now.

His eyes fell back to the creased paper in his hand and studied it as though it might now magically offer more than the four words in block letters. He didn't know what he expected. An explanation? Further information? Anything?

But no. Nothing. The spiky letters remained the same. Loshak's jaw clenched and unclenched.

It was hard not to think that the killer could have left this note. Stood here. Lifted the windshield wiper of the rental car. Slid the paper beneath it. Who else?

Spinks had taken a couple of steps around the front of the sedan, looking up and down the street for whoever had left the note. The reporter turned back, eyebrows high on his forehead.

"You know who does shit like this, right?"

The weirdness of the situation had thrown him, so it took a second for Loshak to catch on. When he did, he couldn't help but roll his eyes.

"I know who *you* think does shit like this."

Spinks shook his head, his eyebrows showing no signs of lowering.

"I'm not even going to say it."

"Good," Loshak said, reaching for the rental's door handle.

"Not even going to speak it aloud. No way."

"Great."

"The Illuminati!" Spinks threw his whole body into this finger-jab. "That's who does stuff like this. And you best believe that if they're leaving cryptic notes, then we're onto something here. Something big."

"First of all, so much for not saying it," Loshak said. "Second of all, this is really what you think the Illuminati is up to? Controlling the world from the shadows by way of leaving cryptic notes on nondescript sedans? Wherever do they find the time?"

Loshak opened the door and sank into the driver's seat.

Spinks gazed down the street for another beat, seemingly oblivious to the notion of leaving. The reporter did a double take as the car started, hustled around the front end and folded himself into the passenger side. His door hadn't even shut before he started in again.

"This is serious, man. Whatever we're getting into here, it's big."

"*Big*, as in an elaborate serial murder case?" Loshak nodded. "Yeah, pretty big. *Big*, as in part of a centuries-old conspiracy to secretly rule the world? Doubtful."

"See? That's how they get away with it," Spinks said in an I-told-you-so voice. "Doubting Thomases like you. Too cool for school, you know."

Loshak couldn't tell how much of this Illuminati nonsense Spinks was serious about and how much was another one of the reporter's bits, so he decided the best course of action was to change subjects.

"How long do you think we were inside?" he asked.

"Twenty minutes?" Spinks guessed. "Not that long. Think they were following us?"

Feeling that tingling chill on his neck again, Loshak glanced at the rearview mirror. He hadn't noticed anyone tailing them on the way over. Not much traffic out here in the residential area the Dents were situated in. Still, with the timing of everything, the possibility that they'd been followed persisted.

"They almost had to be," he said finally. "Unless they were staking out Mrs. Dent."

Spinks leaned forward to look get a better view of the half-remodeled house.

"Hadn't thought of that. Do you think it was the killer returning to the scene of the crime? That's a thing, right? A recurring behavior among these psychos, I mean."

Once more Loshak stared down at the sheet of paper in his hands. Turned it over. The jagged letters, the careless tear. The note looked like something thrown together on the spur of the moment. It was always possible that whoever left it had meant for it to look impulsive, but his gut told him it hadn't come from their killer.

He shook his head.

"Doesn't square with the murders. Those show signs of careful planning. Precision. Patience. Meticulous staging. This note? Not so much."

That didn't deter Spinks.

"But if he's an organized type like you said, those guys get off on playing with the cops — Bundy, BTK, that kind of thing. This could be the beginnings of our correspondence with this guy. Who else would, one, know we were investigating, and two, care enough to leave a note like this warning us about the locals?"

"You mean besides the Illuminati?"

Spinks flinched a little as though injured by the jab.

"Laugh it up," the reporter said, snatching the note out of Loshak's hands. "But whoever left this must know we're headed to the station to brief the task force tonight."

He tapped the hasty black writing with an index finger, rattling the paper.

"Think about it. *Don't trust the locals,* right before we're supposed to walk into a lions' den of local cops?"

Loshak put the car in drive and pulled out onto the street.

"I don't think that logic follows."

But as he drove away, he checked the rearview again. Just in case.

CHAPTER 9

Since it was right in the middle of rush hour, Loshak tried to stay off the interstates and bigger highways on the way to the Prairie Village Police Station. The first murder had taken place in Mission Hills, but when City Councilman Ken Long had been killed, the PVPD had swooped in and taken the lead.

Outside the car window, the neighborhood went from modest but tidy to the kind of cramped, run-down houses and projects where SWAT teams were serving crack warrants in the middle of the day. Then Loshak drove through an intersection on Troost Avenue, and boom, architectural marvels as far as the eye could see. Modern art popped up on the corners, and they passed a major shopping plaza full of stores with names that sounded like law firms and not even a hint at what they sold.

Loshak vaguely remembered reading something about the neighborhoods surrounding Prairie Village. There were seven or eight of them strung together, all developed by one guy over the course of the first half of the 20th century for the wealthiest, whitest Kansas City residents. It was called the Country Club district, and it was supposed to be the largest continuous planned community in the country. Half the buildings in it had been designed by guys like Frank Lloyd Wright and Louis Curtiss.

Grouped somewhere in that stretch of wealth and prestige were two out of four of the crime scenes. Living in

58

an extended country club hadn't kept the councilman or their car salesman vic safe. It was more of that false security.

They didn't have time to stop for dinner before the task force meeting, but Loshak had Spinks find directions to a local bakery for a double dozen of assorted donuts and a bag of donut holes.

The donuts were crucial for a first meeting with the locals. Not only did it make a good first impression to come bearing delicious treats, but you could tell a lot about a person by the kind of donut they picked. It was something like a Rorschach Test performed by way of pastry, Loshak thought. Chocolate with a sprinkle of nuts on top said you wanted some crunch to sink your teeth into. Blueberry cake donut with no glaze indicated possible healthier leanings. Cream or jelly filling meant you weren't afraid to get your hands dirty.

Though as Spinks munched on his chocolate-iced, Bavarian cream-filled longhorn in the car, Loshak thought he might have to revise that last theory. The reporter ate the messy pastry with meticulous care, not getting anything on his mouth but still wiping his lips with a napkin after every bite.

The Prairie Village Police Department looked more like an Olympic-grade rec center than a police station, all sleek curves and manicured lawn. As they pulled around the corner to the parking lot, Loshak even caught sight of a pool and aquatic center in the back — though, to be fair, judging by the twisting, multicolored slides and number of kids running around, he didn't think it was part of the station.

Spinks let out a low whistle.

"Pretty swanky. I bet all the cops in KC want to work here."

"Hell, I'm thinking of picking up an application," Loshak said.

He found a visitor's spot near the back of the lot, parked, and popped the last of his donut holes into his mouth. Unlike Spinks, Loshak managed to get sticky glaze all over his fingers and a few flecks of dry stuff stuck to the corner of his mouth as though spackled there. He spent a full minute licking his fingers and cleaning up with a napkin before climbing out.

Loshak pulled the box of donuts from the back seat, then locked the rental before coming around to meet Spinks in front.

The reporter was busy scribbling something in his notebook.

They'd barely talked on the way over. Was Spinks writing down that crack about applying to the PVPD? Loshak rolled his head on his neck to ease some of the tension in his shoulders. As soon as he started to forget about the whole book thing, Spinks always went and did something to remind him.

Before he gave in to the urge to ask what Spinks had been writing, however, a big man in a suit came striding across the parking lot, grinning at them.

"Hey, there! You boys the Federales?"

He was portly with an excess of flesh around his neck and face. His suit wasn't cramped or ill-fitting, but the jacket was unbuttoned in the evening heat, and the flapping of its wings seemed to double his bulk. In spite of being an inch or so taller, Loshak felt dwarfed by the guy.

"Hank Pressler, head detective."

He grabbed Spinks' hand in one huge, pink mitt, pumping his arm up and down like the lever on a handcar, then did the same with Loshak's.

"Welcome to Prairie Village, guys. Glad to have you!"

"Thanks," Loshak said, returning his freed hand to stabilizing the donut box. He was about to introduce himself, but Pressler plunged onward.

"It's an honor, a real honor!" the big man said, pink hands working overtime to gesture along with his words.

The guy was like a boulder rolling downhill, all kinetic energy and bounce. The combination of over-the-top hand gestures, dynamic movement, and enthusiasm made Loshak think of Chris Farley.

"Government flippin' agents, direct from Washington DC. The real deal, right here in the Ville!"

"I'm actually a consultant," Spinks said. "But yeah, my partner here is the real deal. Special Agent Victor Loshak, profiler extraordinaire."

Loshak thought about chiming in that the BAU was actually located in Quantico, not DC, but decided to let it slide. Not a great idea to come into a situation with the potential for a lot of territorial squabbling correcting people left and right.

Pressler's huge grin slid away at Spinks' words, his fleshy face turning grim in the blink of an eye.

"Look, can I ask you something?" The big guy stepped in closer, head bent and voice lowered. "Maybe something a little personal?"

Loshak traded glances with Spinks, nodding out of

instinct.

"Go ahead."

"Y'all ain't a couple of them libtards, are you?" Pressler asked. "Being from DC and all, I mean. Creatures of the beltway and what have you."

Loshak's mouth came open, but he had no idea what to say. Beside him, Spinks let out a high-pitched laugh, all pinched and nervous sounding.

Pressler clapped both hands together, tipping back his head and cackling.

"Hoo, boy!" He slapped a hand down on Loshak's shoulder and gave him a shake. "I'm just messing with you, buddy!"

The big detective locked eyes with Spinks and jerked his head at Loshak.

"You should've seen the look on this one's face! Looked like he just swam into a turd at the public pool."

Loshak felt his face heat up a little as Spinks started laughing his real laugh, that hissing sound.

"Honestly, fellas! Maybe use those profiling skills. Do I look like I give a rat's dick about politics? The last time I voted was for American Idol. Reuben Studdard, I think." Pressler scratched his high forehead and squinted up at the sky. "I wanna say that was season three. Maybe two."

He waved both hands.

"The little wife made me watch it for a few years there. Dark times in the Pressler house. Anyway, what are we standing around out here for? We got AC like nobody's business inside. Come on, I'll show y'all to the conference room."

CHAPTER 10

As Pressler led them through the Prairie Village lobby, he tipped a wink and a finger gun at the receptionist.

"Molly B! These friendly neighborhood Federal agents are here to take you in for tax evasion."

"Har-har." Molly rolled her eyes.

The desk officer looked too young to have seen her five-year high school reunion yet, much less be working for one of the wealthiest police stations in the US. There was something about the way she sat — maybe the angle of her neck or the feathery sweep of shiny black hair over her right eye — that made Loshak think of a bird.

"Chief's in Conference Room A with the detectives from Overland Park. They're still waiting for Mission Hills." With a jerk of her head, she turned to meet Loshak's gaze. "Welcome, guys. If there's anything I can do for you, just let me know."

"Well, for starters," Loshak opened the box of donuts and sat it on the counter, "you could take one of these off my hands."

"Aw, I love FluffyBellie!" She perched on the edge of her seat and plucked a cruller from the mix. "These are my favorite."

Loshak smiled.

"Good choice."

An eleven-pound ham of a hand dropped onto his right shoulder, pink and slightly warmer than comfortable through his suit jacket. Loshak looked up to find that Pressler had Spinks by the shoulder, too. Pretty hands-on, this guy.

"Alright, you charming SOBs," Pressler boomed cheerfully, "Let's get this show on the road. You wanna beat the Mission Hills boys to the powwow, don't ya?"

"Lead away, Detective," Spinks said.

Though the reporter, unlike Pressler, was using his inside voice, it sounded as if Spinks was trying to match the detective for aggressive jolliness. Interesting development. Maybe he was trying to ingratiate himself so he could ask about the local Illuminati chapter.

If Loshak had a little green Dick Tracy notebook handy, he would've written that down.

Molly buzzed them through a door and into the desk pool. At a quarter to six, only about half the desks were occupied, but as Pressler led Loshak and Spinks past, nearly all of those residents turned to follow the progress of the donuts.

Along the back wall were a series of wooden doors, each with a maroon sign next to their jambs. Two conference rooms, a file room, and a wire cage glass door to the holding cells.

Conference Room A wasn't made for a meeting of three departments, that much was clear as soon as they walked in. It was already packed to standing room only.

"Looky who I found out in the parking lot," Pressler said as they entered. "This respectably bald gentleman here is Jevon Spinks, and the man with the sweet treats is our profiler straight from the Feebies, Special Agent Loshak."

"Help yourselves, folks," Loshak said, lifting the donut

box a touch as if to prove he had the goods, then setting them on a table against the back wall.

A low rumble of greetings and thanks traveled through the ranks as task force members from two of the departments migrated back to pick out their favorite pastry. Given the time of day, Loshak figured at least half of them had put off supper for this meeting.

A shorter man in a worn white cowboy hat stepped forward.

"Chief Tavares," he said, shaking with each of them in turn. "Good to have you boys in on this."

Tavares didn't look glad to have them there. As he said it, Loshak noted that the frown lines around his mouth and between his brows bit deeper. Even ignoring the verbal attempt to make them smaller than himself — calling them boys and emphasizing his status as Chief of Police — Tavares' body language was confrontational, almost territorial. Hands on the belt, feet set wide, head tipped up to make the hat stand up higher.

Loshak had seen the posture often enough to recognize the subtle differences from the standard cop pose. Most of it had to do with the face. A hardening around the eyes. A downward curl of the lip. Plenty of local departments thought they were handling serial murders just fine and viewed the swooping in of Feds as a personal insult. With the way Prairie Village had taken over the investigation from the originating department, it made sense that Tavares would want to hang onto authority here.

"We'll help out however we can," Loshak said, hoping the subservient tone would go a ways toward diffusing the chief's hostility.

Tavares gave him a curt nod.

"Why don't you two grab some wall. Mission Hills should be here in a jiff. I'll give everybody the rundown on what we've got so far, then if we have time, we'll get you up there."

Loshak was about to thank the chief when Spinks let out a sharp laugh.

"If you have time?" Spinks said. "You got something pressing pulling you away from catching a serial killer, Chief?"

Loshak gave an internal sigh.

Predictably, Tavares' eyes narrowed.

"Spinks, was it? I don't recall reading the memo that said an Agent Spinks would be involved in this investigation."

The reporter smiled and pulled out the little wallet the Bureau had given him.

"I'm a consultant," he said, flipping it open to his laminated ID.

The chief scowled down at the ID for a minute before his eyes jumped back up to meet Spinks'.

"Stay out from underfoot and keep your head down if there's trouble," Tavares said. "I don't need an assload of federal paperwork because some half-cocked 'consultant' ran into a situation and got himself shot."

"Don't worry." Spinks slapped his wallet shut again and tucked it into his pocket. "This guy isn't running anywhere. Exercise is against my religion."

The chief gave Spinks one final scowl, then moved off toward the front of the room. Apparently he wasn't interested in donuts from federal interlopers.

A muffled chuckle got Loshak's attention.

"Against your religion!" Pressler clapped Spinks on the back. "Good one. You sure gave that stick up Tavares' ass a nice little twang."

Spinks was trying not to be obvious about gloating, but Loshak could see that he was pretty pleased with himself.

"Is he always that friendly?" Spinks asked.

"The chief's got terminal SMS," Pressler said then leaned toward Loshak as he explained further. "Short Man's Syndrome. He's gotta make up for being knee-high to a leprechaun by letting everybody know he calls the shots and can kick your ass, too. Always wears that cowboy hat for the couple inches it seems to give him. That's what I figure, anyhow."

Over at the door, a new crowd of faces was filtering into the conference room. Mission Hills, the final department in this task force. A helpful soul directed them to the donuts, pointing in Loshak's direction as he did. The new arrivals waved thanks, one saluting him with her jelly-filled.

Loshak nodded in return.

Once she'd gotten a cup of coffee to go with her pastry-wrapped jelly bomb, the detective came over and leaned against the wall next to him.

"Hey, thanks for the extra calories," she said. "I'll remember to curse your name when I'm trapped on the treadmill tomorrow. It's Loshak, right?"

She looked like the type who would've been on the treadmill regardless just for fun. Athletic, late twenties or early thirties, tanned but not overcooked, with minimal makeup and highlights and lowlights in her dark ponytail.

Switch out the tailored suit for one of those sports outfits and she could've been a contestant on that Ninja Warrior show.

"Loshak with no C," he agreed.

He felt a little stupid for phrasing it like that, but her joke felt like it called for something clever in return and he hadn't been able to come up with anything better on the spot.

She stuck out her hand.

"Rainie Wilson," she said. "Also with no C."

"You're with Mission Hills?"

She nodded.

"We would've been here on time, but my partner took 235 over. I'd say we sat about eight feet from our exit for at least thirty minutes. You're the profiler?" She rolled her eyes, smiling in a self-deprecating way. "OK, so I already know you are. Full disclosure, I'm a huge fan of your work."

"Alright, people, let's shake a leg," Chief Tavares said, stepping up to a clear podium at the front of the room. "I'm sure nobody wants to be here any later than we have to. Someone get that door, and we'll get started."

While Tavares directed someone else to begin passing out the packets, Rainie lowered her voice and leaned closer to Loshak.

"Your book on crime scene analysis is amazing. And nice work on that Zakarian case."

"Uh, thanks."

Loshak stopped himself from shifting uncomfortably. In the moment, shooting Zakarian had seemed like the right move—the only move—but there remained something unsettling about being praised for killing a man.

"That was you?" Pressler leaned across Spinks to punch Loshak's arm. "Holy shit, why didn't you say so? I knew you looked familiar!"

At the podium, Tavares cleared his throat and glared in their direction.

Pressler refused to take the hint.

"This is the same guy who took out that coked-up kid-killer down in Florida," the big detective said, jabbing a thick finger at Loshak repeatedly like one of those flashing neon arrows from the cartoons. "DC sent us the best of the best, ladies and gentlemen, the crème de la crème. That's French for *the cream of the cream*."

"Virginia," Rainie said.

Pressler turned to look at her.

"The FBI Academy is based in Quantico," she explained.

"Fascinating as this geographical discussion is," the chief drawled, "we've got a string of execution-style murders going around town like the flu. If nobody objects, I'd like to get to solving it before this guy can kill somebody else."

Just a barrel of pleasantness.

The dull rumble in the room quieted down, and Tavares held up a handful of papers.

"Rubio's coming around with your packets. I shouldn't have to tell you that these pages are not seen by or talked about with anybody outside the immediate task force. Any leaks I will personally seal myself with a pink slip — even if you don't work for me. With Kansas City Councilman Long's death, this whole case became about ten times more sensitive in the eyes of the press than it would have been. Now, I'm not suggesting that he's the most important out of all the victims, I'm just telling you like it is. The newshounds are hungry for any little scrap of information they can get, but they sure as hell better not get it from any of you. Got me?"

The detective with the handouts, a young guy with gelled hair, passed a copy to Loshak. Looking at the detective, Loshak wondered whether it just seemed like everybody on the force was young because he was getting old.

"If you're approached by a member of the press," Tavares continued, "everything you're allowed to disclose is on page three of your packet. If it's not covered on page three, then you have no comment."

Tavares closed the packet and held it up again. Loshak wondered if anybody could actually see the text. Tavares tapped the front page.

"Page one and two is the chain of information, along with contact info for everybody on this task force. When in doubt, bring what you have to me or to your department chief and they'll get it to me. There are no jurisdictional squabbles here, people. From now until this guy is in the bag, we're all one big loop."

The chief sat the bundle of papers down on the podium.

"What we've got on the murders so far is in pages four, five, and six. We would've had the profile Agent Loshak worked up included in the packet, but he didn't send it in time."

Spinks shot Loshak a skeptical look. Loshak gave the reporter a barely visible headshake. If this was the way the chief wanted to assert his dominance, then it was better to let him than to escalate the antagonism. There wasn't anything to be gained by turning the locals against them. And if he and Spinks really couldn't trust the locals like the mysterious note had said, then better to have the locals close where they had a chance of seeing anything underhanded rather than operating blind.

"Once he's finished giving us the rundown on our killer, we'll get a copy and have it emailed to each of you," Tavares continued. "For now, you can take notes on the back of your packet if you need to. Agent Loshak?"

Loshak pushed himself away from the wall and took Chief Tavares' place at the podium.

"Thank you, Chief." He glanced down at his notes, then out at the crowded conference room. "Behold the true believer. The zealot. We have what's known as a mission-oriented killer on our hands. Unfortunately, we don't know what he believes. But let me take a step back."

Loshak drummed his fingers against the side of the podium.

"First, we'll note the lack of evidence at the crime scenes and the cold, efficient style of the killings. These facts suggest a highly organized killer. Then we consider the staging of the bodies, the glove placed over the right eye of each victim. This is someone sending a message. To the world? Maybe. To his other targets? Probably. What's the message? We don't know. Bottom line: If we solve the message, we solve the case."

A murmur swelled through the room, but it died quickly when Loshak raised a hand.

"In any case, this is someone on a mission. For

whatever reason, either perceived or real, this guy feels like he's doing the world a public service by executing our victims. There's a good chance he'll contact the police or the media to gloat or amplify his message. If we're lucky, he might even make his end goal known. He may even believe he can convince others that what he's doing is right. There's either a tangible connection between our victims or he perceives there to be a connection."

A few of the detectives had found pens and were scratching down notes as he talked. Loshak waited a second for them to catch up.

"The probabilities suggest we're looking for a male in his mid-to-late thirties. Educated, gainfully employed, stable domestic life with a wife or partner, probably a longtime resident of the area."

Loshak hooked his jacket back and put his hands on his hips.

"Let's dispel a few misnomers while we're at it. People often confuse mission-oriented killers with visionary killers — those are the type that are unbalanced, hear voices, think murder is their divine calling, et cetera. Our guy is more likely to be sane with above-average intelligence. He's likely to be attractive, even charming. Given the lack of forced entry, there's every chance he talked his way into these vics' houses. We're not talking about someone acting on impulse or driven by lust or seeking thrills. We're talking about someone very, very organized, very focused. They think they are making the world a better place."

His irritated eye started acting up, eyelid fluttering and tear ducts working as if he'd just gotten something new in it. He didn't want to rub it, but he also didn't want to start leaking all over the place in front of everyone. Gingerly, he nudged the lower lid as he went on with the profile.

"You've heard people say, 'I can't believe so-and-so was a serial killer. He was so nice, he was so friendly. I never thought—' Well, odds are good that's what we're going to find here. Perfectionism is a likely trait, maybe even to a compulsive degree. Unless he slips up or something goes wrong for him, we're unlikely to find evidence at the crime scenes that points to him. He planned these murders out step by step and almost definitely already has his next victim picked out. Maybe the next two or three."

Loshak let that settle over the conference room for a moment, then said, "That's the other thing — our guy's not going to suddenly drop off the map and leave us wondering what happened and where he went. There will always be one more victim he perceives to be part of his mission, somebody else who needs to be disposed of. We're talking about someone who is highly motivated, highly skilled, and very clever. Someone who is passionate. Driven. Obsessed. Precise. Meticulous. Consumed with these killings — what he thinks of as his life's work. No, there will be no slowing down, no shrinking back to hide in the woodwork. The subject will keep murdering people until he's either apprehended or killed."

CHAPTER 11

The rest of the task force meeting proceeded smoothly. New potential leads were floated, and angles of attacking the investigation got locked into actionable plans.

For his part, Loshak mentioned checking out Todd Flickinger, the special teams coach that Mike Dent allegedly had an argument with. Rainie volunteered to handle the interview since nobody else wanted to make the drive to Warrensburg.

The rest of the leads were divvied up between the detectives, and then the less glamorous, ground-pounding, phone-answering jobs got handed out. With all of the decisions made, the task force meeting was adjourned.

Being so close to the door, Loshak and Spinks found themselves among the first ones out of the conference room.

"You know who gets defensive when somebody points out their attempts to avoid solving a crime?" Spinks said in a low voice as they passed through the desk pool.

Loshak rolled up his information packet and slapped it against his palm.

"Saying I'd give my profile 'if we have time,' was Tavares' way of showing he was still in control, not an Illuminati tactic to cover up a murder."

Before Spinks could respond, a voice called out from behind.

"Hey, Agent Loshak."

Rainie fell into step beside them, and Spinks tactfully let the conspiracy theorizing drop.

"I was wondering if you wanted to sit in on my interview with Flickinger. It's going to be a drive, but after all of your stuff I've read, I'd really be interested in seeing what you make of him. Anyway, it's your lead."

Loshak smiled, recognizing the friendly gesture. Among detectives, the lead was sacred. A good lead could bring about a collar, and the more collars you had, the faster your career advanced.

"Yeah, alright."

After hearing Tricia Dent describe her husband as being one person at home and a completely different person on the field, Loshak was intrigued by the idea of talking to a guy who'd been on the receiving end of Dent's harsher personality — the Mr. Hyde of Mr. Dent. Loshak gave Rainie his number.

"Let me know when you've got a time for the interview set up, and if I can make it, I'll go."

"Sweet," Rainie said with a grin.

She had a snaggletooth on the right side. Paired with the ponytail, it made the detective look about ten years old.

Spinks stepped through the lobby door out into the pale evening light, then stopped to hold it open.

"After you," he said in the joking, half-singsong tone of a radio deejay.

"Thank you, sir," the detective said, matching it.

Out in the parking lot, she started backing toward her car and pointed a finger at Loshak.

"I'll holler at you tomorrow, let you know what's going on."

Loshak nodded.

"Thanks."

"Bye, Rainie," Spinks said, twiddling his fingers in a cutesy wave.

"Later," she called back.

Spinks chuckled as they headed for the rental.

"What?"

"Nothing." The reporter shook his head in big, exaggerated sweeps and whipped out his little green notebook. "If you can't see it, then nothing."

CHAPTER 12

Loshak sighed as he entered his hotel room and closed the door behind him. He slipped his shoes off, balled and unballed his toes a few times. A big breath sucked into his lungs and eased itself out in slow motion. He let his posture sag a little as the wind vacated his chest, all the muscles in his neck and shoulders loosening.

Relief.

The bulk of the work necessary on this case still lay ahead, but he always felt relieved upon getting that first big meeting out of the way — the meet and greet, the donuts, the ceremonial shaking of hands, the element of theater that always accompanied the presenting of his profile. The pomp was over, mostly. The dog and pony show all dogged and ponied out. Now they could dispense with the pretense and focus themselves on the real work.

From next door, he heard the muffled boom of Spinks' door shutting.

When the case had come through, Loshak offered to get a double room with the reporter to save money, but Spinks had declined, saying he needed the solitude to catch up on his writing. Now that they were actually there, though, Loshak was grateful for the separate rooms. He wanted some time to decompress, and he'd never been able to do that with people from work in sight. They were a visual cue his brain couldn't or wouldn't ignore.

Loshak went to the bed, still balling and unballing his

feet. He emptied his pockets onto the nightstand.

Long day. It had seemed longer than usual, being as packed as it was with tasks. The flight in, talking with two of the widows, and then the task force meeting on top of everything else.

He'd suffered busier days with the Bureau, but something about these killings was wearing on him. It was a puzzle, and his brain refused to put the pieces down. Even while he was presenting his profile of the killer to the task force, he'd felt his brain turning the clues over, trying to find a new angle.

No known connections through their work, the geographical locations were a bust, and none of them had mutual ties to the same organizations. The closest they had to something in common was that each of the victims had been well-off financially. The first vic had been from old money; the city councilman and Mike Dent had both scraped and saved their way up to the upper-middle-class; and the last guy, Griffin, had blown up a few years back when his car dealership opened a second location.

Loshak sank onto the cheap satin comforter and tried to relax.

Maybe this interview with Todd Flickinger would shake something loose. Or maybe they would get a lucky break from the tip line. Unlike most of the places Loshak had worked, Kansas City already had an anonymous hotline set up for information pertaining to homicides. A nonprofit organization not affiliated with the police had instated it back in the day as an attempt to crack down on the unsolved murders in Kansas City, which were through the roof compared to the rest of the country due in part to the violent anti-snitch mentality of the area.

As if it realized he'd forgotten about it, Loshak's eye started itching. Not burning or stabbing, either of which would make sense with a scratched cornea, but the kind of corkscrewing itch that would only be satisfied by really digging into the affected area with fingernails. Since he wasn't quite ready to go the scratch-it-out route — not yet, at least — he had to make do scrubbing the eyelid with his knuckles. Not a great substitution.

Maybe if he ran a little cold water over it?

He sat up, intending to go into the bathroom, but a flash of blue light on the nightstand caught his attention. His phone's message light blinked on and off. He'd missed the notification because his ringer was still on silent from the meeting. He picked it up and thumbed on the display.

It was a text from Jan. A picture of her mailman petting the ugly little dog she had adopted from the shelter in Santa Fe and the caption, *World's worst guard dog.*

Loshak smirked and started to type, *If you tell him he's a bad dog, is that mutt-shaming?*

It was taking forever. He hated texting, had never really gotten the hang of zipping his thumbs around a screen, but Jan liked it, so he put up with it.

Before he could finish picking out his joke, though, a scratching, shuffling sound by the door distracted him. He glanced over, expecting a takeout menu poking up from under the sweep. Instead of a brightly colored flyer for pizza or Chinese, however, a folded, blue and white lined piece of paper slipped through.

Loshak frowned at it for a second before understanding dawned. Notebook paper.

He lurched out of bed and bolted for the door. The handle turned without a problem, but when he jerked, the door slammed to a stop with a loud *clunk*.

Shit. He'd forgotten that he flipped the security latch in place when he first came in. He snapped it off and yanked the door open. He ran out into the hall, head swiveling left to right.

Empty.

To the right was a dead end and a window that didn't open. To the left was the turn that went to the elevators.

No choice, then. Go.

In his sock feet, Loshak sprinted down the hall, grabbed the corner, and swung himself around.

No one there.

He checked the floor lights. The elevators were both on L, neither one moving.

The stairs. He crossed the little lobby and pushed through the steel door to the stairwell, this time moving quietly, staying up on the balls of his feet. He leaned over the railing and peered down, slowing his breath and trying to listen for footsteps.

Nothing.

Either they had outrun him, or they'd outsmarted him. Loshak headed back to his room, considering the possibilities. They could be in one of the rooms in his hall or have access to the cleaning closet and holed up there.

Loshak padded back the way he came and let himself into his room. Some kind of embarrassment groped around in his head, attempting to take hold, but the tension wouldn't quite flee his shoulders. The initial jolt of fear out-muscled whatever sense he had that he'd been made a fool of here.

The note still rested there, waiting for him on the carpet just inside his room. But something jutted out from inside the folded sheet of college-ruled. Another piece of paper, this one yellowed with age and covered in newsprint.

He started to reach for it, then stopped himself. Went to his suitcase and dug out a pen. He didn't want to muck up any potential prints.

With the end of the pen, Loshak flipped open the folded notebook paper. The article was upside-down to him. He craned his neck to read the headline.

LOCAL PHILANTHROPIST DEAD IN APPARENT SUICIDE

Sticking out around the back of the article were a series of black Sharpie marks. Loshak nudged the clipping aside with the pen to see what their mysterious correspondent had to say this time.

THEY BURY IT AND BURY IT
BUT IT WON'T STAY DEAD.

CHAPTER 13

A pang of disgust tempered the sense of wonder the note inspired in Loshak. Why would someone go about contacting the police this way? And why did it intrigue him so much?

After placing a call to the OPPD, he found himself staring down at the note again. He'd meant to go get Spinks as soon as he made the call but found himself stuck in the orbit of the creased scrap of paper as though caught in a whirlpool, transfixed, somehow unable to pull himself away. His thoughts tumbled around in his head, his body going totally motionless apart from his eyes dancing over that lined piece of paper again and again.

And he found the tension inside his skull ratcheting up and up as he studied those spiky letters, that doomed feeling from the Griffins' kitchen recurring once more. A creeping gray sensation.

Something was off about this case. Something even more maddening than that missing piece, that chasm where what tied the victims together should be, where what motivated the killer should be. Something dark. Hidden. It stayed just out of reach. Somehow this made him as nauseous as that stench of dead meat under the kitchen sink, the flies circling and circling.

Finally, he broke his gaze from the note and caught his reflection in the lifeless screen of his phone, noting the grimace etched onto his face. Yep. That stink face staring back at him snapped him out of the trance all at once.

His mind replayed the call. The OPPD had agreed to send a tech over to collect the note and talk to the hotel staff about security footage. Yes. Good. After reassuring himself that everything was set in that regard, he finally got Spinks.

The two of them crouched in his room, staring down at the note and its clipping.

"*They* could be a certain secret society that likes to bury what it doesn't want brought to light," Spinks said, eyes on the jagged Sharpie letters.

"They could also be the locals we're not supposed to trust," Loshak said.

He switched over from the note to the article. He'd already read through it a few times. The piece was about a local millionaire, Carter Dupont, who had committed suicide about a year-and-a-half ago. This article had been written before the police investigation, and only mentioned a few lines about the actual suicide. Apparently, Dupont had shot himself in one of the city's many parks, in a little gazebo on the edge of town. Some college kids who'd snuck into the park after hours to drink had discovered his body.

The majority of the article talked about all the community organizations Dupont was part of and how he'd been a generous contributor to dozens of local charities. It made him sound like a Midwestern Bruce Wayne, minus the Batman persona.

Spinks tugged at his chin.

"I mean, this is crazy isn't it? These notes. These murders. Have you ever had something like this when you were on a serial case?"

"Yes," Loshak said. "We talked about this as a behavioral phenomenon, remember? Berkowitz. Zodiac. BTK. Killers have been taunting the police dating back to Jack the Ripper. They like to prove how much smarter they are than us."

"So, you think what? That this is our killer leaving these notes?"

"It's not out of the realm of possibility," Loshak said. "But killer or not, secret society or not, somebody clearly thinks that this guy's death is related to our murders."

"Pretty exciting though, right?" the reporter said, wiggling his eyebrows.

Loshak frowned down at the scrap of note paper. He hated that he was so intrigued by these notes. It was as if just by being interested he was giving credibility to this ridiculous method of leaving a tip.

If whoever was leaving these had something to say about the murders, why didn't they just call the homicide hotline? There was good money in a tip that led to an arrest. But apparently, their tipster wasn't in it for the reward.

Either they'd seen one too many spy films or this actually was the killer communicating with them. There was no overt taunting, no self-identifying, but that didn't mean it wasn't the killer. Those things could come later.

Either way, they needed to follow up on it.

"So, what are you thinking?" Spinks asked. "Check this Dupont guy out?"

"Somebody wants us to."

Loshak pulled out his phone and thumbed through the contacts.

"What are you doing?"

"Calling the station to see if they can find the next of kin's contact information."

Spinks sucked in air through his teeth, his face scrunching up.

Loshak paused with his thumb over the call icon. "What?"

"Are you sure that's a good idea? I mean, think about the first note."

"I've already got an evidence tech on the way. By tomorrow, the whole task force is going to know about it. Besides, if we can get a usable print, we might be able to track down the note's author or match the print against any future crime scenes. Trusting the locals is our best bet, especially if it's the killer leaving these notes to screw with us."

Spinks blew out a long breath and scrubbed both hands up and down his face.

"This conspiracy shit is giving me a migraine," he said. "I don't know how the Illuminati have stuck with it for so long."

Loshak refrained from comment and hit the call button.

CHAPTER 14

Whatever mix of feelings Loshak had experienced upon finding the note eventually filtered down to naked curiosity.

Who was Carter Dupont, and what did he have to do with this case? That was the compound question.

From the article, Loshak knew about Dupont's suicide, of course. Looking him up online revealed a little more background on the man. He was a multi-millionaire — perhaps close to turning that *m* into a *b* — who apparently made his fortune in the "publishing industry," though Loshak couldn't pin his line of work down any more precisely than that bit of vaguery.

He was another philanthropist and serial social club participant, not unlike Neil Griffin, but where Griffin's gift of gab dominated any discussion of his persona, a pair of feature stories about Dupont gave a sense of him being a loner. Someone quiet. Someone soft. Involved in the community in outward ways, yes, but perpetually at arm's length personally. Distant. Apart. Loshak couldn't help but connect these impressions of Dupont to the seemingly unknowable people he'd been acquainted with through the years, decades' worth of enigmatic faces flashing through his head rapid fire, making him feel old.

A bone dry obituary added little color to the portrait of the man forming in the agent's head, but Loshak thought maybe that was to be expected. Suicide made obit writing tough, didn't it? What could anyone say?

If he wanted to know more about how Dupont might fit into all of this, he'd need to talk to someone who had known him.

After some interdepartmental digging, Loshak got the number for Carter Dupont's sister, his legal heir and next of kin. She'd been surprised to hear from a federal agent regarding her brother's suicide, especially after more than eighteen months had passed, but she agreed to meet with Loshak and Spinks the next morning.

From the description of Dupont in the clipping and the address in Mission Hills, Loshak was expecting a wealthy residence, maybe something like the Griffins, but as he and Spinks pulled up to the wrought iron security gate, any notion of a McMansion dried up and blew away. Mansion wasn't even the right word for it. This was a *residence* or maybe an *estate*.

A thick screen of primeval looking trees and plants with huge leaves blocked off the house from the bustling city around it. Rain had started to fall on their way over, and the way the foliage flashed and shivered with the drops made it feel like they were driving into the middle of a jungle.

A paved drive lined with a forest of honest-to-God bamboo brought them to a house that looked as if it had been designed by Frank Lloyd Wright or a very good copycat. Long, straight lines, at least four full stories with a few interrupted tiers along one side, and endless walls of nothing but glass.

A silver SUV sat running by the front door. As Loshak pulled in behind it and parked, Spinks let out a low whistle.

"You know what they say about people who live in glass houses," he said.

"Don't throw stones?"

"Don't walk around naked," Spinks said. "But I guess that's not a concern when you can afford to surround yourself with your own personal rainforest."

For once, the reporter wasn't talking about a secret society or conspiracies, but his observation triggered something in Loshak's mind, a primal suspicion of people who wanted to hide themselves from prying eyes. The property was probably a hundred years old if it was a day, and the Duponts probably weren't the original owners, they might not even have had a hand in its landscaping.

Still, Carter Dupont had chosen to live his life here, this semi-tropical hideaway tucked into the middle of the city, surrounded by people but hidden completely from view. Whether that decision had been conscious or unconscious, choosing to stay tucked back in here pointed to a dislike of being observed.

Of course, that didn't mean anything. Lots of people didn't want their neighbors breathing down their necks or felt more comfortable with barriers between themselves and the rest of the world. But it was yet another replay of that tingle of unease he'd felt at the Griffin house — as unreasonable as it turned out to be, the damn feeling wouldn't go away.

As Loshak and Spinks climbed out of the car, a woman in her early forties got out of the SUV, opening a polka dot umbrella to keep off the rain.

"Mrs. Goodrich?" Loshak asked.

"Call me Rachael."

She nodded, switching the umbrella to her left hand and reaching out with her right to shake.

"Come on, let's get in out of this."

She pulled a jangling keyring from her purse as she led them up the steps.

"Sorry I didn't already have it open."

"No need to apologize," Loshak said.

Rachael unlocked the door and shouldered it inward.

"We haven't really done anything with Carter's house since he died, and I know it's silly, but it creeps me out to be in there alone."

She glanced from Loshak to Spinks and hurried to assure them, "Not that I think it's haunted or anything like that. It's just... My brother lived here alone, you know, this huge house and no one in it but him. Thinking about him up here, lonely, maybe planning what he was going to do, I start wondering if there was something I could have done, signs I should've seen..."

She shook out her umbrella, closed it, and leaned it against the wall.

"That kind of thing gets inside your head," Spinks said in a soft voice. "It would be hard to want to be somewhere your brother spent so much time after losing him like you did."

Rachael smiled gratefully at the reporter.

"Sorry to go off on you guys."

She led them through the atrium, their steps echoing through the empty house.

"I need to do something with this place. I keep telling myself I just haven't gotten around to it, but the truth is, I don't think I can bear to give it up yet, even if I don't use it for anything. It's kind of like having a piece of him and having nothing of him at the same time."

"Were you and your brother close?" Loshak asked.

"You wouldn't think so," Rachael said. "We were fifteen years apart. He was almost out of the house by the time I was born. But our parents died when I was thirteen — car accident — and Carter let me move in with him. He was like a dad and a brother all rolled into one."

They turned in to a massive den walled on three sides in river rock. The fourth was all glass, looking out the back of the house onto an abandoned-looking infinity pool. The pool's cover dipped in the middle, supporting a small pond's worth of stagnant water and leaves, the raindrops dappling its surface and adding weight that would eventually rip the fabric.

At Rachael's urging, Loshak and Spinks took seats in a pair of Eames style lounge chairs while Rachael tried out the variety of light switches until the recessed lighting in the ceiling came on. Loshak wondered if the chairs were the real deal and figured they probably were. There was something strange about settling his ass into a chair that cost more than he made in a month.

"What did your brother do for a living?" Loshak asked.

Rachel laughed, settling on the loveseat across from him.

"We always joked that he was a spammer. You know the WestMO Trader? Or the SEMO?" She pronounced it like *see-Moe*. "Pretty much all of the Traders — Carter started those."

At their looks of confusion, she explained, "They're like newspapers, but with nothing but ads. People and

90

companies could buy a spot so they can sell stuff, seek out stuff, offer trades. Like Party Line, but in a weekly paper. It's not so popular anymore, with the internet and that sort of thing, but the old folks still like it. Anyway, Carter would get a Trader going in one part of the tri-state area, like, make them really profitable, hang on for a year or two, then sell them for stupid amounts of money to a local, and go do it all over again somewhere else. Luckily, he retired before something like Craigslist could destroy him. Carter was really good at sensing which way the wind was going to blow before it started blowing."

"That sounds really labor-intensive," Loshak said.

"Yeah," she said. "He was always on the go, but he loved it. It was like a game to him. He always called me after a sale. He would be so excited."

She stared down at her hands, her smile fading.

"I think… and looking back this is easy to say, but I think those were his high points. I think maybe he would get low in between. I always kind of wonder if maybe he'd kept at it… because he would've found something else profitable. He just had that knack."

"You mentioned Carter lived by himself," Loshak said, avoiding the word 'alone' because of the way she'd dwelled on it before. "Did he have any other family? A wife, kids?"

Rachael shook her head.

"No, he never even had a girlfriend — or boyfriend. When we were growing up, you know, it was just normal to get married and settle down. People probably suspected Carter was gay, but he never dated anybody that I knew of, male or female. I think if we'd been growing up nowadays, he would've identified as an asexual. He just lived in his

91

own little world, apart from everybody else. Except me." Her shoulders sank. "I thought he was happy. He was such a gentle, friendly guy. Soft. Sweet. He was always reminding me to enjoy the simple things in life."

"I'm sorry to have to drag you through all this again, Rachael," Loshak said.

"No, it's OK."

She put on a smile but couldn't hide the sadness at the corners of her eyes.

"It's only that it feels like I should've seen more, you know? But I thought it was just classic Carter behavior."

"I know there was no note found at the scene." Loshak had read as much in the report the Mission Hills PD had sent him the night before. "But I'm wondering if Carter ever talked to you about anything specific that might have happened to push him into suicide? Stress or financial trouble or anything?"

Already she was shaking her head no, but Loshak kept going.

"Did you find anything around the house afterward? In a lot of cases, people contemplating suicide will draft the note several times even if they eventually decide to go ahead without one."

"Honestly, I haven't gone through the house," Rachael said. "I picked out a suit for his funeral. We had a viewing. The funeral home did a great job with the reconstruction."

She blinked a few times, then returned to the question.

"I know the maid cleaned the food out of the fridge and the cabinets. Other than that, I don't think anybody's touched anything in here since Carter."

"Would you mind if we looked around for a few

minutes?" Loshak asked as gently as he could.

"Of course, yeah, that's fine," she said, then hesitated, as if she were wrestling with herself over something. "If you find anything about… about suicide… will you let me see it? I just want to know if there was anything I could've done, you know. I think that's better than wondering."

CHAPTER 15

While Rachael played on her phone in the den —
Bejeweled, from the sound of it — Loshak and Spinks split
up and searched for anything that might connect Dupont's
death to the murders.

With the size of the house and number of rooms, it was
thirty minutes before Loshak finally found a cluttered
office on the second floor.

A cabinet full of framed photos and trophies had been
built into a wall across from an enormous L-shaped
rosewood desk that dwarfed the leather rolling chair and
file cabinets behind it. Loshak scanned the photos in the
built-in — mostly pictures of a man with the same nose
and gray-green eyes as Rachael cutting ribbons, making
toasts from podiums, and shaking hands with people.
Nothing that jumped out at him.

He turned to the desk. Papers were scattered across its
top, haphazard piles of them. For some reason, based on
Rachael's description of her brother, Loshak had assumed
Dupont was a fairly neat person, but this place was a
disaster.

Loshak caught himself rubbing at his irritated eye and
stopped. Damn it. That was becoming a habit.

The messy desk seemed like their best bet at finding
something to link Dupont to the other murders. Loshak
stuck his head out into the hall and called Spinks' name a
few times but got no answer. He had to resort to his phone.

Spinks answered with, "The call's coming from inside the house!"

Loshak chuckled.

"Are you still on the second floor?"

"No, I headed up to three. So far it's more empty bedrooms, but I did find a gym full of workout equipment. Like, almost a full-sized, no-joke gymnasium."

"Well, I've got an office down here full of more papers, pictures, and general debris than I can sort through."

"On my way."

While he waited for Spinks, Loshak started sifting through the papers on the desk. It was a strange experience. He was looking at the random, weird artifacts of a life stopped short. Folders full of community betterment projects and events half-planned. Letters from charitable organizations thanking Dupont and tax receipts for his donations. On top of one pile, Loshak found a *Popular Mechanics* folded open to an article about drones. Had the guy made it to the end or had he been saving the reading for a less busy day?

Loshak had just unearthed Dupont's day planner when Spinks walked in.

"Wow," the reporter said. "I guess the maid wasn't allowed in here."

"All the more likely that we'll find something he didn't want anyone to see," Loshak said, glancing over the open page of the planner.

Dupont had killed himself in the middle of the month. There were at least a dozen appointments, a gala, and three organization meetings scheduled for the days after his death that he'd never attended.

Usually Loshak had a file to jot notes down in when he did a walkthrough on a crime scene. But since Dupont's death had been ruled a suicide, he had no such file. Instead, he had to resort to punching the names and dates into a memo on his phone. It was a slow, painful process, but texting with Jan had certainly improved his skills with the tiny keyboard. And one of these people might be the connection they were looking for to the current murder spree.

His more pessimistic side couldn't help thinking, *Or whoever left that note might be sending on us on a snipe hunt, and this is all a waste of time.*

"Sure liked to see himself getting congratulated," Spinks said. "It's like a shrine to what a great guy he was."

Loshak glanced up to find the reporter hunched over in front of the built-in staring at the photos.

"His sister said he spent most of the time he wasn't building up those advertiser papers alone," Loshak said. "Maybe charity work and community events were the only way he could see himself as being part of the world. Or maybe they made him feel like he wasn't just taking."

Spinks made a sound in his throat. "Must not've been enough."

Considering this, Loshak turned back to the planner. Dupont had killed himself on the fourteenth. There was a reminder on the thirteenth that said *RBS tutors awards banquet.* If Dupont had already been depressed, he might've hung on until the banquet hoping it would bring him out of the funk, then killed himself afterward when he realized that black ache inside of him was still there, the way people did after major holidays.

He added another note to his phone — *ask sister about moods post-event.*

"Whoa." Spinks swiped a framed photo off one of the built-in's shelves and brought it to Loshak. "I think I just connected our billionaire to Griffin."

The picture was of Dupont and a lean, red-faced man standing shoulder to shoulder, both toasting the camera with highball glasses of some yellowish alcohol. Whoever had taken it hadn't heard that you're not supposed to use the on-board flash for pictures; the light made the men's eyes red and their cheeks shine like they were coated in grease.

"That's not Neil Griffin."

"Not the tall guy." Spinks tapped the left side of the photo. "Look. Recognize this heebie-jeebies factory?"

Then Loshak saw it. Behind the men was a display case of rare butterflies and moths encased in glass.

"You think this was taken in Griffin's house?"

Spinks shrugged.

"How many people in this city do you think have cocktail parties in a room decorated with dead bugs?"

They headed back downstairs with the picture. Rachael was still in the den. She looked up from her game as they came in.

"Do you know anyone named Neil Griffin?" Loshak asked.

She shook her head and pushed the button to send her phone to sleep.

"Doesn't sound familiar."

"Your brother never mentioned him?"

"Not that I remember," she said.

Spinks passed her the photo.

"Do you know the man your brother's with in this picture?"

She glanced at it, then up at the reporter.

"No. Is he this Griffin guy?"

"No." Loshak shook his head. "But Griffin was into a lot of charities and projects around the city. We think it's possible this picture may have been taken in his house during a party."

"Well, if he was involved with half as many local organizations as Carter, then they must've crossed paths at least once or twice," Rachael said.

"Would it be alright if we took this picture with us?" Loshak asked.

She gazed down at the photo of her brother for a long beat, then let out a breath.

"Yeah, I don't see why not," she said with a shrug. "If it helps, then it's what Carter would've wanted."

CHAPTER 16

Loshak hesitated in the car outside of the Griffin house. Let his gaze scan the brick facade. Licked his lips.

Why did he feel so off about this place?

He didn't know. Like so many things about this case, he did not know. He scowled a little at the thought, which made his eyelid hurt.

Motion caught the edge of Loshak's vision when Spinks moved to get out of the car. After a beat, the agent followed suit. It felt strange to budge, to advance in the face of the bad feelings this place gave him.

His fingers found the door handle and pulled, but he kept his eyes trained on the house all the while as though it might sneak off if he looked away.

Just like the day before, as they walked up the sidewalk to the Griffin house, Loshak's palms started to sweat. His skin crawled with the feeling that he was being observed, that he trod now in the presence of something dark. Sinister. Unknowable. The feeling seemed to intensify with every step.

This photo of Dupont in the Griffin house could mean nothing. Even if Dupont attended a fundraiser or cocktail party in the Griffins' house, what would they do with that information? It may have been a one-time meeting, a passing of boats in the night. In fact, it was probably nothing.

But it felt like something.

Loshak entered the code the OPPD had given him and opened the door, letting Spinks precede him.

First they would make sure the photo was actually taken in this house. See if the butterflies in the case matched up. If they did, they could take the photo to Pam Griffin and see if the widow knew the man next to Dupont.

If.

Spinks seemed much more confident about this whole endeavor. The reporter moved through the foyer and down the darkened hall toward the cocktail room, arms swinging, strides long, feet kicking out with each step, as if he couldn't wait to get there and prove that his theory was correct.

As Loshak passed the kitchen, that smell hit him again. The smell of death. Again, it triggered the irrational caveman part of his mind and made the hairs on the back of his neck stand up. He knew it was only the garbage rotting away under the sink. Nothing to be afraid of. No reason for this uneasy feeling in the pit of his stomach.But he couldn't shake that weird nervousness.

By the time he got to the cocktail room, Spinks was already staring into the display case with his nose nearly pressed to the glass.

"I think it's the same one," he said without looking away. "I think these are all the same moths and butterflies."

He passed the photo off toLoshak. Loshak held it up. Glanced from it to the display case. Moved back to gain some perspective.

In the photo, the case was behind the men and to their left. But here in real life, something was off. A wet bar stood where the men would have. No hint of it in the photo. And the wall the case was against, it was too long, didn't match up with the one in the photo.

"I don't know…" Loshak shook his head. "It doesn't quite match the room in this."

Spinks grabbed the photo out of his hands. "It has to match. I'm sure these butterflies and moths are the same. Positive. Look, the big green one is in the exact same spot. And that really wide one there. What are the odds anyone else has their butterflies pinned in the exact same order as Griffin?"

"Something's off," Loshak insisted.

Spinks looked from the photo to the room. Photo. Room. He backed up, turned around, then turned back.

"They moved the furniture," he said. "Rearranged stuff sometime since this was taken. They moved the display case behind the wet bar, and now it doesn't match up."

Loshak leaned over Spinks' shoulder to get a better look at the picture. It was possible.

"Help me move this thing," he said.

The display case was light but awkward. It took both of them to keep from tipping it over as they moved it across the room to the long wall.

And it still didn't match the photo perfectly. The wet bar was in the way.

Loshak opened the wet bar's doors, moving bottles aside so he could check in the bottom corners. It wasn't anchored to the floor. The thing was insanely heavy, though. Between him and Spinks, they were struggling to move it. Eventually they were able to scoot it back enough to get a clear view of the display case and the place where the men would have been standing.

"Look," Spinks said. "The pictures."

Apparently when Pam and Neil Griffin had decided to move their furniture around, they'd left the pictures on the wall in the same place. Over the Dupont and the red-faced man's shoulder in the photo, Loshak could see framed pictures on the wall, each one in the exact same place it was today. The flash glared off the glass in the frames, making it impossible to make out what was in the photos, but each one was the same shape. Even the three offset panels connected to one another.

Spinks saw the expression on his face and nodded. The reporter brought his fingers to his mouth and kissed them loudly like a cartoon chef.

"Perfecto," he said.

It matched.

CHAPTER 17

After staring at the scene for a minute, Loshak let out a long breath. The whole thing was a let-down somehow. All this build-up, but what did this reveal really mean? What did the connection lead to?

The picture matched. So what? It was the same house. Dupont had been here. All of that still meant basically nothing. This didn't tell them who the killer was. It might connect a suicide case to one of their murder victims, but that didn't tell them how their anonymous tipster thought Dupont was connected to the case overall.

That two-word question repeated in Loshak's mind like a refrain:

So what?

"Huh," Spinks muttered, staring at him.

"What?"

"Nothing." The reporter pulled out his notebook and started flipping pages. "I just thought you'd be more excited is all."

Loshak shrugged. "It didn't exactly break the case, did it?"

"No, but—"

A shrill scream came from Loshak's pocket. He dug the phone out. It was Rainie. He thumbed the button and answered.

"Hey, I just got a time set up with Flickinger," the young detective said. Loshak thought he could hear a pen tapping in the background. "Tomorrow. One-thirty in the afternoon. We'll have to leave here at about noon to make it. Are you still game?"

"Yeah, sure." Loshak jerked his head at Spinks and started down the hall toward the foyer. There was nothing else they could do here. "Meet you at the Mission Hills station?"

"That would be perfect."

"Thanks for the heads-up."

"Yep."

As Loshak hung up and tucked the phone back into his pocket, motion in the corner of his eye caught his attention. Spinks had taken a hard right into the kitchen.

"What are you doing?" Loshak followed.

"It reeks in here, and apparently nobody's going to do anything about it."

Spinks wove his way around the island toward the garbage can cabinet.

"The woman just lost her husband. She shouldn't have to come home to a house that stinks like a diaper full of rotten meat."

"Look, Spinks, I understand that you want to help her out, but this place hasn't been released yet. You can't—"

But the reporter was already pawing open the cabinet and rolling out the garbage can.

They both stared down at the black plastic bin, speechless.

It was empty.

Loshak sniffed.

Was it his imagination or was the smell actually fainter in here than in the hall?

And then it was back, that creeping dread. Some electric impulse he didn't understand tingling through the core of his body.

He rushed back into the hallway, sniffing as he went, following the stench like a bloodhound. Away from the foyer and front door, toward the back of the house. He made it to the mud room looking out on the patio and realized he'd lost it. The smell had faded again.

He backtracked to where it had been stronger. Right in front of the laundry room.

In spite of the relatively early hour, the sun wasn't shining in through the slatted wooden blinds. The washer and dryer stood in the shadows, like monsters poised for the ambush. Some primal unease made him recoil at the idea of going in while it was dark like that.

Loshak reached in and felt around the wall for the switch. He flipped it on, flooding the little room with yellow light. That sapped a little of the creepy feeling from the room. Just a little.

When he stepped in, the smell hit him full in the face. He held his breath and walked around a hamper full of clothes and towels, glancing in between the washer and dryer, then leaning over them to make sure nothing had crawled back there and died.

Other than lint, it was clear.

"Oh, jeez." Spinks gagged and turned away from the laundry room, hand over his mouth. "What is it? Dead rat?"

Loshak didn't answer. He'd smelled dead rats before, and he'd smelled this, and they were nothing alike. His instincts had recognized it that first day they were here, but

105

he'd pushed the warnings aside, told himself it was the meat rotting in the garbage because that was easier to comprehend in a place like this. In a way, he'd bought into that false suburban security as thoroughly as the Griffins had.

The laundry room door didn't open all the way. It bumped on the washing machine. Loshak swung it out, blocking his view of Spinks, and letting light in behind it.

There. A hatch cut into the tile on the floor between the door and the washer, most likely a crawlspace.

Loshak hooked his finger through the handle and opened the access door.

A cloud of buzzing flies burst from the gaping blackness beneath the house. The smell of death was overwhelming.

CHAPTER 18

The officer in charge of the scene made a big show of making all the uniforms draw toothpicks to see who had to be the first one to climb down into the crawlspace. Even so, rookie Bud O'Laughlin thought there was a pretty good chance the game was rigged. Surely some trickery must be at play, some sleight of hand to haze the new guy, to make him think everyone had an equal chance of going down in that black hole.

Because of course he drew the short toothpick. He knew it before he even saw the splintered end leave Greisbaum's fist.

Now Bud squeezed down the hallway past the rest of the uniforms, trying not to hook gun belts. His sidling steps made him feel stupid, and his legs were going numb from the nerves.

It almost felt like an out-of-body experience. Mind blank. The world oddly distant. He watched the scene with the camera in his head somehow zoomed out.

All the milling police gawked at him, the chosen one, though they avoided eye contact. Every face held a slightly queasy expression. Pursed lips. Wrinkled noses. And no wonder. It reeked like roadkill, even all the way out here.

Snider and Trendt were coming out of the laundry room, packing a sump pump and a bucket. There'd been a small amount of standing water resting atop the earth floor of the crawlspace. Obviously, they had cleared that. Bud wouldn't have to wait around to go in.

No lines at The Crawlspace, a cartoony carnival barker crowed in Bud's head. *No waiting here, folks. Step right up! Hurry, hurry!*

"Here ya go." Instead of a ticket to ride, Greisbaum forked over a pair of latex gloves, an LED headlamp on a stretchy band, a ventilation mask, and a garden trowel.

"Thanks."

The word came out slowly, and his voice didn't sound like his own. He swallowed after speaking it, something clicking in his throat.

Bud stuck the trowel in his belt and pulled on the gloves, then the headlamp. He had one like it at home for coon hunting, though his was a higher wattage. The ventilator was trickier, and he ended up having to take off the headlamp and pull the mask on over his head before putting the lamp back on.

The laundry room was big enough that Greisbaum and the pair of Feds only had to scoot back to let Bud inside. Two more sidling steps, and he was in, shoulders squared toward the next threshold.

Behind the door, the hatch stood open. A yawning black square, like a mini version of those blackout rooms in haunted houses.

Bud's breathing sounded unnaturally huge in the ventilator, and his hands shook a little as he clicked on the light. The LEDs lit up the black hole, showing earth the color of used coffee grounds instead of impenetrable darkness.

"Alright," he said because it seemed like everyone was waiting on him, watching him. The words didn't break up the tension in the laundry room like he'd hoped they would.

Bud sat on the floor with his feet in the hole. They dangled. The ground was farther down than it looked. He grabbed either side of the hatch and lowered himself until his shoes hit dirt. They sank almost a full inch before stopping. Thick muck. Almost fudgy. He should've asked them to wait while he ran back home and grabbed his hip waders.

He paused there a moment, still boxed in by the tiny square of light streaming in through the hatch, protected in some small way from the dark. He took a few breaths, the ventilator rasping a little. His heart thundered in his chest, thrummed against his ribs. He squeezed his eyes shut.

If he just stayed here, halfway into the crawlspace, none of this would become all the way real, would it? He wouldn't see whatever terrors gave off this wretched stench, wouldn't etch any nightmare images into his memory for keeps. Whatever was down here, it couldn't touch him.

When he opened his eyes, though, the muck and the dark still lay before him. The nightmare had failed to vanish, no matter how hard he willed it so.

At last, he lowered himself the rest of the way. Better to get it over with. He'd be fine. He swallowed, a lump the size of a racquetball bobbing in his throat.

The floor joists were too low for Bud to duck-walk through the crawlspace and save his uniform pants. He knew a rookie who was going to the dry cleaner's tonight.

After another beat of hesitation, he lowered himself onto hands and knees. The ground was cold. Its wetness seeped through to touch his knees right away. He couldn't help but shudder.

He gritted his teeth. On with it.

Bud wormed forward in a half-crawl, prodding at the dirt with the trowel every couple feet. The smell was so much worse down here, even through the ventilation mask. Like that time in high school when he'd been jogging past a dead possum out on 291, and a truck had driven past and popped its bloated corpse right in front of him, except this was multiplied by a few hundred.

The humidity inside the mask didn't help. Tendrils of vapor steamed in and out with every breath, or so it seemed. Warm and wet and foul. Felt like he was breathing in extra chunky soup, in the new Roadkill flavor.

The image of a soup bowl full of chowder with stringy black hair floating on top swam through his head. Made him gag.

He brought the back of his wrist to the place where the ventilator covered his mouth. Had to stop thinking before he barfed.

Focus. Get it over with.

Just prod with the trowel, lift, and turn. Prod, lift, turn. Nothing else.

The trowel hit something solid, ringing out an almost musical note. On the lift, a white stick poked up out of the dirt.

Bud set the trowel aside and swiped the crumbles of wet dirt away from the stick with his gloved fingers. When he reached the end of the first stick and saw that it was butted up against another one of approximately the same size and shape, he started unconsciously nodding his head. This was what they'd been expecting, after all. And here they were.

Bones. Fingers, if he wasn't mistaken. And he didn't think he was, even though this was the first time seeing human remains in the field. What was the Latin term? *Phalanges.*

Bud blinked, realizing his vision was blurring out. He had to sniff hard to clear his sinuses enough to breathe. He was crying.

Chest heaving. Shoulders rocking. Water pouring from his eyes. Strange whimpers streaming out of his mouth.

Weeping like a little baby.

He needed to get it together. Needed to find his way back to the hatch and let everyone know. Needed to breathe.

And from somewhere in the blurred heat of his blubbering, a distant part of him offered a comforting thought:

At least he hadn't thrown up in the ventilator.

CHAPTER 19

From the start of the actual demolition process, it took two hours for the police to rip the laundry room floor out to get at the crawlspace. Loshak watched it all from the periphery.

In addition to the uniforms, officers in plain clothes had been called in on their day off to help. They disconnected the washer and dryer, lugged them down the hall into the mudroom. Chipped out tiles and pulled up brand new looking subflooring, leaving behind a gaping emptiness where the floor should be. A void. A weird drop from where Loshak stood down into the wet black earth below. It was like leaning over the edge of the Hoover Dam or Grand Canyon in miniature, a scene somehow totally wrong when found inside of a house. Forbidden. Perverse. This mud pit in the center of a house was something that should not be, should not exist. It remained disorienting no matter how long he stared down into it.

Spotlights shined down into the crawlspace, illuminating wet dirt flecked with bones. A full skeleton lay visible off in the corner, curled in a semi-fetal position, all but its surface still submerged in the dirt. Presumably, the water had washed the top layer of soil away, exposing just its profile like those perfect dinosaur fossils on display in every museum.

One body toward the middle looked reasonably fresh, its skin gone waxy and yellow-gray as it rotted. Probably the primary source of the odor. It sprawled facedown in the dirt. Prone. No facial features to look at, arms folded unnaturally under the bulk of the torso.

At first, Loshak thought this fresh corpse had been buried in boots. A second glance, however, let him know he was staring down at heels bloated to many times their regular size by decay and standing water. He couldn't stop looking at those swollen, dead feet.

After the first full sheet of subflooring came out, Spinks had had to step outside. The smell had become overwhelming, billowing up at them like warm updrafts on the highway, and the reporter's nose and stomach were too sensitive to take it.

Good thing he'd gone. A ventilation mask shielded Loshak's face, but now that all of the crawlspace under the laundry room had been exposed, he felt like he was standing in a thick fog of death. He could feel the smell working its way into his pores.

But the first wave of poking around provided a fresh revelation: The burial site didn't end at the edge of the laundry room. The mass grave continued on, seemingly spread under the entire footprint of the house.

Loshak watched, a silent spectator. The Overland Park Chief made the call to take down the wall between the laundry room and the living room after confirming it was not load-bearing. It would give them easier access to the remains and help clear a path so they could move the bodies out in bags when the time came.

Decision made, police personnel swarmed around Loshak to commence further demolition. Sledgehammers and Sawz-Alls were brought in. Without hesitation, the symphony of destruction kicked its volume all the way up.

They brought in wide planks to lay over the floor joists and allow easier movement through the now floorless laundry room. Loshak crossed one to move to the hall, trying to stay clear of the white dust spreading as a sheet of drywall caved in.

Chunks of the wall seemed to fall out of the way on cue, giving him access to watch the proceedings once more. From his new vantage point, he peered through the growing opening into the grave, still finding it bizarre and even a touch nauseating to look down through a gaping hole at mud from this fresh angle.

Cameras flashed as crime scene techs documented the exact placement of everything in the crawlspace and the room next door. A couple more techs squeezed back and forth between everyone, filming. No one wanted to miss anything. It all had to be properly documented before they could begin bagging evidence. And bodies.

CHAPTER 20

After a while, the crush of personnel started to feel stifling. Suffocating.

Loshak fled the laundry room, where the techs currently slogged through the processing and bagging of the eleventh set of remains.

He slipped down the hall to a cavernous and unoccupied living room. It felt good to move into an open space, to avert his eyes from that damn death pit beneath the house, to be out away from the churning mass of police working the scene. Something loosened in his chest, made it easier to breathe again, though the ventilator still rasped a little with each inhale.

Through the blinds, he could see the front lawn. A crowd had gathered outside, neighbors standing along the police tape border. Soccer moms. Polo-shirted dads. A few slacker-looking teenagers. All of them fidgeting. Jumpy. Restless. A herd of cattle waiting for the smallest scare to spook them into stampeding.

The creaking of a gurney wheel let Loshak know that the next body was on its way out. A few seconds later, the front door opened.

In the crowd, eyes opened too wide, blinking slowly. Trembling hands lifted to chins and brows as if they could shield themselves from what had happened. Here. On their very street. Inside the walls of their beautiful gated community. One older woman started shaking her head, puff of blue-gray hair flopping a little, her lips quivering.

She probably felt entitled to something better than this. They probably all did. It was like they'd been swindled into paying out the nose for a place here, promised safety and protection. A defense against traffic sounds, ugly streets, loud neighbors. Against anxiety. Against murder.

But Loshak knew better. It was a violent world, every square foot of it, no matter how many walls or gates you built. No matter how far humans advanced, some part of them could never be tamed. A mindless, raping, awful thing etched somewhere in our DNA. Chaotic and savage and indiscriminate. No amount of money could protect you from it.

Loshak let the wood slats fall back into place. He couldn't stay in here. He needed to get away from the crowd, away from all that panic filling the air, surrounding the front of the house.

With some maneuvering, he made it back through the hallway and out into the back yard, peeled the ventilator off his face.

He shut his eyes and inhaled the fresh air. He could still smell the death. Could still see that freshest of the bodies, face down in the crawlspace. Its heels, so bloated that they looked like boots.

Loshak walked out onto that heaven of patios, running his eyes over the massive barbecue pit, the outdoor flat screen, the resort-quality chairs and tables. Along the wall of the house, there was a beer garden with a little tiki hut bar. He took a peek behind it. A keg.

How often had the Griffins entertained with all those bodies tucked away in the crawlspace a few feet away?

Loshak tried sitting in one of the chairs, but he couldn't find a position that didn't feel awkward and tense. He got up again and walked from the tiki bar to the barbecue pit and back. It felt strange to be alone, but the pacing seemed to calm him.

Slowly, the facts began to tumble through his head with some measure of clarity. Emotions came next, his conscious mind becoming aware of them a little at a time. It felt as if he'd been holding his breath for a long time, but now he could finally start to breathe again.

Shock was the first thing anyone felt when faced with horrors like this. Loshak had seen it on the faces of the police working down in the dirt. Vacant looks. Emptiness behind the eyes. Even that rookie who'd started crying hadn't really had an expression on his face, just a blankness, a distance.

A grisly scene such as this one wasn't something the human mind could process right away. That initial horror was always partly undermined by sheer disbelief, the brain rejecting what the eyes were seeing.

But time passed, and the depth of that revulsion crept over you little by little. Made you squirm and twitch.

Words echoed in Loshak's head. The same words that his mind had spoken over and over as he watched the remains excavated from the muddy slop of the crawlspace:

The victim was a killer.

Neil Griffin, the model citizen who'd given so much to the community, who'd been murdered in his own home, must have been a serial killer of some kind. It was the only explanation for a scene as awful as this, a damn cemetery under the floorboards of an upscale suburban home.

Goosebumps plumped on his forearms just thinking about it.

The victim was a killer.

The victim was a killer.

The victim was a killer.

How *the fuck* could that make any sense?

Could that be why he'd been killed? The graveyard under the floorboards was too big of a coincidence in relation to his death to even fathom. But if Griffin's murder was in some way connected to the bodies, what did it mean about the other recent victims? Each one posed with one eye covered?

Loshak wasn't sure, but the gooseflesh spread over his shoulders and down his back as he pondered it.

The screen door opened, and Spinks came out onto the patio from wherever he'd been hiding. He shuffled over to where Loshak had stopped in his endless circuit of the bar and barbecue pit.

"Hey."

Spinks' voice was hushed, and his shoulders were sort of hunched up, as if he were waiting on an explosion or some big scare. The drop of some other shoe.

"You alright?" Loshak asked.

"Yeah. Yeah." Spinks inhaled a deep breath through his nose, then let it out. "I mean, it's pretty weird, right?"

"What's that?"

"We were in there, you know?" The reporter glanced over his hunched shoulder at the house. "Yesterday we walked through this place, and we had no clue what lay beneath our feet. How could we just not know? How did we not even feel it? All that…"

118

Spinks waved a hand, then shook his head, for once finding himself at a loss for words.

"All of it."

Loshak's mind jumped back to the bloated heels of that freshest body, then to his own attempts to push down his instinctive caveman reaction to the smell of death.

"Sometimes I think we just see what we expect to see," he said. "The darkest things have a way of hiding in plain sight, it seems like. The shadows, you know? Even when we're looking for them, we don't see what's really there until it bludgeons us in a way that we can no longer ignore."

"Like a house full of bodies," Spinks said.

Loshak nodded. "Just like that."

CHAPTER 21

The ground beneath the house looked wounded now. Pocked. Excavated. Empty. It lay vacant of its previous occupants, indentations left where the bones had been dug out.

Loshak found himself staring down into the muck for long stretches. He didn't know why. He didn't even know why he was still here. Nevertheless, he stood on the edge of the hole and stared down into the shadows, into the hollowed places carved in the dirt.

The crime scene techs worked until after midnight, logging and bagging evidence and carrying out bodies. They marched in and out of the muddy trench beneath the house, fulfilling their various duties like ants patrolling their hill.

Eventually the crowd dispersed, inside and out. The suburban types out front with their bellies pressed tightly against the police tape thinned until none remained.

With the demolition work complete, most of the officers were sent home as well. Even Spinks headed out, calling a cab for a ride back to their hotel.

Loshak stayed for all of it. Watched as the body bag count continued to rise. It was as if he were holding some sort of silent vigil by the work lamps that had been brought into the house, shining their harsh glow down into the hole.

Finally, the techs wheeled out the last bag. The

ambulance drove out of Prairiefire Estates, siren off, no lights flashing. Loshak was alone except for the pair of OPPD officers stationed outside to keep watch over the crime scene.

The floor had been stripped away throughout most of the house for complete access to the mass grave now. Loshak had to walk on the paths made by the narrow plank bridges as he made his way into the living room. Once there, he stopped and just stood, staring down into the tiny squared-off pits in the dirt. They'd had to bring the sump pump back in twice while the techs were working, and already the pits were gathering new water. Pooling. Turning into tiny lakes.

Loshak's phone vibrated against his side. He pulled it out and read the screen. It was Jan.

He'd never gotten around to texting her back yesterday, he realized. He thumbed the call icon.

"Hey."

"He lives," Jan said cheerfully.

"If you call this living. Sorry I forgot to text you back. I had a pretty good joke about mutt-shaming lined up and ready to go."

She chuckled. "Sounds iffy."

"It was." He glanced down at his watch. It was almost 2 AM. "What time is it out there?"

"Just after midnight. I figured if I wanted to catch you off work, my best bet was the wee hours."

Loshak couldn't think of anything to say. He rolled his lips together, glancing down at the slowly deepening puddles beneath his feet.

Jan sighed. "I didn't catch you off work."

"Technically, I don't think I'm on the clock right now. Nobody approved me for overtime, anyway."

"What are you doing, Vick?" she asked in that disapproving, concerned tone of voice that said she already knew the answer.

He could see her shoving her fingers into her blonde hair, combing it back in frustration.

"I'm thinking," Loshak said. "My job is basically to think, isn't it?"

She ignored this.

"What is it there? Two in the morning?"

"Not quite," he hedged.

"You need rest."

They're kids. The words were on the tip of his tongue, trying to get out, but they wouldn't have any context for Jan. No meaning except for the obvious shock value of knowing he was working a serial killer case and now it was about kids.

The forensic people hadn't identified any of the bodies yet, but they knew for sure almost all of them were under the age of twenty. About half male and half female from what they could determine so far. Odds were good that there would be at least one body down there Shelly's age. As if this case needed any added horror.

Loshak realized he hadn't said anything for a while.

"I didn't figure I would get much sleep anyway, so I'm just going over a few of the details to see if I missed anything."

He heard Jan exhale softly on the other end of the line. What was there to say? She probably felt like she didn't have any right anymore to get after him for working too much. Maybe she didn't. They were divorced, after all. But it still felt like she did.

While he thought, Loshak's eyes kept returning to those dark spaces down below where the work lamps didn't reach. Corners and ends and little pits where bodies lay just a few hours earlier, now pools of shadow and water.

How could he make sense of all this? How could he look into those dark places and find meaning? How could anyone?

"I'm going to turn in soon," he said finally.

"OK."

She didn't sound convinced.

Loshak couldn't blame her. He didn't believe it, either.

CHAPTER 22

Loshak stood in the hotel shower trying to wash the stench of decaying corpses off his hands and arms when he heard slapping feet on the tile floor. The footsteps drew closer, louder. Right behind him. They sounded spongy, too soft to be made by living tissue.

When he glanced over his shoulder, the shower curtain had grown shorter. He could see under it.

On the white tile stood a pair of waxy yellow-gray feet, so swollen that they looked like boots, the nails coming loose, ready to fall away at the slightest touch.

Panic paralyzed him. He cowered under the hot spray of the shower, unable to look away from those dead feet, unable to blink, unable to breathe as they came closer. They stopped an inch away from the tub.

"Dad?"

A shrill scream pierced the hotel bathroom. It was him. The voice plus the feet plus the fear, it was all too much. Loshak tried to twist away, to run, but he stayed rooted to the spot.

The scream came again. Except it didn't sound human. It hadn't the first time, either, he realized. That was… his phone?

The epiphany broke whatever spell the bloated corpse feet had over him. A weight lifted from him right away, let him out from under it.

Loshak struggled up from the depths of the dream,

slapping around the nightstand for his phone. His hand connected, knocking it to the floor. He leaned over the edge of the bed and picked it up.

"Loshak," he answered.

"Hey Agent, it's Rainie. Detective Wilson. Did I wake you up?"

Loshak cleared his throat.

"No, sorry, I just got out of the shower."

"Oh, OK." She sounded satisfied with that answer. "I was just calling to let you know that with the emergency task force meeting today, the interview with Flickinger got pushed to Thursday. You still in?"

Before he thought better of it, Loshak rubbed his tired eyes. The left one flared up instantly. He stifled the accompanying wince.

"I'm in," he said, then thought of how many unforeseen turns this investigation had already taken. "Assuming there are no more surprises in store for us."

"Cool."

Rainie could've ended the conversation there, but instead of signing off, she hesitated.

"It's really awesome what you did. Finding the, uh, bodies and whatnot, I mean. There's no telling whether anyone ever would've known they were there if you hadn't."

"It was my—" Spinks wasn't really his partner, so what was he supposed to call the reporter? His biographer? Jesus, that sounded conceited. "—consultant. He sniffed them out."

"Well, anyway, it's great. It's like we've got so much more to go on now."

Loshak didn't see a cemetery's-worth of unidentified bodies showing up just in time to complicate an already convoluted case quite the same way, but he kept that to himself.

"Yeah," he said.

"Anyway," Rainie said again, "see you at the meeting."

"Sure thing."

He hung up and checked the time on the phone. He had a little over an hour to get dressed, find Spinks, and get over to the Prairie Village station.

With a groan, he shoved the covers off. Sat up. Stretched, popping pretty much everything from the back of his skull to his toes. It all ached. It felt like he'd gone five rounds with Royce Gracie, the angry stabbing in his eye included.

Jan had been right, of course. He wasn't a rookie anymore. He couldn't pull late nights like that and expect to make it out unscathed.

Loshak lurched out of bed and stumbled into the bathroom, slapping on the light. He only had a vague memory of the dream he'd been having when the phone rang — mostly feelings of dread and deep, disturbing, gut-churning sickness, the kind of nausea that reaches all the way down to afflict the emotions, what people call being sick at heart — but the brightness made him feel a little better.

He ran some cold water in the sink, splashing a little onto his eye. That just made it hurt worse. He dabbed at it with one of the sandpapery wash clothes and checked it in the mirror. The lid looked puffier than ever. Swollen and fat and purplish like a wad of grape gum that had been chewed up and stuck to his eyeball. The sight made him grunt a little, not much more than a catch of breath in the back of his throat.

Stubble coated his jaw, going more toward the salt side of salt and pepper, and the lines at the corners of his eyes seemed extra deep today. The bags under them looked like they could hold ten pounds of flour. Little red veins crisscrossed the whites of his eyes.

Haggard. He looked haggard as hell.

Wasn't much he could do about that. He turned on the shower, searching out that sweet spot of just a little too hot. The water probably wouldn't do much to improve his looks, but maybe it would help ease some of the stiffness in his muscles.

CHAPTER 23

It was standing room only again in Conference Room A. Loshak hung near the back with Spinks, Rainie, and an overfriendly Pressler who kept whispering with the reporter. They huddled along the wall, making themselves skinny over and over to let people past. There seemed to be a lot of that: movement, fidgeting, people shuffling around the room like they were playing musical chairs.

Restless. Agitated. This task force meeting seethed energy, anguish, a sense of drama — already more animated than the first meeting before it even began. The spectacle of the crawlspace grave proved too stimulating to deal with, Loshak thought, somehow set everybody off like a bunch of preschool kids jacked up on candy and Kool-Aid.

Nobody seemed to be able to sit still and be quiet, even after Chief Tavares stepped up behind his lectern and boomed his opening speech over the din.

The chief laid out the new information just in case anybody in the tri-state area missed that they'd pulled thirteen sets of human remains from beneath their fourth victim's house, then called the consulting forensic anthropologist up to address them.

When Dr. Marion took the podium, however, the room fell silent. Funny how that worked. This was the main event, Loshak realized. Everyone here wanted an explanation, some kind of logic or cause and effect interpretation that could make sense of all those bodies they'd unearthed beneath Neil Griffin's house, place them into the context of the recent murders, satisfy the maddening curiosity that plagued them all.

"Thank you, Chief Tavares," she said, shuffling through her papers. "We don't have a lot of information yet, and we haven't been able to make any identifications. I'll be direct about this: Without a lucky break, I suspect it will take weeks, maybe even months before we start putting names and faces to these remains. Some of them might even go unidentified despite our best efforts."

Loshak's gaze ran through the crowd. He saw clenched jaws and furrowed brows. No one in law enforcement liked even a single Jane or John Doe. A baker's dozen of unidentified corpses being dumped in their laps was overwhelming, almost too much to stomach.

Dr. Marion adjusted her glasses and continued.

"Here's what we do know: We've got adolescents of both sexes, six female, seven male. The ages range from about ten or eleven years old at the youngest to approximately twenty at the oldest. All but one have been deceased for several months to several years. A more definitive time of death for each set of remains will take longer to pinpoint, but the latest victim is a Jane Doe of about twelve or thirteen, dead less than a week. The pathologist has his own report with specifics on that victim, so I'll keep my presentation focused on the others."

Dr. Marion gestured at a thin older man sitting in the front row. A pair of sleepy-looking eyes peered out from under dark, bushy eyebrows.

"Eight of the victims were found with ligatures still

around their cervical vertebrae, indicating the cause of death as strangulation. Five of the ligatures were made from a braided blue and white nylon cord. We found an identical spool in the Griffins' garage."

She lifted an eight-by-ten crime scene photo showing the rope next to a numbered evidence marker.

"In addition to the evidence of perimortem strangulation, a majority of the remains have antemortem fractures in various states of healing: wrists, ribs, one collarbone, and countless fingers."

"Does that mean they were tortured before death?" someone near the front asked.

Dr. Marion chewed her lip, gazing at the ceiling while she spoke.

"It could, but it's difficult to rule out other possibilities. For example, the fractures could mean that the victims were held captive for some time before being killed, and the injuries were sustained when they tried to loosen bonds or escape. Or they may have struggled with the killer at some point. It's likely we'll never know for certain."

The anthropologist reshuffled her notes and then clutched the pile of papers to her chest.

"I'll be doing a full work-up on each set of remains in an effort to pinpoint age, stature, and race. I've also contacted a forensic odontologist to assist with attempting to identify the victims through dental records. If no one has any other questions, I'll hand things over to Dr. Alexandrou."

She traded places with the lanky pathologist, who wasted no time launching into his findings.

"As Dr. Marion mentioned, the most recent victim is an

adolescent female. Approximately twelve or thirteen years of age. Dark brown hair. Five-feet-two-inches tall. The postmortem interval is somewhere in the range of five to six days."

The pathologist spoke with just a hint of a European accent.

"Ligature marks indicate strangulation as the cause of death. Additionally, the pattern of diagonal grooves left in the skin matches that of the blue-and-white nylon rope found on the other victims. I also found evidence consistent with sexual assault: the cervicovaginal swab was positive for semen. A sample has been sent to the lab for DNA testing."

He lifted an arm and ran a finger from the inside of his wrist to his elbow.

"The victim also had fresh antemortem fractures to the left radius."

Loshak's mind wandered while the medical examiner went on. Both he and Dr. Marion had sent copies of their findings early that morning so Loshak could do something he'd never done before: profile a victim.

"Alright, thanks, Dr. Alexandrou," Tavares said, shaking the medical examiner's hand before he returned to his seat. "Agent Loshak?"

Loshak squeezed down the side aisle and took the podium.

"Assuming Neil Griffin is our killer in the cases of these adolescents—"

In the back, Pressler let out a loud snort.

"Sure as hell wasn't Mrs. Griffin," the portly detective said. When everybody swiveled to stare at him, he raised his hands and added, "I'm just saying. Half these kids were bigger than she was."

Loshak nodded.

"From a profiling standpoint, we classify child sexual abusers into two typologies: Preferential and Situational. The Preferential group is motivated by a specific sexual attraction to children. These are your textbook pedophiles. The Situational group, on the other hand, is not explicitly attracted to children. They end up abusing them for other reasons."

He held up a piece of paper.

"I've included this chart in my profile, which details the difference between the two typologies, along with the seven behavioral subtypes. Knowing what we know about Griffin, it's possible he could fit into one of two of the Situational typologies. The Morally Indiscriminate type is — for lack of a better word — a garden variety sociopath. He uses and abuses anyone he perceives as weak or vulnerable, which makes a child an obvious target. Then there's the Sexually Indiscriminate type, who is interested in children as a way to check off another box on their quest for sexual experimentation."

Pressler piped up again from the back of the room.

"Are you trying to tell me Griffin wasn't a pederast? 'Cause he sure looks like one from where I'm standing."

"I'm getting to that, Detective," Loshak said. "When we don't know the relationship between the offender and the victim, it can be difficult to determine the correct typology. And that's the scenario we're dealing with here. That being said, the evidence suggests a narrative. Griffin's social and economic status; the ritualized manner of the killings, with the repeated use of a particular ligature; the fact that he was obviously skilled at concealing his crimes... all of this leads me to suspect he fits into the Sadistic subtype of Preferential molesters. This is the most dangerous — and thankfully the least common — type. They are specifically attracted to children, and they enjoy causing pain. Based on the forensic evidence we have so far, he was an organized perpetrator, motivated by the need to show his dominance or control over his victims. We see that with strangulation as the method of killing."

Loshak glanced over at a picture of Neil Griffin pinned to the wall. He was smiling in the photo, all bleach-white teeth and dimpled cheeks.

"We need to take another, closer look around Griffin, at anyone who's gone missing who might have come into contact with him through a club or one of his charities or even just near his home. Power killers don't usually go very far outside their geographical location to find victims. Along with missing persons, we'll need to search kids reported as runaways."

Loshak let his eyes move over the faces of the other task force members as he spoke.

"There's always the chance that Mrs. Griffin was complicit or even a willing helper in these murders, but it's more likely that her husband acted alone, without her knowledge. This kind of secret double-life isn't uncommon in power-control killers. They feel they have to maintain the façade to continue feeding their sadistic side, sometimes as a way to prove to themselves that they're normal, sometimes as a way to throw off any outside suspicion."

Rainie had moved closer to the front for Loshak's profile, and he watched her busily typing notes into her phone.

"Odds are that as a child Griffin was abused by a parent or parental figure. As an adult, he was obviously likable, charming, a successful businessman, and part of several charitable and community organizations. All the interviews with friends and family reiterated these ideas. Griffin, like many other power-control killers, was able to kill for years before anyone found him out."

"Except this time, somebody killed him for it," a detective near the back piped up.

"Maybe," Loshak said. "Our original killer could be a vigilante who learned what Griffin was up to, or he could have killed Griffin for another as-yet-unknown reason and just so happened to take out that one-in-a-million serial killer. How the other victims figure into all this will hopefully clarify that, one way or the other. Four seemingly unrelated people killed and posed the same way? There is meaning there we haven't uncovered yet."

"The glove over the eye thing," Rainie said. "It could be like, 'an eye for an eye.' A message."

"It's possible." Loshak agreed. "But we don't want to jump to any conclusions before we know more about these new remains. We have to stay patient. The evidence will tell the story."

The itch in Loshak's eye flared up then, and he resisted an urge to rub at it.

"These types of killers often take trophies of their kills so they can live out the fantasy over and over again, so we may find trophies in and around the house or at his car lots that will help ID the victims. We should take a fresh look at the house, his car, and his office with that in mind. Also, Mrs. Griffin says they've only lived in Prairiefire for the last five years. That means there could be more victims buried at his previous residences. Chief Tavares is in the process of getting in touch with the various agencies in those areas so they can launch their own investigations."

The room lapsed into silence then, the detectives and officers lost in their thoughts. Loshak could almost see the horrors found under the Griffin house playing on a loop inside their heads. Even the ones who hadn't been there for the excavation had seen the crime scene photos. Images of bones and half-rotted bodies pressed into the mud. Images none of them would ever forget.

CHAPTER 24

Spinks still sat in the little observation room when Loshak came back with his refilled coffee. It was the agent's third since the task force meeting and, he was pretty sure, the only thing keeping him standing.

"Sheesh," Spinks said, cocking his head to get a better look at Loshak's injured eye.

Loshak rested his cup on table and pulled a chair closer to the two-way mirror. He wasn't sure he could get back up if he sat down, but at this point, that was a risk he was willing to take.

"Is it getting worse?" he asked.

Spinks moved his finger in a circular motion around his own eye. "The sclera's all bloodshot now."

"Great." Loshak settled into the chair, knees creaking. "Should've worn my sunglasses."

"Can't complete the hungover starlet look without them," Spinks said.

The door swung into the interrogation room, and Detective Pressler led Mrs. Griffin inside.

"Here you go," the portly detective said, pulling out a chair for her in a surprisingly delicate motion for such a big guy. "I'm gonna grab me a Coke before we get started. Can I get you anything? We've got coffee, soda, water…"

"Coffee cake," Spinks whispered to Loshak in spite of the fact that the sound system in the interrogation room only went one way.

"Oh, no thank you," Mrs. Griffin said, settling in the chair.

She rested her oversized purse in her lap and wrapped her arms around it, then peered up at Pressler.

"Well, actually, if you have Diet Coke—"

"I know for a fact we do. Be back in a snap." Pressler actually snapped his fingers before backing out of the room.

Spinks crossed his arms over his chest and cupped his chin. "She looks kind of defensive, hugging that purse awfully hard. Think she knows what's going on?"

Loshak studied the widow for a few more seconds, then shook his head.

"That's more of a comfort motion, like hugging a pillow," he said. "Could be related to losing her husband or dealing with the police again when her most recent memories of them are connected to his death. And sometimes women put things in front of their upper body out of insecurity about their weight or how they look in certain clothes."

Jan had told him that back when they were still dating, bestowing it on him like the secret key to an ancient treasure.

"It'll take more information before we can say anything for sure," he said.

"That's your jam lately," Spinks said. "More information."

Loshak's mind jumped back to game theory, poker, and games of incomplete information. By this point in a case, he usually had a better feel for things. A lot of murder cases were surprisingly simple up close. Once you sorted out the who, what, where, and when, the why and how had a way of making themselves rather plain.

Not this time, though. Something about this one didn't want to give up the goods. The case kept throwing revelations at them with no time to sort through the old ones. The evidence kept piling up, but none of it led anywhere. It was somehow more disorienting than a simple lack of leads. Jarring. A little wrong.

"Here we go," Pressler's voice brought their attention back to the two-way mirror.

The detective sat a Diet Coke in front of Mrs. Griffin, then popped the tab on his own. He took a drink, then let out a satisfied sigh.

"Can't beat a Coke in a can. I had to quit the hard stuff and switch over to Diet last year, though. Got to watch my girlish figure."

The detective patted his round gut. Mrs. Griffin smiled politely and opened her own can without comment. Pressler pulled out the chair opposite the widow and lowered himself into it.

"Course, people say aspartame's just as bad for you as regular sugar. Making us fatter and diabetic and what-all," he said. "I say if it means I can drink ten sodas in a day and have cake that won't send me into sugar shock, then I'm not too worried about it."

Mrs. Griffin perked up visibly, and Loshak smiled humorlessly. Pressler had just hit a home run with the cake comment, whether it was intentional or not.

"I tried using it for baking," the widow said, shaking her head. "It just never tasted quite right. Neil always pretended like he enjoyed it, but let's just say my coffeecakes with artificial sweetener always hung around a lot longer than the ones I made with sugar."

Pressler nodded, his expression turning to grim understanding.

"Hey, you tried to keep your man healthy," he said. "That's more than some people can say. How are you holding up, anyway?"

She took a breath and opened her mouth as if she were about to speak, then let it out.

"I don't know. I just… First Neil and now all those bodies. It feels like none of this is real," she said, blinking at Pressler hopefully. "Like it's a joke? Or some kind of nightmare?"

It took Loshak — and Pressler, too — a second to process that she really wanted confirmation.

Pressler let out a long sigh.

"I'm afraid not, hon," he said in a soothing, almost apologetic tone. "No, it's really happening, awful as it is."

Her shoulders slumped, and she stared down at her soda can.

"I just don't understand how this could be. We *lived* there."

"How long?" Pressler asked. "That house is a fairly new construction, isn't it?"

"Four — no, five years now. Because the builders finished it right before Christmas. We kept calling everything a Christmas present as we unpacked it."

"And you didn't ever smell anything?" Pressler asked.

"Of course not," she snapped, raising her head and pushing her back into the seat a little.

"You never caught a whiff of dead animal and asked

Neil to go check if something had died up under there?"

Her arms crossed over her purse again.

"Well, there was the cat."

Pressler's eyebrows scooted up his forehead.

"Cat?"

"It crawled under the house to die last summer. Cats don't like to be seen at the moment of death. They panic and find a place to hide so they can die alone. But Neil found it and buried it behind our shed. There was no smell after that."

"So you saw the cat? Personally?" Pressler asked, nodding as if he weren't suggesting she'd been deceived.

"He didn't have time to go hunting for it before I left for Florida. He had to work. But he found it over the weekend while he wasn't at the car lot."

"Florida?"

"My sister lives in Palm Beach with our mother," Mrs. Griffin said. "I go stay a few days here and there, whenever I can. Mom can still take care of herself for the most part, but I don't want to leave it all up to Andi."

In the observation room, Spinks turned to Loshak, frowning and shaking his head.

"See, that's why their relationship could never work long-term. She was more of a people person and go-getter, while he was more of a psychotic serial killer."

Loshak grunted, too tired to give the joke the laugh it deserved.

In the interrogation room, Pressler took a casual sip of his Coke.

"How often do you get down there to visit?"

"At least once a month."

"That's an awful lot. Neil didn't mind you being gone so much?"

Mrs. Griffin glared at Pressler.

"Neil understood that you do for family. Your parents created you. Caring for them in their old age is the least you can do," she said, folding her arms a little more tightly around the handbag. "I could've just sent checks and told Andi 'good luck' like so many other kids do, but that wouldn't have been any better than sticking Mom in a nursing home and throwing away the key."

Pressler rested one thick arm on the table and leaned in.

"Why didn't you guys move down there so you could be closer?"

"The car lots, the community projects — we'd built so much here that we couldn't just pick up and leave."

"Did you ever notice anything strange when you came back from Florida? Maybe the furniture was rearranged or Neil had picked up a new rug as a surprise? Blankets gone or tools missing?"

"No. Nothing like that."

Pressler nodded again, leaning back in his seat.

"You can see what it looks like, Mrs. Griffin. You being gone all the time, no idea what your husband was getting up to—"

"Neil would never hurt anyone," she insisted.

"Look, somebody killed all them kids and buried 'em under your house," Pressler said. "If it wasn't you, and it wasn't Neil, then who was it?"

"I don't know!" Mrs. Griffin cast her eyes around the room. "Maybe it was one of the builders. We didn't check up on them much during the construction. They could've

141

been burying bodies there the whole time."

"Could be," Pressler said. "Can you give me the name of the company y'all used?"

"I have to look it up." She pulled her phone out of the purse and tapped it a few times. "It was called 'PDM.'"

Pressler made a show of jotting down the letters, then pushed himself back from the table.

"Alright, I'm gonna go give these guys a call. I'll be right back."

Mrs. Griffin nodded primly.

A second later, the door to the observation room opened, and Pressler squeezed in.

"What do you think?" the big detective asked Loshak.

Loshak rubbed his jaw, the stubble rasping under his fingers.

"I think she's being truthful. She was gone too much to know if anything was going on. Sounds like she was concerned about her mom, and he told her what she needed to hear to get her out of the house."

Spinks held up a finger.

"Or maybe she had an inkling what he was up to and came up with plenty of reasons to be away from home so she could keep the denial going," he suggested.

Loshak bobbled his head from side to side, unconvinced.

"Maybe."

"She was awfully quick to lay the blame on the construction company," Spinks pointed out.

"More likely because even now, she can only see in her husband what she expected to see," Loshak said. "It's a way out, a way she can keep believing he was the man she thought she knew."

"That's what I'm getting, too," Pressler said. "I don't have anything else to ask her. Y'all need to know anything?"

"Ask her for a list of her husband's friends and the people he worked with on the boards and community projects," Loshak said, thinking of the photo of Carter Dupont in the Griffins' cocktail room. "Anybody he might've been spending time with while she was gone."

Pressler gave him a thumbs up, then slid out of the room. When Pressler made it back to the widow, he had a yellow legal pad and a pen, which he slid across the table to her. They spent the next several minutes watching Mrs. Griffin write down names and organizations.

After Pressler escorted her out, Spinks and Loshak left the observation room. Loshak checked the clock on the wall as they passed it. One-twenty. If not for the grisly discovery below Griffins' house, they would be talking to Flickinger right now.

"I did tell you our interview with Dent's special teams coach got pushed to Thursday, right?" Loshak asked the reporter.

A wide smile broke out across Spinks' face.

"I wasn't invited to that interview, partner."

"Detective Wilson knows you're consulting. She probably assumed she was asking us both."

"No," Spinks stretched out the word thoughtfully. "I think Rainie wants one-on-one time with her secret agent crush. Some interview and chill."

Loshak rolled his eyes, then immediately regretted it. Felt like he had pulled some muscle behind the irritated one. That was just what he needed.

"She's half my age," he said. "Probably literally. What's half of fifty-three? Twenty-six and a half?"

"Some women like the older guy thing," Spinks said.

"What're we talking about?" Pressler stage whispered, stepping between them and hooking one arm around each of their necks conspiratorially.

Loshak immediately pulled away. He suspected Pressler was strong enough to keep him in the semi-headlock, but the bulky detective let him go without a fight.

"Our suspicions that Detective Wilson likes Loshak," Spinks said.

For some reason, Loshak didn't like Spinks talking to his new bosom buddy Pressler about this. Something about the detective just rubbed him the wrong way.

"That little hottie from the MHPD?" Pressler elbowed Loshak in the ribs with a little too much enthusiasm. "You dog!"

Loshak frowned. This conversation was making him feel like a middle schooler, and he was too worn out to come up with a way to derail it.

"She doesn't," he said.

Spinks hooked a thumb at him and told Pressler, "Can you believe this guy profiles people for a living?"

Pressler laughed a lot harder at this than Loshak thought was necessary.

"Did you get that list of Griffin's acquaintances?" Loshak cut in, gesturing to the paper in the detective's pink fist.

"Molly's compiling their contact info now."

"Is Carter Dupont on the list?"

The detective scanned the names.

"Nope."

"Doesn't mean he and Griffin weren't friends," Spinks pointed out. "Just that Mrs. Griffin didn't know about it. You could say that was kind of the theme of their marriage."

Both the reporter and Pressler stood up straighter and looked to Loshak's left. Loshak's eyes tried to shift over that way, but that stabbing pain shot through the irritated one again. He had to turn his whole body to see who it was.

"Glad I caught you," Chief Tavares said.

Under the fluorescent lights of the desk pool, his cowboy hat cast his eyes in half-shadows.

"CS was able to pull a partial print from your first anonymous note."

He held up a manila file folder, tapping it with his middle finger.

"And wouldn't you know it, we got a hit. Jeffrey Trufant. Got a black and white headed over to pick him up now."

CHAPTER 25

While he waited for the next interview subject to show up, Loshak hit the john. He relieved himself, washed his hands, and then stood in front of the sink for a moment to better admire his puff-ball of an eye in the mirror.

He wondered if there were some eye drops he could pop in there to take down some of the redness, because Spinks was right. The blood vessels were so inflamed they looked like they might pop.

His eye watered at the very thought of putting a drop of anything in there. It would sting like hell, he could guarantee that much.

Just as Loshak rejoined Spinks in the hallway, Pressler breezed past wiggling his phone in the air.

"Molly just buzzed me from the front desk," he said, wiggling his phone in the air. "Trufant is in the building. You ready for this?"

Loshak nodded and followed Spinks back into the little observation room. A few moments later, Detective Pressler led the subject into the interrogation room next door.

Jeffrey Trufant was a pale, middle-aged man with feathery, thinning hair. He couldn't have been taller than five-eight or so, but the way he swaggered to the table seemed to dwarf the much larger Pressler.

Trufant pulled out the chair facing the two-way mirror and lowered himself into it with an elegance that suggested the chair should be thankful he was gracing it with his presence.

Pressler dropped a folder on the table.

"Before we get started with all this junk, I'm gonna grab a Coke. What do you say, bud, can I get you a soda or coffee while I'm up?"

Loshak cringed. Even without the air of self-assurance and arrogance surrounding Trufant, "bud" would've been a serious misstep. To anyone over sixteen, the nickname was condescending. One man saying it to another implied that the speaker perceived a mismatched power dynamic and saw themselves as the dominant party.

Of course, there was always the chance that this was intentional on Pressler's part, a tactic to put Trufant on the defensive right away. They hadn't suspected Mrs. Griffin of anything, not really, and so Pressler had worked to put her at ease throughout their talk.

But with Trufant's print on the note making him the most likely deliverer of the cryptic messages, and the indication that the sender knew something undisclosed about the murders, there was the possibility that he was the killer of Griffin, Dent, and the others.

Of course, there were two killers in this case, weren't there? It seemed likely. This case, already odd, went downright wonky as soon as the crawlspace bodies were found.

Serial killer A and Serial killer B, Loshak thought.

In the interrogation room, Trufant chuckled. Loshak had to remind himself that Pressler had asked the man on the other side of the interrogation table if he wanted a drink.

"What pairs well with a criminal investigation,

Detective Pressler?" His voice was smooth and cultured. "Something in the claret family? Or perhaps a barrel-aged scotch? Even considering the tax bracket here in Prairie Village, I doubt your department pulls down enough to afford anything decent. Probably safer to stick with the water. Do you have bottled or does everyone gather around the bucket and drink from a tin ladle?"

When Pressler turned toward the door, Loshak could see a sneer pulling at the detective's lips.

As soon as he was alone, Trufant smiled squarely into the two-way and waved. Spinks flinched, then crossed his arms.

"He can't see us," the reporter said, as if to reassure himself. "With Law & Order and CSI, everybody knows how interrogation rooms are set up these days."

Loshak grunted in agreement. Still, it was unnerving. Like Trufant wanted them to know he was toying with them.

"Alrighty," Pressler said, reentering the interrogation room with a Diet Coke in one hand and a Styrofoam cup of water in the other.

He dropped into his seat and leaned over the table to put the cup in front of Trufant.

"Sorry, the Cristal machine was all out of bottled water. Hope you can stomach tap."

Trufant grimaced and made a show of pushing the cup away from himself at an angle. Somehow the gesture was more insulting than if he'd simply refused the water.

As if he hadn't noticed, Pressler scooped up the file folder and flipped it open.

"So, Mr. Trufant, it says here you've been picked up

quite a few times around KC. Possession, DUI, indecent exposure, lewd acts, all sortsa speeding charges."

Trufant nodded along with the accusations, looking off into the upper corner of the room as if he remembered each one fondly, openly smiling at the mention of "lewd acts" in particular.

"How come I don't see any jail time on these sheets?" Pressler asked.

"Given your bourgeois attitude, I suspect you already know the answer to that," Trufant said. "I have a disgusting amount of money. Just obscene, really. I could probably stab you in the eye right now with everyone watching."

He jerked his chin at the two-way mirror.

"By tomorrow morning, my family's lawyers would have convinced the judge that you started it, and I'm the real victim here."

"That's an interesting theory, there, partner." Pressler was trying to sound disinterested, but his shoulders had stiffened up, and he'd started flipping through pages in the file in an unconvincing attempt to look like he was searching for something specific. "You ever test something like that out in real life?"

Trufant let out that condescending chuckle again.

"Yes. I'm a vicious serial killer who murdered all your victims and ate their livers with some cannellini beans."

Pressler's shoulders loosened.

"That's fava beans, bud." He flipped the folder shut. "Let's cut the crap and get down to business here. We found your print on a note left in an investigator's hotel room—"

"Special Agent Victor Loshak's hotel room," Trufant

corrected him. "And I believe he prefers to be called a profiler."

He made a show of glancing up at the two-way.

"Is that the correct terminology, Agent Loshak?"

In the observation room, Spinks glanced sidelong at Loshak, one eyebrow raised.

"What," the reporter said, pausing for dramatic effect, "the hell. Is up with this guy? Big-time Hannibal Lecter fan?"

"Probably." Loshak touched the puffed-up eyelid of his injured eye. "Sometimes you get people obsessed with serial killers coming in on these things. They want to be close to it, so they make up ways to get involved."

The men fell silent as Trufant continued.

"While we're laying all our cards out there, I should come out and say that I won't be answering any questions from you, Detective. Not with any degree of seriousness. My notes were intended for Agent Loshak. If he's interested in conducting my interview, I'll gladly tell him everything I know."

"Listen here, Richie Rich—"

Trufant grinned.

"Really, Detective, class resentment? In this economy?"

From Loshak's angle, he could only see the back of Pressler's neck and the sides of his cheeks, but both were quickly turning red.

Leaning his bulk forward, Pressler jabbed a finger at Trufant.

"I've got more than enough evidence to hold you as a suspect, not to mention charge you with harassing an officer of the law."

"I notice you've stopped asking questions," Trufant said, raising an eyebrow. "I take it that means you've realized I'm serious about not answering any more from you."

Pressler stood up so fast the chair scraped back and toppled into the wall under the two-way mirror. Without another word, he stormed out of the interrogation room.

The door to the observation room opened.

"You called it, Feebs," the portly detective said, squeezing past Loshak and leaning against the table. "The whackadoo's demanding you talk to him."

Loshak nodded. He'd guessed as much would happen. The notes indicated that, for whatever reason, the man had fixated on Loshak. Before the black and white had brought Trufant in, he and Pressler had talked through the possibility of switching interviewers, and they'd both agreed it was likely to yield more information. If Trufant was the killer, he would want to gloat. If he had real information, he might feel Loshak could use it best. And if he was just a nut job, then at least Loshak could weed him out.

"Alright, I'm going in," Loshak said.

When Loshak walked into the interrogation room, Trufant stopped staring into the two-way and watched him take a seat.

"Hmm," Trufant murmured, cupping his chin. "You're taller than your press clippings let on."

"Have you been following them long?" Loshak asked.

"I admit I'm a fan of your work, though my interest is more recent. The police stations in town were buzzing when they found out you were coming to Kansas City."

"Is that how you knew I was coming?"

Trufant waved a hand dismissively.

"I'm a member of all the necessary clubs an influential, land-owning white male in the highest tax bracket should be a member of, and so are some very important members at the top tier of our fair city's law enforcement branches. One hears things."

"Really? Top tax bracket?" Loshak asked. "Maybe I should quit the BAU and get a job out here."

"Don't bother. These acquaintances made their money the old fashioned way, just like I did — by inheriting it."

"Carter Dupont," Loshak said. "He was doing pretty well for himself, too. He wouldn't happen to have been a member of these same clubs?"

Trufant's eyes sparkled.

"I knew you would catch on faster than that portly wildebeest."

"Were the two of you friends?"

"Ish," Trufant said. "You aren't really close with someone like Carter; you're just in the same room when he is. Of course, he had the money to be that way. Distant. Standoffish. Most people don't, and we call them dickheads for it."

"What is it about Dupont's suicide that makes you think he's connected to all this?" Loshak asked.

"Well, that's the sort of connection certain… wealthy individuals… would rather keep secret. Hence my warning about trusting the locals," Trufant said, drumming his fingers on the table. "Those rich, white, land-owning male clubs aren't terribly forthcoming with information on their membership. In fact, some of them are downright closemouthed about it."

Loshak cocked his head.

"But you can talk to me about it?"

"What are they going to do? *Murder* me?" Trufant rolled his eyes.

"Someone is murdering people," Loshak said. "That's why I'm here."

Trufant shrugged.

"I hear running for your life is good cardio. Frankly, I could use the exercise. Maybe your whale friend, Pressler, could join me."

"About Dupont and the case?" Loshak prompted.

"Oh, right. Among the ridiculous secret clubs I belong to, there's one that's a little too *Eyes Wide Shut,* even for me. The upper floor is a bar, one of those dreadful places with the dead animal heads stuck on the wall like some sort of upscale Bass Pro Shop that serves liquor. The drinks are abysmal, and the company is enough to make a man want to put out his eyes just to liven up the conversation. I've only been three times in all the years since I inherited my membership. But I've heard rumors that the lower floors are debauchery unbound, nothing off limits. If you can dream it, you can screw it. Personally, I've never taken a closer look."

"Really?" Loshak asked, allowing the skepticism to bleed into his voice. "Why not?"

Trufant snorted.

"I'm gay, Agent Loshak. Fat, saggy, naked old men living out their most disturbing fantasies is the last thing on Earth I want to see," he said with a smirk. "It might scare me straight."

"And how does all this relate to the case?"

"I believe one of your serial killer's victims was Neil Griffin?" Without waiting for an answer, Trufant continued. "Griffin's a self-made man, but you don't get the kind of wealthy this club requires by working for your money. The man had nowhere near the funds to join, and yet somehow he was a member."

Loshak's brow furrowed.

"You saw him in there?"

"His membership was a subject of much speculation in the bar," Trufant said. "This isn't the sort of crowd you can blackmail or bully into giving you something. Griffin got in, but nobody really knew how."

Loshak nodded slowly, the wheels grinding to life in his head. If what Trufant said about the club was true, it might have offered Griffin a sexual outlet for his deviant impulses when he couldn't bring someone home to murder.

"And how does Carter Dupont's suicide fit into this?" he asked.

"Carter was a member of the same club," Trufant said. "And he killed himself a month after Griffin joined."

CHAPTER 26

The interrogation room quickly turned into a conference center with Loshak, Spinks, Pressler, and Trufant gathered around the table.

"If the rumors you've heard about the lower floors are true," Loshak said, "then it's likely Griffin used the place as an outlet during the times he wasn't murdering, a place to enact his fantasies. If we can get inside, maybe we can talk to someone who knew both Dupont and Griffin. Someone who saw the side they were keeping hidden from their families."

"Hells yeah we're going in," Pressler said, leaning over his gut to slap the table with a pink palm. "I want an undercover wired up and talking to everybody in there."

Trufant cleared his throat, somehow managing to make the sound both cordial and derogatory.

"Getting any local inside poses a problem," Trufant said. "There are people from the top tiers of the law enforcement and judiciary, and they're as likely to recognize you or your officers as they are to recognize me. Unless you've got undercover officers who've inherited multiple millions before deciding to go into law enforcement, they'll never pass. And we've covered the fact that I've already heard chatter about Agent Loshak's imminent arrival from within. They're bigger fans than I am. His presence is bound to attract attention."

"What about me?" Spinks asked. "I rarely even get a

155

headshot in at the end of most of my pieces. I'm virtually a faceless voice."

"While I normally enjoy insulting people, Mr. Spinks, I prefer to do it in ways tailored to their individual shortcomings rather than by generalization tied to race, sexuality, or creed. So forgive me if this comes off as racist, but I did mention that most of these secret clubs are for rich, white men. Emphasis on white."

Spinks nodded.

"Sure. But could you get a black man in if he was with you? Say, as a boyfriend or significant other. You're rich enough to warrant that kind of special treatment, aren't you? Or does obscene wealth not buy what it used to?"

Trufant assessed the reporter, then smiled.

"You're not gay, are you?" He asked, then heaved a dramatic sigh without waiting for an answer. "The boys who're my type never are. Well, what the hell. At the very least, it'll be entertaining. Shall we go tonight?"

"Now just a flippin' minute," Pressler said. "We're not sending a civilian in with a civilian. Neither of you has training in how to behave in a hostile environment, and you don't know what you can and can't say to keep the evidence admissible in a court of law."

Spinks raised one finger.

"Actually, I've worked with several departments in Miami in this capacity. The audio I got from infiltrating the New Jack City Cowboys near Liberty Square led to the convictions of two enforcers and an executive member of the gang."

Loshak thought it was likely that Spinks had more experience with undercover work than most of the officers in the Prairie Village PD, but the reporter was smart enough not to step on the detective's toes by mentioning it.

Trufant, however, didn't mind at all.

"You see," the man said, gesturing to Spinks. "He's probably more qualified than you are, Detective."

Pressler worked his jaw as if he were trying to bite through a piece of gristle. It must have been a tough spot to be in. The detective seemed to like Spinks and want his approval in an almost juvenile way, like a kid hanging on at the periphery of the cool kids. At the same time, however, it was clear he couldn't stand Trufant. If Pressler gave in, it would be like letting Trufant win. But if he stood firm, he might lose whatever cool he thought he'd developed with Spinks.

Loshak didn't like the idea of sending Spinks in without police backup, either, but it might be their only chance to gain some insight into one of their victims, maybe even figure out how Dupont's suicide really fit into the picture.

"You'd have to run the operation, Pressler," Loshak said, going with his gut feeling that Pressler would react best to a combination of peer pressure and inflated importance. "Spinks knows what works in Miami, but he doesn't have any experience with Kansas City."

"That goes without saying," Spinks said with a nod. "And I'm willing to submit to any stipulations you might have."

Pressler's thick shoulders were relaxing by the second.

"We need time to do a drive-by, get some info on the place," he said and pointed a finger at Trufant. "That means we need an address, interior layout, and description of the staff from you. I don't give a rusty shit whether the other guys in this place are liver-spotted mummies on life support, we treat this like a sting operation. Full workup beforehand, and no fooling around once you're inside."

Trufant glanced over Spinks, eyes glimmering.

"I'll attempt to keep my hands to myself."

CHAPTER 27

Loshak let himself out of the conference room where Spinks was doing the final prep for his undercover assignment. They'd head out any minute now, the anticipation thick in the air around them. After the false start of getting Pressler on board, everything had proceeded at breakneck speed, and the agent couldn't take it anymore.

His pulse pounded in his ears, his heartbeat seeming to build steadily as the operation drew near. He needed to get some air. Maybe something to drink. Needed to calm the fuck down, Darger would probably say.

He jogged down a flight of stairs and hustled for the vending machine outside the lobby. The thing slurped down his dollar and spit out a Fanta that he didn't really want. The can felt sweaty in his fingers.

He cracked the top and took a slurp. It was wet and orange and far too sweet. Oh well.

Nothing about this should be terribly concerning, Loshak knew, but here he was. Stressed. Pacing. Drinking a Fanta.

He ran the plan through his mind, not sure if he was trying to calm himself or find some justification for calling the thing off, some technicality he could use to make them stop.

Accompanying private club member Jeffrey Trufant, Spinks was going to head into The Wooden Nickel to

159

uncover what he could about this allegedly sinister club for the ultra-rich. Spinks. They were sending in Spinks. He wasn't a cop. He was a writer.

In so many ways, however, this was routine — any Joe on the street could be an informant for the police, wear a wire into "enemy territory," and most of the time, Loshak would think nothing of it.

On top of that, the assignment was basically to walk into a bar. Maybe try to get access to the basement. Nothing dangerous.

So why was Loshak freaking out about it?

He paced back and forth in the hall next to the vending machine. Tried not to think about what would happen next, though there was nothing else to think about, nothing else to do at all short of drinking more of this carbonated orange candy.

Truth was, he felt left out. Undercover work wasn't his area of expertise, so he'd taken a backseat during the planning stage. So far, they'd taken a preliminary look at the rudimentary building floor plan Trufant had sketched out for them, consulted with an engineer and picked out audio equipment, and drawn up a tactical approach for the men outside. Meanwhile Loshak huddled in the back of the room with nothing of value to offer. Taking up space, mostly.

Feeling left out made him worry. And the fact that it was Spinks heading into danger only enhanced the anxiety, turned it personal, gave his misgivings some element of fatherly concern that made Loshak uncomfortable. Embarrassed, really. Spinks was a grown man. Nearly the same damn age he was.

Pressler was wiring Spinks up now, the large detective and diminutive Trufant taking turns peppering the reporter with last-minute coaching and pep talk. Loshak had partaken in this for a while, but he kept getting the urge to chime in with his fears, second guess things the others were saying, express doubt about the plan as a whole.

He knew that wasn't doing any good, so he left. Wandered out here to pace around like an anxious weirdo and disgust himself thoroughly with a can of Fanta for no good reason.

He breezed out into the parking lot and weaved between cars at random, his path tracing strange patterns that vaguely circled the lot in crooked laps. Pacing always seemed like it would calm him down, ease his nerves. He wasn't sure it actually helped, but it was something to do to fill the time.

The orange can hovered along beside him like a trusty companion, now seeming to weep condensation into his palm. He didn't drink any more of the sweet brew — two sips was more than enough Fanta for one lifetime — but he did gesture with the can periodically, accenting his internal monologue with little flourishes and can thrusts. It wasn't a great prop as these things went, but maybe it was better than nothing.

The door squeaked a little when it opened behind him, and when Loshak turned back, he found Pressler nodding his way, a big ridiculous cowboy hat on his head. Was that part of his undercover gear, or just his normal casual attire? Spinks and Trufant filed out of the building behind the big detective.

Loshak hustled over to the trash can next to the door to ditch about three-quarters of a can of Fanta.

It was time to go.

CHAPTER 28

Spinks crossed the street with Trufant, keeping pace with the shorter man easily.

"Do we hold hands?" Spinks asked.

Trufant gave him a disgusted sidelong look.

"I'm gay, Jevon, not *gay*."

Spinks laughed, nervous energy tingling along under his skin.

"Hey, I don't know if I'm about to blow our cover if I don't ask, right?"

"I suppose that's true," Trufant said.

He sounded cooler than the other side of the pillow, but his eyes sparkled. Spinks got the idea he was having a little bit too much fun with this.

The club sat diagonal from where they'd parked. Spinks resisted an urge to glance back to where Loshak and Pressler waited in the rental that time forgot. Thanks to Trufant's obscene wealth, Spinks was wired with the latest in bug-style devices, a button-mike pinned on in place of one of his actual shirt buttons. "A must-have for any spy operation," according to Trufant.

The consulting audio guy had been positively giddy over the thing. Even Spinks had to admit it was definitely an upgrade from any of the police-issue wires he'd used on the job before.

There wasn't a flashing neon sign over this infamous club, just a cheapo plastic banner hanging over the

basement entryway that read, *The Wooden Nickel.* A piece
of printer paper was taped to the metal security door below
to make sure everyone knew *No One Under 21 Allowed
Entry.*

Trufant breezed down the stairs and through the
security door, leaving Spinks to catch it as it swung shut. A
big guy in a muscle shirt sat on a stool in front of a second
door.

"Ain't seen you in a minute, Jeffrey," the guy said.
"How's it been going?"

"Trivial, shallow, meaningless, X-rated — all the best
life has to offer." Trufant jerked his head at Spinks. "He's
with me."

"Alright. You two have a good one."

"Certainly not," Trufant said and flashed the bouncer a
dazzling smile. "I prefer the bad ones. They're much more
fun."

On the heels of this statement, he swept into the club.

Spinks had to hot-foot it to catch up. He leaned down
and hissed in Trufant's ear, "Are you trying to pick up
other guys on our fake date?"

"Psh, Donny's straighter than you are," Trufant said,
waving a dismissive hand. "Though not quite as handsome.
Jealousy becomes you."

Spinks followed the shorter man to the bar, trying to
ignore an attack of the weirds attempting to twist his face
muscles and give the game away. Better to focus on the
layout. This place sure did favor the dead animal style of
decoration. He only half-listened in as Trufant ordered
them both high-dollar scotches, taking in the trophy
basses, a zebra head, a rack of moose antlers, and a moth-

eaten old Grizzly standing in the corner. Someone had duct taped a beer can into its paw.

It was probably easier to appreciate the hilarity of the beer-bear when you weren't on a mission. Trufant and he had both argued with Pressler and Loshak that this place and its clientele weren't dangerous, but Spinks' heart was still hammering away in his chest. A combination of nerves and excitement. He'd gotten the same way the other times he'd gone undercover. There was a big story here. He could feel it. All he had to do was keep his cool until he found it.

From the bar, it sure didn't look like anything big was going down in The Wooden Nickel. Spinks could count the number of patrons on one hand, and they were all drinking quietly alone, except for two at the end of the bar nursing Stella Artois glasses and watching football on the big screen above the liquor shelves.

"Come on, Jevon, let's sit over here, where we can get to know each other better," Trufant said, handing one crystal tumbler of scotch to Spinks.

They sat at a table in the corner, up against the only wall in the place that wasn't brick. If Spinks had to guess, he would've said the bland red color the decorators had chosen for the accent wall was probably called Elk Tongue or Turkey Wattle. Something classy like that.

"Is this place legit?" he asked, keeping his voice low. "I mean, coming in with exactly no knowledge, I would've guessed this was a blue-collar bar on a slow night, not a secret hideout for the super rich."

Trufant grinned.

"You were expecting more New York chic? Don't you think we get enough of that in the endless swirl of parties and galas and art openings we're always being invited to? Sometimes a man just wants to feel like someone else, someone less fortunate but more wholesome with the whole working poor hard work thing going on." He sighed and rolled his eyes. "I've got to be honest with you, I'm not really committed to this joke. I have no idea why anyone would want to hide a secret club down in this dump. Maybe it's so ugly and impoverished that they assume no one will ever find them out."

Trufant took a delicate sip of his scotch, sighing appreciatively, then sat back in his seat.

"See that door over there?" he asked.

Spinks followed his gaze across the bar to a much bigger bouncer, this one more farm boy with extra helpings of gravy than Muscle Beach body builder. Set into the brick behind the overfed farm boy was a door painted the same Elk Tongue red as the accent wall.

"That's our point of ingress," Trufant said. "When the time comes, I'll get you past him."

"How?"

"Easily." Trufant plunged on before Spinks could point out that he hadn't actually answered anything. "The trick will be blending in once you're down there. Basically, act superior to everyone around you at all times. Except when you first meet someone. If you're introduced to someone, the moment you hear their name, you must always exclaim, 'My God! Of course!' That will make it seem like you've heard of them, and perhaps more importantly, that whatever you heard left quite an impression. Most of the time after that ego job, they'll go along with anything you want."

"Yeah, that's great advice, but how are you going to get us past the bouncer?"

"I didn't say us, I said you. Don't you worry your pretty little head about it. Not when we could be having some of the best steak in three states." Trufant gestured his scotch toward the door to the kitchens. "They've got a chef back there hoarding three Michelin stars. Tell me, can I buy you one or two, Jevon?"

"One, I guess."

"A cheap date."

Trufant snapped his fingers until he got the bartender's attention. She came over and took their order—two steaks and a fresh scotch for Trufant—then disappeared into the kitchen.

"Hope you love eating loogie," Spinks said.

Trufant snorted.

"They wouldn't dare in a place like this. There are cameras monitoring every square inch. That's one thing you learn quickly with the ultra-disgustingly rich. They keep an ever-watching, Panopticon eye on their staff. It keeps them resentful and submissive."

Spinks brought the scotch to his lips to drink, but caught a whiff of the stuff. Didn't matter how smooth people claimed the extra expensive brands were, they always smelled like kerosene laced with rat poison to him.

The bartender came back with Trufant's refill, leaving it without comment. It was behavior Spinks had seen before at some of the highest-roller parties across the US. Staff was expected to be silent until addressed directly. He felt a sneer tugging at the corners of his lips, but managed to resist.

"Just look at them," Trufant said, narrowed eyes sweeping over the few other patrons in the bar. "Fat, comfortable, complacent bastards. You don't want to know how many young, stupid ex-wives old Jonesy there prenupped out of child support payments. Probably puts a warm feeling in a young boy's heart buying bread with food stamps while his dad eats pâté. And Ray and Tony T. at the bar? They both play the good ol' boys on Sunday, trying to outdo each other at who can put the most money in the offering plate, but come Mondee mornin' Ray's boinking half the women at his company, and Tony's foreclosing on little old widows and stealing settlements from orphans. They could use a shakeup like this. Every damn one of them."

At first Spinks thought Trufant meant their infiltration of the club and the investigation looking to uncover all the deep dark secrets of the local upper crust. But Trufant wasn't done.

"Sneaking through the city at night, swatting down the rich and powerful like flies." He grinned, a cold baring of teeth like a shark about to attack. "Yessiree-bob, a reckoning's coming. Better scatter, little rich boys."

"It almost sounds like you're on the serial killer's side," Spinks said.

The way Trufant's attention jerked to him, he felt pretty sure the smaller man had almost forgotten he was there.

"On the serial killer's side," Trufant mused. "No, hunting the most dangerous game just doesn't do anything for me. But that doesn't stop me from enjoying all the skirts he's blowing up and all the wrinkly old balls he's exposing."

Spinks was about to say something else, but the bartender was back with their steaks. She set the plates down and made to go.

"Thanks," Spinks said, a little loudly.

She looked startled, but covered it with a friendly smile. "You're welcome."

Across the table, Trufant was grinning down at his plate like a lunatic. The arch in his brow paired with the grin looked unquestionably demonic.

The weirds reared up once again, and Spinks wanted to just call it a night, get out of here. Before he could mention it, however, Trufant leaned closer to him.

"Be ready," he said, his voice pitched low. "It's showtime."

Snakes coiled in Spinks' gut. "What exactly do you have in mind for—"

Trufant grabbed the steak knife from his plate and jammed it into the flesh of his wrist. Spinks leapt out of his seat, knocking his chair over backward. Blood welled up around the blade in bright pearlescent red. That crazy bastard Trufant looked like he was about to giggle.

Instead of letting out an insane peal of laughter, Trufant grabbed the knife and jerked it back out of his wrist. He winced, that sick rictus still frozen on his face.

"The hell?" Spinks choked, his voice coming back.

The blood poured now. It sounded like rain dropping onto the tabletop in spurts.

"Oh dear God!" Trufant shouted, standing up with way too much poise for the amount of blood he was leaking all over everything. "I've cut myself."

He ran to the farm boy bouncer and shoved his

streaming wrist into the man's face.

"Help me! You've got to help me!"

"Hold still! Just hold still!"

The bouncer tried to grab Trufant's arm and steady him, but the bleeding lunatic kept lunging and smearing the blood all over the poor guy.

"I'm going to faint!" Trufant crowed, the grin now impossible to hide. He stumbled, streaking red across the bouncer's cheek and neck. "I need an ambulance. I've lost too much blood."

"Just stay calm!" The bouncer finally snagged Trufant's arm. "Come on, stay calm and we'll get some pressure on this."

The bouncer dragged Trufant toward the kitchen, shouting for clean towels. The bartender went running to find some. Every eye in the bar followed them.

Spinks slipped through the Elk Tongue red door and down the stairs unnoticed.

CHAPTER 29

Loshak sat in the passenger seat of the unmarked car, twisted toward the laptop carriage. Colorful bars spiked and jumped in the black square of the audio program Pressler, Trufant, and Spinks had set up with Trufant's spy gear. The peaks and valleys were meaningless, but Loshak couldn't look away. In the driver's seat, Pressler mirrored his posture, eyes glued to the spikes.

"The hell?" Spinks hissed, his voice coming through appalled and a little wheezy in the laptop's speakers.

Loshak leaned forward, glaring at the little spikes now as if they would suddenly resolve to show them what was happening inside the bar.

"Oh dear God!" At the sound of Trufant's gleeful shout, both Loshak and Pressler shifted in their seats. *"I've cut myself!"*

Scraping chairs. Loshak thought he recognized Spinks' harsh breathing. It could only be the reporter. Who else would be so close to the button mic in his shirt?

Then, from farther away, Trufant screamed, *"Help me! You've got to help me!"*

"Hold still!" Another voice. Deep. Male. Out of habit, Loshak's mind immediately latched on to the accent evident in the second word — *stee-ull* — and catalogued it as if he would have to testify to it later on. *"Just hold still!"*

The crowing from Trufant grew quieter, as did the half-angry, half-desperate shouting from the unidentified male

171

with the backcountry accent.

"They're drawin' away," Pressler said, his voice a strange half-whisper. Then, as if embarrassed that he'd blurted that out, the big detective added, "That's why it sounds like they're fading. Or our man Spinks is drawin' away from them."

Loshak nodded absently. For whatever reason, he didn't feel like he could look away from the screen while this drama was playing out.

In the far background, someone was shouting for clean towels — *unidentified male with accent*, Loshak thought — while another unidentified voice, this one female, shouted something he couldn't make out.

Suddenly, Spinks' breathing stopped. Fabric rustled, and the small pops of a mic on the move made the bar spike on the audio program's black rectangle. A metallic click, more pops, another click, then the chaos and shouting disappeared.

Spinks started breathing again.

"*I am in through the red door,*" the reporter whispered, the wheeze still hissing along his airways as he spoke. "*There's a staircase here, leading down. No one here that I can see.*" A series of low ticks started up in the background, their spikes hardly hitting the halfway point. Something about the sound reminded Loshak of tiled school floors. "*I am descending the stairs.*"

That cartoon Spy Vs. Spy flashed through Loshak's mind, only with Spinks creeping exaggeratedly down a staircase, the reporter's knees lifting almost to his head before he stepped forward on just the point of one toe.

A pause.

Loshak's stomach roiled, and he stifled a nervous burp. Those two ill-conceived swallows of Fanta were coming back on him with a vengeance.

"No one in the hall. I count three doors on my right and four on the left." More footsteps. Another pause. *"Racquetball court. Or is it squash? I don't know how people tell them apart. Two white males well on their way to massive coronaries smacking a little blue ball around with racquets. Make of that what you will."*

The tension in Loshak's shoulders started to unwind. It didn't all go — too many stings gone wrong wouldn't let it — but if Spinks was back to making jokes, the situation couldn't be completely wrecked.

An unidentified male asked a question, but a strange echo garbled the words.

"Hmm?" Spinks' voice had the sharp edge of a response. *"No, I'm sorry. I thought this one was the squash court. Jeff Trufant was supposed to meet me down here for a game."*

More echo-y words.

"Racquetball?" Spinks chuckled. *"Well, you know Jeff."*

The teacher from Charlie Brown, Loshak realized as the other unidentified male. That nasally *wah wah wah wah* was what listening to this one-sided conversation reminded him of, except this time the teacher was in an all-tile bathroom.

"Third one? OK, thanks, man. I appreciate it." As the footsteps picked up again, Spinks mumbled under his breath, *"Personal masseur on the premises. Very small shorts. Shorty shorts, you might say. Bulge presented with the all too clear outline of a pair of plums. Nothing left to the imagination."*

173

In the car, Pressler let out a hearty laugh. Loshak found he was smiling, too. Spinks had made contact with someone, and they hadn't kicked him out or immediately opened fire.

"Sauna. Locker room." Spinks listed off the doors as he passed them. *"Authorized Members Only, huh? Let's see where this rabbit hole leads, Alice."*

A door creaked, and even in the car, Loshak cringed. But no accusatory shouts rang out.

"Down, down, down," Spinks said. The door creaked again, and there was the clicking of the mechanism catching. *"I am descending another staircase. There's a nice creepy bare bulb hanging on a wire at the bottom. No axe murderers immediately obvious. Probably busy on the racquetball courts, which as it turns out is the game with the paddling of blue balls. Make a note of it."*

Tension crept back into Loshak's shoulders and neck as he listened to Spinks' monologue. Loshak could sense the unease, could hear the reporter trying to fill the silence and drive away his own discomfort with sheer volume of words.

Spinks' voice dropped to a low rumble that sounded like it was coming from his chest instead of his throat. Loshak had to strain to catch every word. Across the console, Pressler was craning one ear closer to the laptop as if he was having trouble hearing.

"Well, this hall isn't the scene for some creepy murder basement in a horror flick. Everybody's fluorescent lights give off a constant hum like that. That's a sign they're working as the manufacturer intended. Nothing weird about that or the concrete or— Oh, shit."

174

Loshak jerked up in his seat, the car bouncing a little under him. His instinct was to reach for his gun — his hand even went that direction — but then Spinks' voice was back.

"Definitely could've done without that image," Spinks whispered. *"Late sixties, early seventies white male, either in pony play or BDSM gear. I'll never be able to identify his face, but I'll be seeing those wrinkly danglers in my nightmares for the rest of my life."*

Pressler guffawed, then clapped a wide pink hand over his mouth as if the people in the bar might hear him.

"OK, Jangleberries McStuffins is gone. I'm leaving my little hidey-hole here and heading back out into the murder hallway."

This time, Loshak was sure Spinks was tiptoeing in that cartoon way. Something about the intervals between footsteps. They were more careful, like he was inspecting every spot before he set his foot down for a trap or a patch of noisy floorboards.

"Not sure if you guys can hear this, but…" There was some fumbling with the mic, then a loud scratching that blew the top off the audio program's highest points. For a second, Loshak thought, *That's going to blow the speakers.* It sounded like Spinks was scraping a nail across the surface of the mic.

It ended, and the reporter breathed, *"Did you get any of that? Jesus. I think…"*

The *snick*ing sound of a handle being cranked spiked the lines on the laptop.

Then Spinks snapped, *"Stop! Whatever you're doing to…"* His voice trailed off.

175

"Who the hell are you? How did you get down here?" Unidentified male #3.

Furniture scraped, then the mic started popping and rustling.

"Hey!" Spinks yelled, his voice cutting in and out of the popping. *"Get your hands off—"*

It was a fight, Loshak realized. Spinks was being overpowered. He'd seen something, and now he was in a fight.

Loshak's hand was already on the door handle when he realized the car had gone silent, the audio program showing nothing but a flat line.

Spinks' mic had cut off.

Loshak lurched out of the vehicle, drew his weapon, and ran across the street for the bar. The heavy thuds of Pressler's footfalls followed him.

CHAPTER 30

Loshak took the stairs down to The Wooden Nickel three at a time and plowed through the security door.

"Hey, whoa, no—" The bouncer, a white male in his mid-twenties wearing a skin-tight black t-shirt jumped off his stool, ready to throw himself between the man with the Glock and the door. "What the hell?"

Loshak whipped out his badge. "FBI. Step aside."

"Prairie Village PD!" Pressler roared, his thick shoulder bumping against Loshak's. "Out of the way."

"No fucking way," the bouncer snapped, crossing his arms over his wide chest. "I don't have to let you guys in if you don't have a warrant."

"We don't need a warrant if we have probable cause to search the premises," Loshak said, his voice calm and professional in spite of the anxiety and toxic orange soda pumping through his gut.

Spinks could already be dead, and they were screwing around out here with an armchair lawyer who had his fists shoved up against the backs of his biceps to make them look even bigger.

"Get out of the way, or I'll arrest you for interfering with a federal investigation."

The metallic jingle of handcuffs got the bouncer's attention. Pressler dangled them in front of his face.

"If he don't stop posturing on me, I'll arrest him for threatening an officer of the law," Pressler growled. "Now step aside."

With a disgusted grunt, the bouncer moved about three inches.

The door behind the bouncer swung open, and a much bigger, wider specimen from a Strongman competition chugged out.

"What the hell is all the yelling? You cool, Don?" *Unidentified male with accent,* Loshak's mind put the voice to him. He could still hear this one pronouncing "still" as "stee-ull" in his head, the tone turned slightly tinny by the tiny microphone.

"FBI and Prairie Village PD," Pressler snapped, waving his star. "We have probable cause to search the premises, so move your enormous ass."

"Fuck off," the Strongman bouncer said, taking an aggressive step forward and giving Pressler a shove in the meaty shoulder.

The portly detective moved much faster than his size would seem to allow for, ratcheting a cuff shut on the Strongman's outstretched wrist.

The Strongman lost his shit. Drew back a huge fist and threw it toward Pressler's face.

Pressler's nose exploded, blood and snot gushing, but he kept hold of the bouncer's cuffed wrist.

Loshak grabbed the bouncer's haymaker arm, trying to wrestle it up behind his back, then suddenly he, Pressler, and the Strongman were on the ground.

Their limbs tangled. Elbows and knees jabbed Loshak in the ribcage.

The agent fought his way to the top, but he couldn't drag the guy's free wrist close enough to the cuffed wrist to complete the circuit.

Pressler yeehawed like a bullrider while the bouncer twisted and raged beneath them. His ridiculous cowboy hat went tumbling and got crushed under a thigh as wide as a telephone pole.

Then the Strongman bouncer cranked Loshak's wrist hard the wrong way as he tried to tear free. Pain shot through the joint, up the forearm bones and down the hand, sudden and blinding. Loshak let go. The Strongman's next buck sent him flying off.

In the small space of the basement hallway, Loshak smacked up against the wall, half sitting, half slumped over. He cradled his wrist against his chest.

"Look out!" Pressler cried, ecstatic. "He's gonna death roll!"

The Strongman managed to flip onto his back across Loshak's legs, but the move pinned his free arm. Loshak hooked his good arm around the guy's throat, then smashed his fingers against the pressure point under the nose, trying to ignore the throbbing in his wrist and pushing until the Strongman was shouting in pain.

A ratcheting snap signaled the end of the fight.

"Hoo!" Pressler bounced up to his feet, a snot and blood-smeared grin stretched across his face. "Oh son, you done fucked up! Must be your first day on the job. Didn't you pay attention at all in bouncing school? No touchie. That's rule number one. You don't lay a finger on them 'til they reach for you."

He rolled the Strongman off Loshak's legs and maneuvered him to kneeling using the chain between the cuffs.

"Oh, yes sir, you done fucked up. I got all sortsa charges for you, boy."

"Spinks," Loshak said and bolted to his feet, knees popping and protesting.

The other bouncer stood back, hands raised high.

"I don't want any trouble. I was complying. You saw me."

Loshak sprinted past him, tearing open the door to the bar proper.

"Spinks?" he yelled.

Every eye in the place turned to him. A half-dozen old drunks and a bartender with an empty Pilsner glass stared at him open-mouthed.

Then someone cackled.

Loshak spotted the source of the sound immediately. Trufant was in the corner, hugging an arm wrapped in white towels to his stomach while he laughed like a lunatic, face going bright red.

Loshak glanced around the room, suddenly disoriented. Laughter wasn't the right response. It didn't make sense in this situation.

"Where the hell is Spinks?" Loshak snapped.

Trufant trailed off into giggles, then started up again. Now everyone in the bar was staring at the nutcase who couldn't stop laughing. Tears squeezed from the corner of Trufant's eyes. He scrubbed them away with the towel-bandage.

A red door on the far side of the bar flew open, banging off the brick wall. Feet scuffled on tile stairs, then Spinks and an older man in a suit appeared. The man in the suit was probably in his mid-sixties, but he had the barrel gut

180

and stocky build accustomed to hired muscle. He gave Spinks a rough shove that sent the reporter sprawling.

"Get the fuck outta here," the man said.

He threw something at Spinks. Something small. It bounced over the reporter's long leg and rolled to a stop at Loshak's feet.

It was the button mic.

"And be sure to take that shit with you."

CHAPTER 31

Loshak, Spinks, and Trufant sat around Pressler's desk at the Prairie Village station, not talking. The reporter's eyes were huge. He hadn't said anything the whole drive back.

A grin still curled on Trufant's lip, and the small man snorted every now and then. He'd given Loshak the play-by-play on stabbing himself as they drove back to the station. He would probably need medical attention — at the very least a tetanus shot — but for now he seemed thrilled with all the white towels he was staining red.

Loshak massaged his own throbbing wrist. He'd taken a handful of aspirin for it as soon as they got back, but it wasn't helping yet.

The door to Booking opened. In unison, the three of them turned toward it.

Pressler crossed the desk pool and sat gingerly behind his own. He had a wad of gauze shoved up each nostril, and the delicate skin under his eyes was already starting to swell. Beyond that, he looked nauseous. A far cry from the triumphant cowboy hog-tying the Strongman bouncer. Now that the guy was in a cell, Loshak supposed, the comedown was getting to the detective.

Trufant giggled.

"Will you shut up?" Pressler snapped. He chewed his lip a moment before he turned to address Loshak and Spinks. "We screwed the pooch on that one, boys. Just unzipped and bared our asses."

"They don't know why we were there," Spinks said. "I didn't tell them anything."

"But they know we were there for something." Loshak wrapped his hand around his wrist and squeezed. Sometimes pressure helped. "If there's anything at all going on there, no matter how small, it'll be cleaned out by the time we can get back in."

"What if we got a warrant?" Spinks asked.

"For what?" Pressler shook his head. "We got fuck-all to go on."

Spinks took a breath like he wanted to say something, then stopped.

"What?" Loshak asked.

"I— I saw something." He took another breath, then let it out. "But it might not be anything. It was like… Well, you know I saw the old guy in the bondage gear."

"That's legal in Kansas," Pressler said. "Consenting adults."

"But… but it might not have been." Spinks swallowed hard, then glanced from the portly detective to Loshak. "You heard that when I held the mic up to the door, right? You could hear the kid crying?"

Loshak shook his head.

"We didn't get any kids crying."

"It was a kid," Spinks said, his eyes going wide again. "I'm sure it was. Sounded like a girl, but it could've been a young boy. I think… I thought they were, like, doing bondage stuff to the kid, hurting him or her. It sounded bad."

"Did you see anything?" Loshak asked, leaning toward the reporter.

Spinks scowled and looked away.

"I kind of threw open the door and busted in on a guy. But like, immediately, the sound cut off. And there was just me and him staring at each other over this computer station. It was one of those weird moments where every second stretches out into an hour, and you have this nonverbal communication, except you have no idea what the other person is saying. Like they're shouting at you from inside a soundproof booth, but you can't even read their lips. Then I think I yelled at him… Or maybe he yelled at me? Then he was coming at me and wrestling me out the door. And… I didn't see a kid. I didn't see anything in the room but him and that desk full of monitors."

The four of them sat in silence for a moment. Loshak shut his eyes, replaying the scene as Spinks had described it. He came to a conclusion just before Trufant spoke up.

"No one's going to say it?" The smaller man grinned as if he were on the verge of cracking up again. "He was watching porn."

Spinks squinted. "Maybe." He didn't look convinced.

"Or CC footage of another room," Pressler said.

Loshak sat forward.

"We can get a warrant for videos. Real footage or child porn — either one, we can make arrests on that."

CHAPTER 32

Paperwork occupied the next several hours. Pressler insisted. Everything needed to be in order and properly documented before he would reach out to a judge.

"We gotta dot every 'i' and tail every capital 'Q', boys," he said more than once, voice all soft as though talking to himself more than them. "Them's the rules of the paper game."

With all the reports written, Pressler went about making arrangements for requesting a warrant.

In the meantime, Loshak and Spinks took the opportunity to stretch their legs. They milled around in the breakroom of the PVPD. Neither could sit still for more than a minute or two, so they alternatively paced and stood before a bulletin board covered with flyers for random upcoming events.

Loshak's mind wouldn't slow down. He was still jacked up from bursting into The Wooden Nickel. Residual adrenaline coursed through his system, brain flitting from thought to thought at an almost unbearable pace, utterly lacking in smooth segues. Jarring, even.

His eyes kept snapping to a neon green sheet of paper on the bulletin board. It touted some big country music festival coming up at the Platte County Fairgrounds, sporting a long list of artists that Loshak had never heard of. The only country music he liked was Hank Williams. Senior not junior. "Your Cheatin' Heart." "Lost Highway."

Little snippets of the songs played in his head as he thought of them. His flitting mind remembered that Hank's real first name was Hiram, for some reason. And then he remembered that Junior's nickname was Bocephus after some popular puppet from the 1940s or so.

The knuckles of Loshak's good hand flexed, his grip tightening on the paper cup of coffee he was holding. Spinks had gotten each of them a cup out of a machine in the hall, eschewing the Mr. Coffee in the break room for reasons unknown. The stuff was terrible, but Loshak couldn't stop sipping it. Maybe just to fill the time.

He watched Spinks take a sip of his terrible brew and grimace. And still he found himself overcome with the urge to drink some more.

He gazed down at the cup of muck in his hand. Why? Why was he doing this? He simultaneously dreaded it and couldn't resist.

After a beat of hesitation, Loshak took another sip of the sludge. Still God awful as ever and now firmly in lukewarm territory.

He swallowed a couple mouthfuls of saliva, as though that might cleanse the bitterness from his palate, and he wondered about the origins of the term "lukewarm." Why luke? Was there a guy named Luke involved in the naming of the term? A half-hearted type, maybe. Luke. That guy's wishy-washy, you know? Classic Luke. Weak personality. Yep. Just Luke being Luke.

The door banged open, startling Loshak out of his inane thought patterns. Pressler stormed into the breakroom, tie flapping to one side like a windsock.

"Get a load of this hot hooey!" Pressler shuffled over to

the bulletin board, shoving a phone into Loshak's face. The screen was black. "We ain't getting a warrant now, that's for damn sure."

Loshak frowned. "Why not?"

Spinks stepped around Pressler and tapped the phone's screen.

It was a local news channel's page, and their top story read, **BREAKING NEWS: FIREFIGHTERS BATTLING BLAZE AT HISTORIC LOCAL BAR.**

A video began to play automatically, featuring a dark-haired reporter in a purple quilted vest. She stood in front of an old brick building almost completely obscured by thick, roiling clouds of black smoke. A slew of police and fire vehicles with their flashers lit up had blocked traffic on the street.

"The fire here in Prairie Village broke out just about an hour ago, and as you can see, crews are still battling to get the fire under control."

The video cut to a shot with flames visible in the lower windows of the building. Out front, firemen hustled back and forth, adjusting hose lines and gesturing to each other.

"The blaze is believed to have started in The Wooden Nickel, a bar located in the basement of 3902 Prairie Lane, and quickly advanced into the upper levels of the building," the reporter continued.

"Damn it," Loshak muttered.

"There's been no official statement on the cause of the fire to this point, but authorities were able to share one bit of good news," the dark-haired reporter went on. "We have been told that no one was inside the building when the fire broke out."

The footage segued into a segment about the upcoming weather forecast, and Pressler thumbed the phone screen off.

"Pretty lucky how nobody was there when they burned the place to the ground, huh?" Spinks said.

CHAPTER 33

Loshak flexed and unflexed his fingers on the steering wheel. He took a deep breath and let it out slowly, but it didn't ease any of the tension squeezing his chest.

His head had gone light after Pressler shared the fire video, and the following moments remained distant in his memories. Dreamlike. He'd excused himself, walked out to his piece of shit rental, and now here he was. Driving through Kansas City for no good reason.

The city blurred past in the false twilight, the blackness of the sky above held at bay by the huge lamps illuminating the highways and streets. The glowing signs still stood out, but the buildings seemed to tuck themselves back into the shadows, reduced to dark silhouettes. Featureless black shapes in the murk.

He drove without purpose. Without a destination.

It felt like he was letting the car pick the path. Letting it sniff out which turns to take, which lanes to coast along in. He snaked through town like that, following the whims transmitted through the steering wheel into the meat of his hands as though it were a dowsing rod.

Aimless.

It fit, didn't it? Everything about this case felt that way. Directionless. No place to go.

He pressed the pedal down a little harder, felt the rental perk up a little on its tires as it accelerated. Sensed a lightness in his belly.

Wind blustered in through the open driver's side window. Messed up his hair. Cooled his cheeks.

That's what he'd said he needed when he ducked out. Air. But now that he was getting blasted with it, he knew it was no help. The air around here was always thick with humidity and caked with exhaust fumes. Never quite clean.

He smelled the smoke before he saw it. That charred odor hit and made him wrinkle his nose.

Scanning the sky, he found it. The oily cloud twirling up from the scene of the crime, tinted orange by the light pollution.

Might as well drive by. See what he could, which wouldn't be much. He wouldn't linger. Just a peek as he passed it by.

Yellow tape cordoned off that block, though, and what seemed like all the fire trucks for 500 miles crammed themselves as close as possible.

The smoke didn't look too thick up close. Translucent. More like a wispy cloud than a wall.

And he couldn't see any flames or any signs of the fire itself now. Maybe they had it mostly contained. He hoped so.

He pressed a little closer. Saw a little more.

Fire hoses trailed across the ground like beige snakes. Crooked lines that ran from the hydrant to the steps down toward the entrance of the building.

The spray itself seemed haphazard. Wetting not only The Wooden Nickel but the buildings around it. Probably to contain it, Loshak knew. Sometimes firemen had to dole out incredible water damage, preemptively dousing the surrounding buildings to keep a fire from raging for blocks.

Loshak hadn't planned to stop, hadn't even weighed the thought consciously, but before he knew it, he found himself parking. Getting out. Walking toward the smoldering building.

His hand still clutched the car keys as though to reassure himself that he was only stopping for a moment, would be leaving any second now. It was just a peek. That's all.

Before he even crossed the police tape threshold, he could hear those jets of water roaring and sizzling, slapping brick and concrete. Loud and obnoxious. Unbelievable water pressure.

A small crowd had gathered to watch in spite of the hour. Loshak flashed his badge at the uniformed officer watching the perimeter of the scene — a scrawny guy with a thin mustache who did a quick double take and then waved him through.

Twelve more steps over wet concrete and there it was.

Firemen huddled at the bottom of the concrete steps where he and Pressler had confronted the first bouncer just hours before. The steel door itself seemed to be gone. Removed?

The building lay open, wounded, and the firemen blasted water into those fissures. Their endless spray touching everything.

Loshak could just make out glimpses of the blackened innards of the club, but it was enough. They wouldn't be able to salvage any evidence from that mess. Not that he'd expected the people who started the fire would have left much to chance.

He stood there at the top of the stairs. Watched for a time. Listened to the water attacking everything.

His eye hurt as though the smoke might be bothering it, though he didn't think it was. Not really. Just another thing happening in his head.

Still, the bad eye kept blinking on its own. And for just a second, Loshak worried that one of the men would glance up just then and think he was winking at them. The ridiculous thought seemed his cue to leave.

Yes. He'd seen quite enough here.

He nodded to himself as he walked away.

CHAPTER 34

It's early in the morning, faintly light out, the air still thick with mist. Dank and heavy.

The shadow moves in the gray. He glides down the sidewalk a ways before cutting between houses, feet kicking up dew from the grass. Better to stay off the street when possible. Walk in the places in between.

He hates to be out in the light like this. Prefers the dark. That happens when you become a nocturnal creature, pushed out of the daytime for good. And it's for the best, ultimately. In the light, you can't disappear. You're more solid than you are at night. More real.

At night, the murk swallows reality up. Lets it shift and morph in the dark. Lets you disappear.

That's what the shadow wants, to disappear. Not to snuff out his life or existence so much as to vanish into a puff of smoke, into a cloud of darkness. Become invisible. Turn his physicality, his corporeality off and on at will and slip through the world like the ghost he is. To operate in the places where no eyes could go, do things no one could see, linger where nothing is quite real.

But this is a special circumstance, isn't it? He's watched this house for weeks. From a ways back at times, and close up at others, creeping right up to the glass to peer through the windows. Studied. Picked up on the routine of the impending target.

He knows the whole morning routine. Up at 5:45 AM,

every single day. A three to five minute shower. Two toaster strudels for breakfast. Raspberry. No icing. A round of flossing after brushing, which seems odd to him. Out the door by 6:15 at the latest, most days before 6:10. The time the target arrives home from work falls in the same type of short window — a seven-minute span from the earliest to the latest arrival shortly after 5 pm, a very tight window as these things go.

That leaves the house wide open all day long. His plan is to sneak in just after the target leaves, when the rest of the world is still quiet, still sound asleep. Entering just after dawn leaves very little chance of a witness.

The house appears up ahead on his left, a classy-looking Tudor, all clean and neat. He crosses through a yard, slides behind a couple of the neighbors' houses so he can reach the back door without ever having been on the street anywhere near the place. The daylight makes these extra steps necessary. Even shadows stand out in the light. Precautions must be taken.

The screen door screeches as it peels open, and the sound sends goosebumps all down the shadow's chest and the back of his neck.

But no lights snaps on in the neighbors' windows, no twitch or flutter shifts the blinds. Good.

He reaches down and cranks the knob of the steel backdoor. Locked.

Strange how often a door stands between us and what we want in life. Blocks us. A rectangular slab of wall that would swing out of our way if only we knew how to make it happen.

The shadow knows a way, luckily.

He pulls the little kit from inside his jacket and squats so that the lock is at eye level. Prods the keyhole with the tension wrench and rake, scrubbing back and forth at the pins slowly but surely. He jiggles the little wrench, finds it better to apply and remove ginger touches of torque.

Finally, the plug rotates freely. The deadbolt snicks out of the way.

A surge of adrenaline washes over the shadow. He huffs a silent laugh out of his nostrils. Why was it so exciting to cross these thresholds? To violate these boundaries drawn up all around us? Was it just that he wasn't supposed to be there? A simple breaking of the rules, that social contract that kept the trains running on time? Maybe these rules apply not at all to someone like him, a creature of the night, an Other. He feels a little like a vampire who'd found a way around the lack of invitation.

But he thinks it's more than that. Something primal. Something connected to the thrill of the hunt, being able to stalk his prey into their own lair and lie in wait for them.

He walks between the worlds. Makes his own rules. Doles out his own version of justice, however roughly.

The thought makes him smile.

Someone's waiting for you. Waiting in your house tonight.

The knob turns under his hand this time, that rectangular barrier gliding inward, and courtesy of nothing beyond his own ten fingers, the shadow finds his way unblocked.

CHAPTER 35

The bedside clock let out a high-pitched shriek, and Loshak flailed a hand out from the blankets to shut it up. He rolled over, savoring the coolness of the pillowcase against his cheek.

He needed to get up soon. Had to get something to eat and then meet up with Rainie for the Flickinger interview. But not yet. He could rest a little while longer.

It felt good to rest. And yet… he couldn't help but feel a sense of loss worming around in his gut. Almost a kind of grief, he thought. Because of what they'd found at Griffin's house. Because of what happened with The Wooden Nickel.

The fire at the club replayed in his head, the oily smoke, the firemen clustered around the basement entry gushing water into the bar.

There must have been something there worth covering up to go to the trouble of torching the place. They had nothing to show for that lead. A full stop on that line of investigation, and they didn't even really know what they might have had there. Never would now. All they really accomplished was tipping off pretty much everyone who had something to hide.

Trufant had helped work up a list of other group members. They could maybe start looking into them if nothing panned out with Flickinger.

Still, it felt like another closed door. Another lead that

went nowhere.

Somewhere in the midst of his drifting thoughts, Loshak fell asleep again. It was a dreamless sleep. Nothing but black emptiness surrounding him.

When he woke, he knew by the crack of bright sunshine peeking through the shades that he was running late.

He hustled out of bed, wondering if he'd have time to grab something from the breakfast buffet downstairs.

CHAPTER 36

The target's home feels cold and sterile, completely lacking in personality. Like a hotel room. Standard living room set, weird abstract art prints on the walls instead of family photos smiling down at him. No knickknacks cluttering the shelves and tables, no clothes or magazines or candy wrappers lying around.

Nothing that makes this place feel like a home.

The shadow strides from the sparse living room into the kitchen. There's a little pantry full of junk food — all Pop Tarts and Funyuns and multiple cases of Sprite.

Into the dining room. More weird art and one of those giant wall clocks manufactured to look old and faded. Instant heirloom. Faux personality.

He sits. Waits. Grows antsy. Clenches and unclenches his jaw and fists. Checks the time over and over on the giant mass-produced clock.

He's got eight hours to kill. Empty time. Nothing to do.

At first he thinks it's going to be hell, but as time starts to pass, the tension dies out in his shoulders and gut. That initial burst of adrenaline from picking the lock and sneaking in wanes. Even the restlessness fades to a calm kind of boredom.

The doldrums seem to settle over his body first and his mind soon after.

Mindfulness seeps into his head. Replaces the thoughts. Awareness.

What Lies Beneath

He observes the things around him in minute detail. Each tick of the clock. Each beat of his heart. Each fleck of color speckling the cream carpet. He does not judge these events, these details. Does not editorialize them in his mind with cleverness or irony.

He merely observes reality as it unfolds. The present moment — that endlessly fleeting now that happens and is gone over and over for eternity.

Something transcendent roils in his mind. Something bigger than him. A universal truth. He holds onto it for a while, though he paradoxically accomplishes this by letting himself go.

In time, sleepiness sneaks up on him. Heavies the eyelids. Loosens whatever neck muscles keep his head upright.

He paces to fight off the drowsiness. Constant motion.

Needs to distract his body, distract his mind. Hold sleep at bay.

He looks closer at the strange abstract prints this weirdo seems hell-bent on plastering the house with. Geometric shapes that raise no feelings inside of him. Orderly but meaningless. Drab colors. More ready-made character to hide the fact that the owner has none of their own.

Thinking about this reminds the shadow that he has a kill coming up in just a few hours, even if it doesn't seem real in the now.

He tries to picture it as it will happen. The gun lisping out two silenced bullets to the back of the head, entering near the brain stem and blowing a big wad of gore out of an exit wound in the face — something perhaps the size of a grapefruit.

He licks his lips when he sees the gory pictures, can almost smell the metallic stench of blood, can almost taste it.

Oh, he's tempted to picture it going other ways. Tempted to really let himself go. To free his hands and bash this little bitch's face in, but that wouldn't be right. Better to stay under control. Better to remain civilized. Find that cold, logical place where all these executions come from.

So many people, whether they be truly violent or not, seem to fetishize expressions of rage. Overkill exaggerated to dramatic proportions. He absolutely understands why. Hate demands catharsis, lusts after the feel of the kill expelled through hands and arms somehow. It wants to be experienced as a physical sensation, internal tension turned to muscle tension, the emotional made real, etched into the concrete world, pressed into being with the hands.

It would've been easy to let that lust for violence run away with him when it came to Griffin. Even more so with the councilman. Maybe he would've let himself go to town on them if this was just about him or Maria, if it was only personal. But so much rests on his actions. Something beyond him, bigger than him. He can't fuck it up with emotions, can't risk it.

Besides, there's something unfairly generous about violence like that, a strange kind of empathy to it. To appreciate the suffering of the victim actually gives them value. It considers their interior world, points a camera at them and zooms all the way in. It's a way of saying their deaths matter enough to give them the full theatrical run, and he won't do that, won't give them that.

These people? They aren't worth it.

He'll make it fast. Distant. As impersonal as the abstract paintings hung up and down these walls. Not out of mercy. Out of something lean and hard. Something icy and animal.

Two quick, cold-blooded bursts. Justice in the squeeze of a trigger, and boom, it's over. Their light snuffed out forfuckingever in the time it takes to blink.

No need to belabor it. No need to be sentimental at all. No feelings. No words. Just action.

While these thoughts pulse through his skull, he opens drawers and cupboards and closet doors, digging through stuff dispassionately. Just killing time until it's killing time.

He opens a drawer by the sink and freezes. There's a picture inside, in one of those big, plastic-windowed envelopes, the kind he used to get his school photos in.

Through the clear plastic, smiling teeth and squinted brown eyes beam up at him. Curly brown hair like a mop, a yuppie suit jacket over a blue shirt.

He lifts the photograph to get a closer look.

It's her. The target. Must be from a few years back. One of those fake-looking photos in front of a backdrop. Looks like something she got taken at a mall or something.

Mitzi Davis. She's an insurance agent. He's seen her updated photo on a business card.

He swallows, unable to shift the odd lump in his throat.

This will be the first woman he's killed. Part of him wonders if that will fuck him up at all when the time comes. Make him hesitate or something.

But no, it doesn't matter if she's a man or a woman.

She's on the list. Her number got called. Today's her day. He'll make it fast like he always does. Boom. Justice.

CHAPTER 37

The sun was high overhead when Loshak pulled into the parking lot of the Mission Hills Police station. Rainie met him in the lobby with her coat over one arm and keys jangling in her free hand.

"Ready to drive forever?" she asked cheerfully.

"Born ready," Loshak answered.

It was a stupid thing to say, he realized after it came out. Didn't make any sense. Something about the young detective made him want to project an air of glibness to match hers.

It made him think of Pressler's apparent need to be accepted by Spinks, and the cool kids versus the periphery kids again. Maybe there were just some people whose personality called to others', who made you want to reshape your own personality to fit with theirs. A charisma that allowed certain people to affect the behavior of others. Or maybe it was Spinks and Pressler insisting that Rainie liked him. Maybe he would be going about his business blissfully un-self-aware if they had kept their mouths shut.

Whatever it was, he was overly conscious of his body language and demeanor as they crossed the parking lot.

"Right here," Rainie said, thumbing the key fob and unlocking a powder blue Escape. "I know it looks like some ho's eye shadow, but it gets great mileage."

She grinned, and Loshak jerked his head at the rental a row over.

"I can't really talk. Most of the time I'm on the road driving rentals older than you are, and when I'm home I'm driving an appletini-green Saturn Vue."

Rainie laughed.

"I didn't know they let men buy those."

"You have to get special permission."

They climbed into the little SUV. When Loshak shut his door and turned to buckle up, he found Rainie studying him.

"I figured you for more of a muscle car type, that's all," she said, starting the car.

Loshak shook his head.

"I'm not going outside at two in the morning in a Virginia winter to plug in a tank heater. And fuel injection's spoiled me. I like the modern conveniences too much. Anyway, the Appletini-mobile was my neighbor's. She lost her license when her eyes went bad — cataracts — and wanted to put it up for sale. But she couldn't work a computer to put it on Craigslist, and my junker went out around the same time. Seemed natural to make an offer."

"That's actually really cool," she said.

Rainie eased them out of the parking lot into the late morning traffic.

"It's dumb how into new cars some people get. Like the newest model right off the lot is going to make driving a more fulfilling experience or never break down, so much so that they can't even imagine buying used. I figure if it gets you from point A to point B, everything else is just an upsell."

Loshak smiled. There was something in all this that reminded him of Spinks' characterization of him as a millennial. That and the rise in opinion pieces that said millennials were killing the economy by refusing to buy big-ticket items new. Maybe the reporter was on to something.

"Did you have lunch?" Rainie asked, glancing over at him. "Because I was thinking of getting something from a drive-through. That way we can scarf it on the way."

"I could eat. By the time I made it down to my hotel's so-called 'Continental Breakfast,' they were already closing up. I had to settle for a Nutri-Grain bar."

Rainie wrinkled her nose.

"Yeah, I don't think that's going to cut it."

She merged, blasting the horn when another car tried to cut her off. Her expression didn't change. Road rage was just an ingrained response with no sentimental ties.

After a few moments of silence, Rainie said, "I heard about last night. About the undercover operation and fire and everything."

Loshak sighed and ran a hand through his hair.

"Yeah, I believe Pressler had it right when he referred to it as a 'clusterfuck with a capital C.'"

Rainie nodded. "On the bright side, at least you solved one mystery."

"What's that?"

"You figured out who was sending the notes. That's gotta ease your mind at least a little, to have one box checked off."

Loshak thought about it for a second. He hadn't realized it, but he did feel slightly less tense. One less thing to worry about, she was right about that.

"Yeah, I guess it does," he admitted.

"How do you feel about grinders?" Rainie's question broke through his musing.

"Good when they're hot," Loshak said. "Less than favorable when they're cold cuts on cold bread with cold cheese."

"That," she said, flipping on her turn signal, "is the right answer."

Ten minutes later, they were pulling out of the Bellacino's parking lot with a pair of long cardboard boxes in their laps. Rainie's contained an eighteen-inch Bayou Chicken grinder, minus onions, plus pickles and bacon. Loshak had gone for a Cuban of the same size, oven-crisp bread stuffed with three kinds of ham — smoked, sugar-cured, and black forest — four cheeses, and spicy dill pickles.

While they were stopped at the next light, Rainie turned the radio on low, thumbing through things on her phone until some sort of psychobilly filtered through the car's speakers.

"I hate eating in silence," she said. "I'm so sure everybody can hear me chewing, and *I* don't even like to hear me chewing. It's nerve-wracking."

"Music is supposed to help digestion, anyway," Loshak said, opening his box and unfolding the foil around the first nine inches of his sandwich.

"That's what I'm going to tell people from now on." Rainie propped her phone on the dash. "'I'm aiding your digestion. You're welcome.'"

They ate to the psychobilly soundtrack, then stored their boxes in the back seat to await the next trash can.

"So, how much do we want to reveal to Flickinger about

the second serial killer?" Rainie asked. "Just stick to the questions about Mike Dent, or should we drop that we've found bodies at the Griffin house? See if that gets a reaction out of him?"

Loshak scrubbed his hands with a brown paper napkin.

"You're assuming someone besides Neil Griffin knew something about his killings?"

"I don't know what to assume anymore," she said. "I just figured he's probably seen it on the news already. Maybe dropping it in our interview will surprise him enough to knock something loose in his memory."

"I'm not sure how effective it would be. Might overshadow anything he remembers or make him start reaching for things to have been suspicious about. But we can keep it in mind, maybe bring it up near the end and see where he goes with it. So, I guess you're in the vigilante camp?"

"For our first killer?" Rainie nodded. "It fits a lot of the evidence. Although I could see this as a partnership gone wrong, too. Griffin screws over somebody working with him on the killings and they take it out on him. That one's shakier, because then why are all these other people with no apparent connection being targeted, too? Really, they're both shaky for that same reason. Why are these other people being killed? Why not just shoot Griffin and be done with it?"

Loshak squeezed his fingers around the napkin in his fist, compacting it into a little ball.

"That's what I'm hoping to find out," he said.

CHAPTER 38

The shadow climbs into a closet in a guest bedroom and obscures himself with a blanket. There's barely anything stored in there, and nothing on the floor. The space proves more than big enough for him to stretch out. He's got time to catch a little sleep.

He sets the alarm on his phone for four-thirty, that way he'll have plenty of warning before she gets home. If something unforeseen happens, he's probably hidden well enough to adjust his strategy and still get the job done.

In any case, he trusts that the target will follow her routine. She seems like the rigid type.

Sleep comes quickly and swallows him whole.

In his dream, he walks through a thick forest in the middle of fall. Dead leaves line the ground and crunch with every step. His breath puffs out little clouds of steam.

The branches around him are bare and skeletal. Bony arms reaching for the sky.

He works his way up a hill, traversing a steep incline in a zig-zag pattern.

Up ahead, on top of the rise, he can vaguely make out a place where the ground flattens out and the going might not be so tough. Looks like the trees thin out up there, too.

When he reaches the top, instead of the clearing he imagined, there's just a black hole in the ground. A hollow place where the earth drops off into nothingness. Almost like a well without any stones surrounding it or walls of any kind. Borderless.

The kind of image that can only make sense in a dream.

As he stares down into the pit, his skin crawls. It feels distinctly like he is looking into nowhere. Illogical. Impossible.

But in the dream it makes perfect sense.

Some distant part of him knows that he's had this dream before. Many times. A recurring dream image that morphs and plants itself in new locations.

Sometimes the black hole nestles in the side of a tree.

Sometimes it gapes in the floor of his old bedroom.

Sometimes it hovers in the sky.

And the aware part of him, the part that remembers these things, is scared.

Because it knows how the dream always ends.

The camera in his skull zooms in on that black nothing little by little until it fills the frame, until it's the only thing. Until nowhere is everywhere. Until nothing is everything.

And he lies there again. Face down in the dirt. Underneath the house.

In the crawlspace.

But in the moment, he wasn't in the crawlspace, was he? He was in The Nowhere.

Only looking back could he piece any of the reality together, what really happened. In the moment, there existed only the dark and his fear. The strange loudness of his breath echoing back at him.

He only remembers fragments of being there. Panicking. So scared and confused to awaken in the dark place.

And the smell. The smell like swollen roadkill

everywhere. The stench of death smeared on his skin. Forcing its way inside him through his nose and mouth, filling him up with every breath.

He pushes himself up onto hands and knees. Bangs his shoulders blade into wooden joists which knock him right back down into the mud.

A tight space. Confined. Almost like a casket.

His head throbs. Waves crash inside. Confusion. Dizziness. Pain. Some chemical taste in his mouth and throat.

He can't remember how he got here, how any of this is happening. Head woozy. Thinks he's been drugged.

He feels his way around and around. Feels mud and rocks and odd shapes he thinks must be bones. His eyes see nothing for so long that they start to imagine oil spills of color rippling in front of him, semi-translucent rainbows that morph endlessly.

Until he sees it. At last. The little glimmer of light. It streams through a crack.

Then that's all he can see. Scrambling toward it, hands and knees pistoning over the stony earth to take him there, desperate to get out. Shoving the panel of metal skirting out of the way, pushing with both hands, then really leaning into it with his shoulder, digging his feet into the wet dirt until panel pops free.

The memories from before the crawlspace are mostly wiped. The faces are blurred. Details of the settings erased. He remembered walking down near the SMSU campus, trying to find a house party to go to, because back then he thought things like that mattered. But the memories fuzz out from there, leaving him behind while he was still on his feet.

The phone alarm only has to vibrate once to wake him. He's not a heavy sleeper. Hasn't been since it happened.

The little rattle against his chest brings reality flooding back so hard that he sucks in a startled breath.

He swipes the alarm to Off and blinks a few times. His chest pulls tight, muscles all constricted, and his hands want to shake as he sticks the phone back in his pocket.

But he's OK. Hunkered in the closet in the target's guest room. The light streaming in through the spaces in the slatted door remind him where he is, remind him that he's OK.

Memories of the black dream swirl in the shadows around him, but just for a moment. They will pass. The fear will fade away. It always does.

They thought he was dead when they stuck him down in that crawlspace under the Griffin house. They must have. And maybe he was close.

Half dead. Half buried.

But he climbed out of the ground.

And he was coming back for all of them.

CHAPTER 39

Coach Flickinger was in his office off the UCM football locker room reviewing game tape when they arrived. The special teams coordinator was younger, just hitting middle age if Loshak's guess was right, and only now starting to go soft around the gut.

"Come on in," Flickinger said, shaking their hands. "Have a seat."

As Loshak and Rainie took the chairs on the player side of the desk, Flickinger shut the office door. The rough, knobby texture of the upholstery and the wooden frames of the chairs reminded Loshak of the seats in a public library. OK for the short term, but not something you'd want to sit in all day. Flickinger's chair, on the other hand, was one of those rolling, ergonomic kinds with the cushioned armrests and Swedish names.

"So, you guys are still looking into whoever killed Mike, huh?" Flickinger asked. "I definitely want to help, I'm just not sure if there's anything useful I can tell you. We just worked together."

Loshak nodded.

"From what Mrs. Dent said about Mike, it sounds like he was a workaholic. You probably spent as much time around him as she did."

Flickinger laughed.

"Well, that much is probably true. Football was life for Mike. If he wasn't here until all hours, he was on the road, recruiting. I'm surprised Tricia ever got to see the guy, as much as he was gone."

"Is that pretty common for a college coach?" Rainie asked.

"Mike definitely took it to an extreme."

Flickinger rocked back in his chair and crossed his ankle over his knee. The move pulled up the leg of his khakis to reveal a neon green, navy, and orange argyle sock.

"Hell, last year the guy went from Soledad Canyon to San Antonio to Chicago in a month. All over the damn country and back again. You can't neglect the schools right here at home, either — Mike was clear about that. He probably burnt up more county roads in Missouri than all the little hicks out in the sticks combined, visiting promising high school players and little colleges like SMSU and Central Methodist, scoping for transfer fodder. Mizzou and Nebraska block us out from getting the best players, and in turn we block all the Division III schools from getting the second-tier guys. It's a vicious cycle."

"Sounds like it," Loshak agreed. "Mrs. Dent mentioned you all lost your last game, the one against Western."

Flickinger grunted in frustration and threw one hand up in the air.

"Shanked a twenty-yard field goal in the last three minutes. Supposed to be a chip shot, but the kid banged it off the upright. Sounded like someone struck a gong or something. You could hear the impact over all the crowd noise and everything. Can you believe that? And what's worse, the kid could hit it again a hundred times in a row if you gave him a hundred shots. It was just one of those nights."

"From what we heard, Mike got pretty upset with you over it. Mrs. Dent said he gave you an earful after the game."

Flickinger frowned in confusion for a moment, then seemed to comprehend.

"What, that? Look, Mike can — could — blow his top if he felt like you weren't taking the game as seriously as he was," Flickinger said before raising both hands as if to stop them from jumping to any conclusions. "Which is a good quality, don't get me wrong. But he didn't always remember that I'm trying to get a bunch of underclassmen field-ready here, not coaching the Chiefs. If anybody's gonna crack under pressure, it's gonna be the specialists. That's just how it is. Opposing coaches ice the kickers for a reason, you know?"

"Did Mike ever blow up at any of his players or the administration?" Rainie asked. "Anybody who might have held a grudge?"

"Nah, no way. I mean, he'd lose it now and then at the players, but it was all to make them better and help us win. The players understood. You gotta have that hunger. Mike always called it keeping a hard edge. An attitude. An aggressive way of doing things. If you don't have it, you might as well go on home."

From the gleam in Flickinger's eyes, Loshak thought it was likely at least the end of the special teams coach's little spiel was part of a go-to pep talk. The man seemed to have some genuine admiration for the late defensive coordinator.

"Was there anything strange about Mike's behavior

lately?" Loshak asked. "Any changes in work habits or routine?"

"Like I said, I wasn't around him all the time," Flickinger said, rocking his chair a little. "Everything seemed pretty normal to me. I guess he was out of the office a little more, but he really kicked the recruiting into overdrive last year. I told you about the rapid-fire recruiting trips over the summer. But he was just really laser-sighted in on that championship. He felt like this year was our year. Probably why he lost it when we went down to Western."

"Any big changes in spending?"

"No, not that I—" Flickinger stopped rocking his chair. "Maybe there was something. Not money-wise. I mean, like his work habits. But—"

He pressed his lips together and shook his head.

"—it's probably nothing. I just thought it was kind of weird, you know? Usually he locks up the whole locker room for the night, but there was one night last winter when... Oh, hell, this isn't anything. My mind's just playing tricks on me, trying to make stuff seem strange when it's not."

Loshak gave him a reassuring look.

"That's alright. Go ahead and say it, no matter how it sounds. It's our job to comb through all the details — all of them — because we'll never know which one will help us catch Mike's killer until we find it," Loshak said.

It never ceased to amaze him how much most people avoided speaking ill of the dead. Of course, he'd come across plenty of witnesses that had no qualms about airing the deceased's dirty laundry, but for the most part, people didn't even want to suggest that anything was amiss with the victim. He'd learned years ago that a subtle reminder that there was a murderer at large was usually the way to ease any misgivings.

Flickinger exhaled, nostrils flaring.

"Well, one night a few months back, he locked up the locker room and his office. I left some papers in his office — just a folder with some scouting reports in it — so I let myself into the locker room with my key. But I couldn't get his office door open — I don't have a key to it. I didn't remember him ever locking it before unless he was staying there, but he wasn't there that night. I guess I just thought it was weird that he locked it up. Kind of a stupid thing to get all bent outta shape about."

Loshak caught Rainie's eye, and she sat forward.

"Do you think we could see his office?" she asked.

CHAPTER 40

The shadow watches her car pull up the driveway from the guest bedroom window. His heart speeds up, adrenaline spiking again.

Time elongates. Hours pass after the car's engine cuts out.

He waits. Listens. Trains his ears beyond the roar of the blood pounding in them. Feels droplets of sweat bead along his hairline.

At last the front door opens and slams shut again.

Mitzi Davis is home.

He hears keys jangle onto a hard surface in what sounds like the living room, then linoleum crackle in the kitchen. Routine sounds that seem almost violent after sitting in the quiet for so long.

He creeps out of the guest room and down the hall. Every step sounds like a bomb detonating. Every breath like a scream. Shrill and dry.

He pauses before stepping into the living room. Forces himself to find that cool, logical place in his mind where these executions must flow from.

In the kitchen, the fridge's seal cracks, followed by the hiss of an aluminum pop tab. An after-work Sprite to take the edge off.

The shadow raises the gun and follows it into the living room, eyes on the kitchen doorway. She's not standing directly in front of it, so all he can see is the sink and the window into the backyard. If she's still by the fridge, she'll be off to the right when he walks through the door. If she's not, then she's off to the left.

Which way?

Better to guess wrong than hesitate. He swivels his body and the gun to the right and steps over the threshold.

Nothing but fridge. Shit.

He's still spinning around when he hears Mitzi gasp. She backs up against the countertop, almost climbing it ass first, and wings the Sprite at him. The throw catapults from her shoulder. Nothing dangerous, but it startles him.

He squeezes his eyes shut and jerks his face away instinctively. The can smacks into his neck, and the gun goes off.

A bullet smacks the upper cabinet, leaving a splintery divot in the wood near the knob.

Instead of screaming for help or running, Mitzi grabs the toaster and swings this at him, too. It's solid. Heavier than it looks.

The appliance slams into his knuckles on a downward arc. Strips the gun out of his hands.

The weapon slides to a stop halfway under the dishwasher.

And already she's grabbing for more shit. There's a butcher block full of knives just a few feet away from her. If he doesn't do something, she'll get to it before he does.

He lurches out. Catches her by the shirt and wrist just as she lifts a cutting board to brain him with. He twists, the torque buckling her at the waist and then the knees, dragging her and the cutting board to the ground.

He sees the flash as her eyes lock on the gun. Pupils

218

swelling like a cat spotting a bird through the window.

She drops the cutting board. Goes rigid for a split-second. Then she's clawing and kicking, her fingernails going for his eyes.

Gouging. Scratching.

He's got to fight and grapple to stay on top, to keep her from getting to the gun.

He bites down. Hard. Not sure what body part his teeth grip and gnaw.

She shrieks out an awful sound. Piercing.

Then she bites back.

Leaned in. Face to his shoulder.

There's so much adrenaline surging through her now that he feels her tearing a chunk of flesh from him. A ragged hole in the meat of him.

Screaming agony.

The words come to him from nowhere. One calm thought in all the commotion:

A fight to the death.

Mitzi bucks and thrashes under him. Wild. Insane.

The rabid look of a trapped animal twists her face into something ugly, something completely unlike the photos of her he's seen. Something savage.

It's a constant struggle to maintain control of their wrestling. He uses his weight to keep her down. Somehow he manages to get a grip on both wrists to mostly control her like a puppet.

At last his hands shift to her throat.

Squeeze.

Squeeze.

Squeeze some more.

He squeezes until cramps roll through this hands and forearms.

Heat crawls up from his core. Grips his neck. Touches his cheeks.

This is the opposite of cold and calculated. This is ending her life in the most vicious, personal way possible.

But it has to happen.

She has to die.

So be it.

Breath heaves in and out of his lungs. Raspy and ragged and dry.

His tongue lolls out of his mouth as if he's a panting Doberman. He feels the wet of it touching his lip. Squirming there.

And maybe now his face twists in that wild way, too. Ugly and savage. Some beast gone feral in a death fight.

She still bucks beneath him, but not like before. Exhaustion. Strangulation. These things catch up. Drain the fight from her.

The flesh of her face goes dark and veiny. Deepens to burgundy. Almost to purple. Fades to gray.

At last she lies still.

He unclamps his hands from around her neck. They're cramped, clawed. He falls off her corpse and leans against the wall. Lies there sucking dry wind in and spewing it back out all wet and hot.

He can feel the blood surging out of the bite wound in his shoulder. It's worse than he first realized.

And little panicked whispers replace the calm words in his head.

Blood loss.

What Lies Beneath

Hemorrhage.
Exsanguination.
He needs to get out of here.

CHAPTER 41

"Nobody's moved anything, as far as I know," Flickinger said, holding the door open and clicking on the light. "Except I did take the TV and the Western game tape out to my office. That's it, though. We'll probably get around to clearing this place out sometime, send Mike's stuff home to Tricia and the kids. Eventually. I'm not sure what the time limit is for respecting the dead, but it didn't feel right moving his things around yet."

Loshak and Rainie wandered through the office, looking over the artifacts left behind by a man obsessed with his work. There was the twin mattress Tricia Dent had mentioned, the makeshift Murphy bed leaned up against one wall, between a set of shelves covered in binders and game tapes and a desk covered in stacks of paper, clipboards, and folders with the year and "Offense" or "Defense" typed on the label.

On the long wall behind the desk hung a whiteboard with a series of plays and defenses drawn out in fading red and black marker. X's and O's with arrows diagramming blitz packages and bubbles to mark the borders of the zone coverage.

While Rainie sifted through the papers covering the desk, Loshak began opening drawers. He did it as gently as he could, considering Flickinger's feelings about disturbing Dent's things.

Loshak didn't know what he was looking for exactly. A

flashing neon sign that said something like *Evidence here!* would be nice. The first drawer contained whiteboard markers, erasers, pens, pencils, a headset with a broken earpiece, staples, and a staple remover, but no stapler. The stapler turned up in the second drawer, sitting on top of a black metal box that sparked some vague recognition in Loshak's head.

He pulled it out and held it up. The box didn't feel heavy enough.

"Is this a pistol safe, Coach?" he asked.

"Well, yeah," Flickinger said, shrugging. "Mike had a C-and-C, but I doubt the gun's in there. I think he kept it in his truck."

"Why would Mike need a conceal and carry permit?" Loshak asked.

"You don't meet a lot of people around here without one," the special teams coach said, each fist propped on either hip. "He got it... oh, within last year or two. Tricia wanted him to have something to protect himself with while he was traveling. He got mugged on one of his recruiting trips — some dickhead busted his nose and gave him a serious shiner — so he bought that."

CHAPTER 42

It's pouring rain now. Dark. The asphalt shiny with the wetness. Glistening under the streetlights.

The shadow is soaked. Shivering. Pressing his wadded up hoodie to the wound in his shoulder.

All of his clothes hang limp from the weight of the water. Heavy. Pressing the cold moisture into him. Smearing. They make a slopping sound when he walks.

The rhythm of his steps awkward and jerky. He can hear his feet scuffing and dragging, but he doesn't feel them all the way. Distant. Almost anesthetized. Like they're on the verge of going to sleep.

The rain brought in the cold. What's it called? A front. It numbs his limbs, that lack of sensation slowly seeping into his core. The chill makes him arch his shoulders. Makes his jaw tremble. The blood loss probably isn't helping, either.

The street around him stares back all industrial warehouses and a distribution center. Cinder blocks. Gravel. Concrete. Everything painted shades of gray.

There's only one house for blocks, a crumbling Victorian with boarded up windows and a rotten roof about to fall in over the porch. Obviously abandoned.

Home sweet home.

His head flutters, going light. Tingly.

Part of him didn't think he'd make it home, and now he wants only to get inside and lie down. Close his eyes. Rest.

He'll clean the wound later, worry about his blood smears at the scene later, deal with everything else in the world later.

He stumbles up the steps, skipping the broken one out of habit, and lets himself in.

It's colder inside — like a cave, this place holds in the chill — and it's even darker in here than it was outside. The streetlights can't break through the boarded windows.

He passes through a dark foyer into a candlelit living room. A group of kids, early teens and down, cluster on the mattresses, draped in blankets to ward off the dank air in this place.

When he staggers in, they all sit up. He was hoping to sneak in, stay quiet so they could sleep, but he must not have been doing a great job of staying light on his feet. Must be more woozy than he realized.

He needs to sit for a moment. Gather himself. Wait for the world to grow all the way solid beneath him once more.

He goes for a gentle descent onto the mattress with only one kid-shaped shadow on it, but his body is too numb. Too stiff.

He loses his balance. Crashes down. Something of a belly flop. Bouncing a little on the worn-out springs. The landing throttles his head and neck. Tries to jerk them away from his shoulders.

But just as quickly he goes still. Peaceful. Sprawled in a relaxing pose. All of the muscles that held him upright, dragged him here? They call all let go now.

He closes his eyes.

"Holy shit, Dylan, is that blood?"

"Are you hurt?"

"Oh my gosh, you guys, that's blood."

He feels the mattress shift as they gather around him. All the childish voices filter down to him, some talking to him, some talking about him.

"What happened?"

"Did someone attack him?"

He hears a flashlight click on — one of their LED solar lanterns — and bright red shines through the backs of his eyelids, the angry shade lighting up the inside of his skull.

"There. See? He's been stabbed."

"No. Stabs are straight, a slit like a line. That wound is ragged. Like... like a bite."

"Like an animal?"

"I mean... maybe?"

Dylan sighs and looks up at the scared faces. The worry makes them look even younger. Kegan, the littlest one, looks like she's about to cry.

"It's not a big deal. I just got caught on the top of a barbwire fence," he drawls, forcing a self-deprecating smirk. "Tore it up pretty good, but I'll be fine. I've survived worse."

They all go quiet for a beat, like they're surprised he could tell them what happened. Maybe the blood made them sort of forget that he knew how to talk.

Sam, a rail-thin fourteen-year-old with a crooked jaw, is the first to jump back in again. He always is. Couldn't shut that kid up to save his life.

"The fence protecting the Dierberg's dumpsters?"

"That's the one," Dylan says.

"You didn't throw anything over the top?" Sam asked, his thick eyebrows coming together. "You gotta throw

226

something over the top before you climb it. A blanket. A floor mat from a car. At least a jacket or something."

Dylan pushes up onto an elbow.

"I'm the one who taught you that, dingus."

"Well, why didn't you do it then, genius?"

Dylan huffs out a laugh. Sam's mouthy attitude got him every time.

"I was in a rush, OK? I got overconfident, and I paid the price. Let this be a lesson to you. Take heed. Learn from my bloody mistake."

That calms them down. Just another barbwire accident during a round of dumpster diving. That's a danger they can comprehend, one they can control and prevent. The damage from something like that isn't scary; it's just inconvenient.

Movement from the opposite side of the living room catches his eye. A girl his own age with long, straight black hair, soft golden-brown skin, and a round baby bump that looks too large for her petite frame.

"Come, let me clean that before it gets infected," Maria says, her pretty accent giving the words a slightly foreign lilt.

Dylan doesn't want to move, but she takes his hand and pulls. She'll keep doing it, too, he knows. She won't let something like this go. Not wanting her to strain herself or hurt the baby, he sits up, then stands, but he's unable to stifle the grunt of pain.

"Is it so bad?" she asks, her dark eyes showing concern in the flickering candlelight.

Dylan smiles and shakes his head.

"Nah. Just being a baby about it."

She *tsks*, picks up one of the lanterns and heads for the hall, waddling a little.

"Y'all need to get some sleep," he tells the kids, then follows Maria out of the living room, the lantern light lurching along the walls around them.

CHAPTER 43

"Should've brought an umbrella," Rainie said, shielding water from her face with a hand cupped at her brow.

The night sky had opened up since they went in to the UCM Athletics' Department, and now rain was blowing across the parking lot in sheets. They jogged to the shelter of Rainie's Escape and climbed in.

"What'd you think of Flickinger?" she asked.

Loshak wiped his face on his already soaked jacket sleeve.

"Not interested in murdering his boss, let alone three other strangers. I'm thinking we check the records for the make and caliber of Dent's gun. Probably won't tell us anything, but it can't hurt."

They were already drowning in information that didn't seem to add up, so why the hell not?

"For sure," Rainie said, starting the Escape's engine. Outside, the precipitation picked up. She raised her voice to be heard over the drumming on the roof. "I'll get that in motion as soon as we get back to the station."

"It's pretty late for that, isn't it?" Loshak asked. The kettle calling the pot a workaholic.

She shrugged.

"The sooner we nail this guy, the better. I'll take all the information I can get, and I'll take it now, please."

"Keep acting like that and you might just make a career out of this police gig," Loshak joked.

"Oh, don't you worry." Rainie twisted around to look over her shoulder as she backed them out of the parking space. "I'm aiming for Chief of Police. Take no prisoners, accept no substitutions."

She shifted into Drive, the rapid-fire clunking of the stick serving as emphasis for her declaration.

Loshak found himself smiling.

"Well, if you decide chief isn't for you, I could recommend you to the Academy."

Rainie looked over at him, that ten-year-old's grin on her face again.

"Seriously? I think that's the nicest thing anyone's ever said to me."

She steered through the parking lot and pulled out onto the road before she spoke again. The rain landed in fist-sized splatters on the windshield.

"Maybe. I could maybe take you up on that," she said, grinning. "I did say accept no substitutions, though, and now I'm considering a substitution. I feel like this is some kind of moral pop quiz."

Loshak raised his hands.

"I'm just offering an alternative. You never know."

"I do know, though. It's all planned out, see?"

She began mapping things out on an invisible timeline, moving her hands a little farther apart each time she added a new event.

"I kick more than the requisite amount of ass. Take various names. In doing so, I get a ridiculous amount of recognition and become the best-known detective in Mission Hills. Get promoted to Head Detective. Old chief steps down, I throw my hat into the ring. They have no choice but to hire me."

"It's a decent plan," Loshak conceded, nodding.

Rainie snorted.

"It's bullshit and I know it. Nothing works out like that. You gotta know somebody in high places to make chief, and I don't have those kinds of connections. Yet. I need to add that to the To-Do List."

She brought the invisible timeline back up, hands wide, then pointed to a spot near the middle.

"Networking. Right between taking names and kicking ass. Maybe throw in some charity work, just to round out my extra-curriculars."

The charity work comment brought Loshak back to the case. Griffin's strange obsession with charity work. Making the city a better place by day and storing kids' bodies under his house by night. And now their first victim had a gun.

"The gun thing could be a coincidence." Loshak felt obligated to point that out, just in case it was all a waste of time.

"Honestly, it would be weirder if he didn't have a gun," Rainie said as she merged onto Highway 50.

The headlights lit up every drop like a sparkler against the asphalt backdrop.

"Everybody and their grandma has a conceal and carry in Missouri. Heck, my little sister has hers, and she's a stay-at-home mom."

When the last words sunk in, Loshak's stomach did a weird flip-flop that went right along with the rhythm of the windshield wipers.

"Jesus. Does she keep her gun locked up where her kids can't get at it?"

"No, she keeps it in their bedroom, in the sock drawer of their My Little Pony dresser. But don't worry, she only loads a few rounds at a time, just in case."

"Alright, alright." Loshak huffed a laugh at the dryness in her voice. "It was one of those knee-jerk reactions. But I've seen more end results of a kid getting on the wrong end of a gun he thought was a toy than I want to think about."

Rainie dropped the sarcasm.

"I get that. Really. But I don't know," she said, shaking her head. "The attitude around here is different. Most people in the rural areas start out teaching their kids pretty much from the womb how to respect guns, same as you would teach a kid that a knife is dangerous. It's just something you grow up ingrained with, like don't run with scissors and don't pee your pants."

"Maybe not quite the same," Loshak said.

She shrugged, face neutral in the blue dashboard light, and turned on some music. Loshak didn't know enough about psychobilly to tell if this was the same band as before. The lyrics kept talking about being pushed out of the light and becoming a nocturnal creature.

They drove for a while with nothing but the sound of the rain on the roof, the thump of the wipers, the splash of the water on the highway, and the twanging, frantic songs.

Loshak wondered if he'd offended Rainie. The sudden shift seemed to indicate a yes. He didn't want to spend an hour drive in awkward silence, but he wasn't sure what to say.

"Did you grow up around here?" he asked, feeling like the uncle who asks his nieces and nephews what grade they're in now every time he sees them.

"Not in the KC metro area," she said. "I'm from Blue Springs. It's a small town — compared to Mission Hills, I mean — over here in Missouri. The kind of place all the cliché kids are dying to leave behind so they can prove themselves in the big city."

She grinned and rolled her eyes.

"But not *too* far behind. Only about a half hour, forty minutes, if traffic's good."

There was something contagious about Rainie's smile. Loshak couldn't stop himself from smiling, too.

"Big fish, small pond syndrome," he said.

"I got it bad," she said, giving the steering wheel cover a little twist and sighing. "I just can't seem to grow out of it."

CHAPTER 44

They call the room at the end of the hall the master bedroom. It's theirs — his and Maria's. They're the only ones who really needed the privacy, anyway. Like parents. Sometimes you need alone time where the kids know not to bother you.

Dylan eases himself down onto their mattress while Maria goes through the little stockpile of medicine stuff. He's getting control back over his body, the numb, tingling feeling fading for the moment.

"Was it her?" Maria asks, digging out the hydrogen peroxide and a couple gauze pads from when Parker cut his knee up real bad. "The Davis woman?"

"She bit me."

He reaches behind his back and pulls out the gun. Slips it under the head of the mattress on his side, then pulls his shirt off.

Maria hisses when she sees the wound.

"*Qué chingados?*"

"I know. She ripped a huge chunk out."

"This is bad. It's…" She makes a circle with her fingers and thumb to indicate the size of the wound. "Maybe you should go to a doctor?"

"Yeah right. Once they find her, they're going to be looking for somebody with a bite taken out of their shoulder. I got blood all over that place. They'll match it to me in no time."

Her brows knit together.

"It won't grow back together on its own, Dylan. If you get sick from it—"

"Then I'll get better. But I won't get better if they arrest me. Jaro didn't get better, did he? He got dead."

They both fall silent. That's how the straight world takes care of strays like them who know too much — trumped-up vagrancy charges and staged suicides in holding cells.

They'd made it look like Jaro slashed his wrists. Funny how he was tucked back in the one corner of his cell that the security camera couldn't see.

Dylan wonders what they'll make it look like if he gets caught. A hanging with shoelaces or sheets? Maybe. It'd be a lot easier to shoot him while they were apprehending him. Say he shot first and they were just returning fire.

Maria sighs and leans over his shoulder again.

"Hold still."

The peroxide stings and bubbles when it hits his flesh, sizzling like bacon on a hot griddle. From the way it sounds and feels, it's hard not to imagine acid eating through the skin and muscle. But he grits his teeth and doesn't make a noise.

Dylan tells himself the searing, burning feeling means it's working, cleaning out all the germs and hatred from Mitzi Davis' last-ditch effort to survive. Kind of like a tiny exorcism.

When it's done fizzing, Maria presses the square of gauze to the wound and tapes it down.

"Don't do this anymore," she whispers. "You've done enough."

He knew it was coming. They go through this every time. She hates telling him their names, showing him the faces. He's always got to convince her that it's necessary. Over and over again. But he can't do it alone. He doesn't remember any names or faces. Whatever they gave him wiped all that out.

Maria knows all the names, all the faces. The councilman had kept records — a little insurance in case the others ever decided to turn on him. But he must've destroyed it all as soon as Maria escaped, because Dylan wasn't able to find anything in his house. Now she was the only one who knew. Even more incentive to finish this up fast. If he can dispose of the last of the trash, they'll never come gunning for her.

"One more," he says. "That's all that's left, right? Just one?"

She frowns. Chews on her bottom lip before finally nodding.

"The last one, then we're done," he promises. Gently, he pulls her down onto the mattress beside him. "Then we'll get out of here. Get the kids out of this awful fucking city."

"Where? Where can we go?"

Her tone is challenging. She doesn't believe him, doesn't know this state like he does. She grew up in the Yucatan, not Missouri. He has to remember when she gets scared like this that it's because she's never been outside the metro area, doesn't know there's small towns where nobody asks questions. Endless acres of woodland they can get lost in.

Even now, six months after she escaped from those assholes, she thinks they're still trapped.

Dylan kisses the top of her head and hugs her to his side.

"We'll head down south to the bootheel and find a place in the woods where nobody can find us. Go off-grid. It's basically the same thing as living here, except there won't be anybody else around. We can grow a garden and hunt and fish and stuff. And it doesn't get quite as cold down there during the winter."

"You know this?"

"I used to live down there," he says, leaving out the rest of that thought. *Before I woke up in a crawlspace three hundred and fifty miles away.* "Mark Twain National Forest's got some abandoned campgrounds and old trails where we can set up until we find a good spot to stay. And it's not too far into town if we need anything."

Maria glances up at him through her lashes, a reluctant glimmer of hope in her dark eyes. She knows he was living rough before they met, has heard how his dad left him with a lady friend and took off for Alaska after some job, then never sent any money or called. How it was easier for Dylan to leave the woman behind, take the burden off her and hit the streets. If anybody can take care of their little family down there, it's him. Maria just has to trust him.

"You'll see," he says, rubbing her arm up and down to warm her up a little. "I just need to finish this last one, then we're gone."

CHAPTER 45

The bed in the hotel was comfortable, firm but not a rock, and the sheets and pillowcases didn't have that over-dried, burning smell some of the bedding in cheaper hotels got. Still, Loshak found himself staring at the blue digits on the clock as they rolled over to three a.m.

He tried to focus on his breathing to clear his head, tried to let that most basic form of meditation take him away from the case, help him relax. Breathe. Focus. No stray thoughts. Only awareness. Only mindfulness of this moment, of his immediate surroundings. Nothing abstract.

Breathe. Focus. Repeat.

It wasn't working.

Curiosity fluttered in his chest like heart palpitations, couldn't stop his thoughts from churning no matter how hard he tried to turn them off. Some blend of intrigue and desire kept all the circuitry burning bright behind his eyes.

He turned on his other side, punched the pillow into a different shape, then tucked it between his head and shoulder.

No matter how comfortable Loshak should be, he wasn't. He closed his eyes, and it felt like they were still open. Like they wouldn't go all the way shut.

His mind wouldn't stop running through all the disparate information they'd come up with so far. It felt like they were so close to breaking something wide open, but it always twisted away at the last second. Left them behind to start from scratch.

The football coach's gun, the posed bodies, the torching of The Wooden Nickel and what Spinks may or may not have overheard in the weird basement sex dungeon, the connection between Carter Dupont and Neil Griffin. A crawlspace full of kids in shallow graves. A second serial killer, as if one wasn't enough.

He tried to focus on the potential positives. The bodies under Griffin's house would start to get IDed at some point — hopefully soon. The techs were working around the clock to put names and faces to bones. That would shake something loose, give them something concrete to move on.

It had to.

Didn't it?

The victim was a killer. That was still something of great significance. Yes. A big puzzle piece snapped into place.

The bodies would be the next piece. They would lead to something. They would link some of the loose ends. The narrative would all come together from there. The bigger picture would come clear at last. Someway, somehow, it would all start to make some kind of sense.

Now he was drifting. His thoughts circling and circling. Repeating themselves.

The bodies. Yes. The bodies. Loshak was sure they were the key to understanding the case. One way or another, all the answers lay under the floorboards of the Griffin house.

CHAPTER 46

Time passes. Hours maybe. It's hard to tell at night without looking at the time on his phone, and he doesn't want to roll over and grab it.

Maria's head rests on his arm, her back fitted against his front, her arm over his arm over her round belly. If the big spoon moves, the little spoon will wake up. She has a hard enough time getting a few solid hours lately with the baby kicking and having to pee every ten minutes. She doesn't need Dylan waking her up, too.

So he holds still, his head on her long hair and watches the window past the curve of her ear. It looks out the back of the house, away from the industrial warehouses. Out front, it's all-night security lights like people are just dying to break in and steal an excavator or a pile driver. Out back tells a different story. Out back, it's dark. Advanced night. Especially tonight, with the rain clouds blocking out the stars. Full dark.

Dylan wishes he could shut his eyes and just drop off to sleep like Maria does, but he can't. He hates nighttime dark. It's different from early morning dark. Around about four a.m., the dark becomes something safe, manageable. But from nine p.m. until then, the dark wields danger, harbors threats.

Some massive black hole blooms in the night that swallows the house, swallows him. There's a distance here that becomes tangible in the lack of light, infinite space between himself and Maria. She's somewhere safe, and he's awake keeping an eye on the emptiness. Someone has to.

It's lonely, though.

He blinks a few times, trying to wet his corneas. They feel dry, tired. He would definitely sleep if he could. But if he did, who would keep watch?

Maria moves, her arm twitching in her sleep. The motion jars his arm, which sets the bite in his shoulder to burning again beneath the gauze.

The wound seems prophetic. The pain somehow foreboding.

I'm going to die doing this.

The thought booms like a loudspeaker in the quiet darkness. This path is going to kill him, seeking vengeance the way he is. He can feel it.

And he sees Mitzi Davis, her wild eyes, her instinct to fight back. He feels her teeth sink into his shoulder and just barely stops himself from flinching at the memory. She almost won. She disarmed him, tore up his shoulder. What if she had managed to get his gun? Or if she had one of her own hidden away in a drawer there in the kitchen? It would've been game over for him.

He knows you can't go crashing into life-and-death confrontations and expect to survive indefinitely. No one goes undefeated.

The concept of death itself doesn't scare him. The idea of leaving Maria and the kids here does. Dying would be like abandoning them. It's his job to protect them, hunt and gather food for them. That's his whole purpose in life — the preservation and protection of their little family. That's what a man is supposed to do.

241

Dylan can feel that truth thrum through his whole body when he's doing something for them — a physical manifestation in his flesh telling him that this is right, this is good, this is real. All the stupid shit from his life before, that was all just nonsense. Kid stuff. This here, taking care of them, this is a man's work, and he's happy to do it.

The list of names runs through his mind, the faces of the men and now woman he's killed, then finally that nightmare in the crawlspace. That overwhelming darkness. The black nothing.

The black lay thicker in that crawlspace, darker even than the night itself, stinking of death. It closed around everything. Coiled itself and clenched tight.

Oblivion hung up right there. All around him.

He could still feel the impossible emptiness of it, the vacancy somehow too vast to comprehend. Could still hear his breath echoing in the confined space. Panicked and sharp. Each inhale sounded so loud down there. Threatened to reveal him.

He clenches his teeth and pushes the memories away. Feels the anger surge to replace the doubts.

Someone has to make these people pay. The price for their crimes is death.

He knows revenge motivates this, at least to some extent, but it's more than that. It's a kind of protection he can offer. He can eliminate the threats to his family, eliminate the evil that no one else is going to stop, make the world a slightly better place for Maria, the kids, and the baby.

There's almost an ambition to it. Other men go to work and move up the corporate ladder, sign contracts, and transact business.

Not him. He destroys evil.

He lays out the bodies, poses them, puts a glove over their eye so they all know he's out there, that they should fear him, that he is coming for them.

I'm going to die doing this.

It's even louder this time, the words like a slap from an Old Testament prophet.

Maybe Maria can feel it, too. Maybe that's why she hates telling him the names, because she knows how it's going to end, knows she'll be left alone to take care of the kids without help from the man of the house.

A man should protect his family and provide for them. But that's in an ideal world. What if, in this messed-up world, you have to decide between them? What if they're mutually exclusive? Which one should you pick?

Thinking about this is like being pulled in two, but Dylan knows what he's going to do.

Even if he also knows he shouldn't.

CHAPTER 47

The next morning, Loshak made his way down the hall to Spinks' room. He stood there staring at the door for a few seconds, not knocking.

While Loshak and Rainie had driven over to interviewed Flickinger, Spinks had stayed behind with Pressler to start going through the names of The Wooden Nickel club members provided by Trufant. He and Spinks had agreed to meet for breakfast at seven to go over what — if anything — they'd learned. It was a quarter after now.

Spinks might have forgotten to set his alarm. Or maybe he'd slept right through it. Loshak wasn't sure what time the reporter had finally gotten in.

Strange how weird knocking seemed when you knew the person on the other side of the door. Loshak could walk up to a crack dealer's house, a murderer's house, a victim's family's house, whatever, and give the three-note cop knock, no problem. Loud, proud, and as obnoxious as possible. But because he and Spinks were in that weird stage of friendship working relationships usually stalled out at, knocking when the guy might be trying to sleep in was almost intimidating.

Maybe it was something about the possibility of Spinks coming to the door in his underwear. The weirdness of seeing someone in that vulnerable state of half-asleep, half-awake, eyes all squinched up.

Loshak checked his texts to make sure he'd gotten the

agreed upon time right. Still seven in the morning. He dropped his phone back in his pocket, took a deep breath, and tapped out *shave and a haircut*, trying not to flinch at how loud it sounded in the muffled, early morning stillness of the hallway.

As the seconds passed, Loshak stuck his hands in his pocket and started nodding. Spinks was asleep. He should head out and grab something for them both, coffee and some donut holes maybe, and see if he couldn't catch the reporter awake when he got back.

He was just about to go when the door opened.

"Well, good morning, partner," Spinks said, a cheerful smile on his face.

He was fully dressed, wearing a pair of crisp-looking khakis and a lavender polo shirt. The guy appeared more awake and alert than Loshak felt. Not even a touch of sluggishness.

"I was starting to wonder if I was going to have to send you a friendly neighborhood wakeup call."

"You had me thinking the same thing," Loshak admitted. "I figured if you got in late enough, you might be sleeping in."

"Nah, I never could do the sleeping late thing." Spinks grabbed his wallet and key card. "I like to get up early and write before the rest of the world starts pushing its way in. That's the best time to get the words flowing, when everybody else is still asleep, not crowding your headspace."

As they started down the hall toward the elevator lobby, Loshak asked, "Working on the book or an article?"

"The book," Spinks said. "I'm taking time off the

column until it's done. Well, not like completely off. I've got some friends who submitted guest pieces to take up the majority of it, and a couple old posts I never got around to putting up to cover the rest. But I'm essentially off until the book is in my publisher's hands."

They stepped into the elevator, and Loshak hit the button for the lobby. He wanted to ask how the book was going, but he wasn't sure he really wanted to know. Asking when someone was going to finish writing a book about you just seemed conceited.

"So, what are we having?" Spinks asked as the car came to a stop on the ground floor. "Continental breakfast? IHOP? Waffle House?"

"Rainie mentioned a diner a few streets over. Feel like some runny eggs and diner coffee?"

"I'm game," Spinks said. "If the locals like it, then it's either good eatin' or the locals have bad taste in food."

They crossed the lobby, nodding to the night manager, and stepped out into the bright sunshine. The asphalt was still wet, and the low spots had puddled from the night before, but the rainwater left behind by the storms smelled warm, like it was being slowly cooked away.

Loshak thumbed the button to unlock the rental. Spinks climbed in the passenger side, but Loshak stopped as soon as he opened his door. A big oval on the left side of the driver's seat was wet.

He cursed under his breath and took off his jacket, laying it over the spot. There would be plenty of time later to go back to the room and grab a dry jacket. In the meantime, he wasn't walking around with a wet ass.

"What happened?" Spinks asked. "Leave your window

cracked?"

Loshak settled into the seat, careful not to push the jacket aside.

"No, I think this door leaks," he said, prodding the stripping between the door frame and the body with a thumb. "Somebody probably locked the keys in at some point, and they had to break in with a hanger or bar."

He started the car and backed them out of the space.

"Lisa pulled that little trick with her BMW a few years back. The seal never did work right again. We had to get the whole thing replaced." Spinks shook his head. "And the hell of it is she could've just called a locksmith. It wasn't like we couldn't afford it. You can take the girl out of the ghetto, but you can't take the ghetto out of the girl."

There was something about the tone of voice Spinks used to tell the story that made Loshak's ears prick up. An exasperated fondness, the kind elderly couples developed over the years. But there was a sadness there, too. Or maybe it was more of a longing.

"How is Lisa doing?" he asked, turning onto the street and heading north.

"Ah, you know." Spinks shrugged. "She's in Texas right now, doing the Habitat for Humanity thing with some of her church friends. She remodeled our house once, so I guess she's an expert at houses now. She likes that kind of thing, though. I think it makes her feel like she's doing some real, tangible good in the world. I can't blame her. You see enough bad shit, and it's like you have to do something, take some kind of action."

He rubbed his jaw and gazed out the window at the passing gas stations and mini shopping centers. The expression on his face tightened.

"And it gets bad this time of year. She likes to be somewhere else. Anywhere that isn't Miami."

The reporter didn't have to specify what time of year he meant. Loshak had a time of year, too, a date he dreaded the other three hundred sixty-four days while trying not to think about how he was dreading it. Then it passed, and Shelly was still gone, and there was still a hole in his life, and he started trying not to think about how he was dreading the eventual return of that date all over again.

"What about you?" Loshak asked. "Is that why you're halfway across the country?"

Spinks grinned.

"Nope. That is so I can catch a bad guy." He whipped out his little Bureau-issued wallet and credentials as if he'd been practicing. "J.R.R. Spinks, on the case."

Loshak chuckled.

"So, it's good old-fashioned wish-fulfillment."

But he didn't say that playing FBI agent was escapism, just like Lisa was using. One escaped to another place, the other escaped to a fantasy.

"What do the Rs stand for?" Loshak asked.

"Same as Tolkien's: Rock and Roll," Spinks said without missing a beat.

He stowed his wallet and leaned forward as if that would give him a better view of the passing businesses.

"So, where's this diner Rainie promised?"

"Should be another block or two."

"How was your guys' not-date last night? I forgot to ask."

Loshak shook his head.

"I don't get why you're so stuck on this. We talked to Flickinger, then drove straight back to the Mission Hills station. It was one-hundred percent professional."

"Look, normally I'd say people were being sexist and assuming because she's a woman that she's coming on to you." Spinks did his dramatic pause thing, then raised a hand as if to stop Loshak from interrupting, in spite of the fact that Loshak made no move to indicate he might. "However. You're ignoring all the basic signs of a little girl with a crush."

He started ticking off fingers.

"She grins any time you agree to hang out with her. She laughs at your dumb jokes — which I can attest are mostly not funny. She tries to stand next to you whenever there's a meeting and makes excuses to follow you to your car when it's over. Have I left anything out?"

Loshak snorted.

"Yeah, drawing cartoon hearts on binders."

"Do you live in the Stone Age? The kids don't use binders anymore, they Snapchat and heart each other's Timeline Stories."

Loshak spotted the sign for the diner up ahead, a retro deal with neon letters and chrome detailing. He flipped on his blinker and pulled into the turn lane.

"Are you making those up?"

Spinks thought about it for a second, pursing his lips.

"I know Snapchat's a real thing. The Timeline Stories might not be. It sounds like it could be a thing, though."

A break in the traffic was coming toward them, just big enough to slip through and into the diner's parking lot. Loshak got ready to hit the gas.

But just as the last car before the gap passed, Loshak's phone let out a piercing shriek. His foot twitched, and his heart rate jumped up at the disturbance. His chance to turn slipped by. He dug the phone from his pocket and answered, watching for another opportunity.

"Agent Loshak, this's Detective Pressler. We got another body — glove over the eye, all that crap," Pressler said, then hesitated. "Only the thing is: This one here's a woman."

CHAPTER 48

Dylan doesn't remember falling asleep. It's hard to be sure of the time without looking at his phone, but he figures it happened around four or five. Safe hours that count as morning and don't require a vigil.

Whenever it was, he still wakes before everyone else. Maria has turned onto her other side sometime in the night, her face pressing against his chest now and her hair tickling his chin. Her soft exhales warm and dampen the skin beneath her nose.

Dylan slips out of bed and dresses. He'll wake someone up if he passes through the front room, so he creeps down the hall to the kitchen and lets himself out the back door. Not a layout you'll find in a new house, Dylan thinks, but this one is old. He figures they built it before air conditioning became a thing. He read something once about people putting hot kitchens as far away as possible from where the family would spend the daylight hours so it wouldn't overheat them during the summer.

Out back, the grass is overgrown, sunburnt, and yellow. It slicks moisture and grass seeds onto Dylan's jeans as he walks, but he barely notices. Plumes of steam puff from his nose on each exhale, little reminders that fall is about to crash down on them.

He tells himself that he intends to have Maria and the kids a long ways away by the time winter sets in, but he doesn't believe it. It's too hard to sell himself on the fantasy when he's alone, when he doesn't have to believe it to make Maria believe it.

The asphalt and concrete are still damp from the night before, and it looks like more rain on the way. The sky has gone light and gray, but the dawn can't seem to break through the clouds, even down at the horizon line. It gives the industrial warehouses and chain link fences around their house a lifeless, strange look. Smoke billows up out of brick tubes protruding from the tops of various factories farther into the city, but nothing else moves.

He makes it to the Haymaker's a few streets over, the bright fluorescent lights inside unnaturally harsh. He senses the faintest flicker in the glow streaming down from the bulb. It makes the little self-contained universe inside the gas station look animated. Like something he's seeing on TV instead of walking around in. He watches his hand grip the handle to the cooler door, opening it and fishing out a half gallon of whole milk.

It's more expensive than the skim, but he read somewhere that kids need the extra milk fat and nutrients to support healthy growth until they're like eighteen. So he doesn't skimp on the milk. He can cut plenty other corners that won't hurt their development.

When he gets back home, Sam and Kegan are stirring on their mattress. Sam is the only one awake enough to follow him into the kitchen to grab their stash of cheap plastic bowls and the box of spoons. He lets Sam pour the cereal while Dylan doles out the milk. The kid is still puffy and pale with sleep, but he likes playing man of the house.

With a start, Dylan realizes he's unconsciously making plans for the scrawny little guy to take over for him. Take over when what?

When this kills me.

In the growing gray daylight, the thought doesn't scare or surprise him as much as it should. He's had all night to accept it. And he can feel that it's going to happen. Pretty soon, in fact. Pretty damn quick here, his dad would say.

Kegan wanders in, scrubbing at her eyes.

Dylan milks a bowl of Cinnamon Toast Crunch and hands it over.

Like the milk, cereal is one thing they don't skimp on. Most of the food they eat comes out of dumpsters. Boxes of leftover donuts every night from the blue metal buffet behind Dunkin's. Random past-date stuff from grocery stores — cheeses, juices, and produce. Whole Foods is the best of the bunch, but Dierberg's is right up there. Cereal and milk they buy, though. Breakfast is important and shit. Everybody agrees on that.

One by one the rest of the kids come in, pushing and talking. Dylan stops a fight between Aleta and Gus and lets Kegan sit on his lap while she eats, but he can't shake the somberness hanging over him. It's like the darkness has gotten inside him. And he knows if he leaves the house today, if he goes out there to find the last name on the list, he is never coming back.

It's too late to back down, though. This is his purpose. Protecting his family, doling out justice. There's no question of whether or not he'll go. Only how he'll spend the last few hours he has with them.

Eventually Maria pads into the kitchen. In spite of having slept all night, as Dylan can attest, there are dark bags under her eyes. He thinks her stomach is riding a little lower today, too. It looks heavier.

She sits beside him while she eats, leaning into his side. When she finishes, he pours her a second bowl. There's just enough left in the box because he didn't eat. The baby needs it more than he does.

Dylan tries to get in some quality time with each one of them. Sitting still and listening to what they're saying one last time. He wants to be present and mindful in this moment with them, but he keeps losing the thread of the conversation. He sees the patterns in Kegan's irises or the pores beside Gus' nose and thinks, *That's why this has to be done, so they can live safely and grow into something.*

Later on, when the sun is up and peeking through the clouds, Maria gathers everybody up for the hike to the library. It's thirteen blocks from their little squat. They'll spend a few hours reading there, a family outing and home school all wrapped into one. Sometimes Dylan goes with them, sometimes he heads into town and spends the day asking for spare change at intersections and outside gas stations.

Today, he'll stay home.

When they're finally out of the house, Dylan finds a notebook and gets to work. He needs two letters, one for just Maria and one for everyone else. Not suicide notes, but close enough.

He needs to say goodbye.

CHAPTER 49

When Loshak and Spinks arrived, the street was blocked off. A wood framed police barricade drew one line of the perimeter, while yellow police tape comprised the other three sides of the square. The space inside the lines was crammed with cruisers, unmarked cars, and crime scene vans.

The usual three-ring circus of press had stationed themselves along the very edge of the boundary, pointing their cameras in. That Loshak was used to. What he wasn't used to was the train of realtors' vehicles circling the block like a swarm of sharks. He found something about it unnerving. Crass.

Loshak parked the rental down the block, and he and Spinks walked up to the barricade, flashing their credentials to the uniform standing watch over the sawhorse barrier.

Two crime scene techs stooped over the front porch of the Davis house, scouring the door and bristly welcome mat for clues.

Another uniform stationed at the front door handed over one pair of gloves and booties apiece, then let Loshak and Spinks into the house.

Inside, cameras snapped and paper booties rustled as techs documented evidence, and voices filtered through what should have been a silent crime scene.

Loshak frowned. He was used to inspecting scenes

alone, often days after most of the action. By the time he got there, the places tended to be as silent as a church, the emptiness saturated with a strange reverence. Having so many people swarming around while he was trying to get a feel for the place felt wrong, almost blasphemous.

Still, something about the heretics swarming the home made the urgency of the case more real. He was on the clock. They all were. There wasn't time to wait until everyone else was finished bagging and tagging, wasn't time for any hushed reverence, wasn't time to even slow down. Somewhere an invisible countdown was running, ticking off the seconds until the killer struck again.

Loshak took a deep breath, tried to block out the bustle going on around him, and stepped into the living room. It was a nice enough house, if not boring. A color scheme of blue-grays and whites paired tastefully with numerous glass surfaces and dark wood. A little red here and there for accents. Overstuffed couch, glass-topped end table. Some abstract art prints on the walls. The kind of art that said what great taste the owner of the house had without actually conveying any emotion or meaning. If this thing with the gray lines and red blobs had been hanging in a gallery, he and Jan would've made fun of it.

The house was closer to the size of the Dent's Painted Lady, but there was something about the decor — the feel of the place — that reminded Loshak of the Griffins' McMansion. How cold and generic it was, maybe. Like Mitzi Davis had pulled the room straight from the pages of a *Better Homes & Gardens* magazine without adding any personal touches. No family photos or bric-a-brac. No coats hanging over the back of the chairs or mail on the handiest flat surface.

What did that say about their newest victim? Was she someone who spent her life trying to recreate the perfect pictures she saw in print, thinking that one of them would make her like her house enough to stay in it? Or did she not have the depth of character to take a scene like that and make it into a home? Did she spend all her time away, maybe traveling for work like Dent, but without the family to keep her house messy while she was gone?

Who was she? How did she attract their killer's attention?

Loshak had an idea then and grappled for his phone. He found Trufant's name in his contacts list, thumbed the name, and listened to the shrill tone of the phone ringing.

Trufant picked up after the second ring.

"Agent Loshak," he said, his smirk clear as day over the line. "I was wondering if you'd call."

"Why's that?"

"I saw it on the news. There's been another murder?" he asked but didn't wait for Loshak to answer before plowing ahead. "Of course, they haven't officially said it's related to the others, but that doesn't stop them from speculating. And who can blame them? I know I can't."

Loshak lifted his free hand and scrubbed at his scalp.

"I trust I can tell you the victim's name in confidence? I'd be curious to know if she was possibly a member of the club."

"*She*? My, that is an interesting twist," Trufant said. Loshak imagined his eyes glittering with intrigue. "And her name?"

"You understand this information is not to be shared—

"

Trufant interrupted. "Yes, yes, I understand. My lips are sealed."

"The victim's name is Mitzi Davis. She's an insurance agent."

"Never heard of her," Trufant said, and Loshak thought he sensed disappointment in his voice.

"You're sure? She couldn't have been around the club as someone's guest or something like that?"

"I told you, agent," Trufant drawled, sounding bored. "This club was very exclusive."

Loshak's eyes roamed around Mitzi Davis' home.

"Looks like she was doing pretty well."

A snort came over the line.

"By exclusive, I mean seven-figures a year, minimum. An insurance agent, you said? If she were an insurance *executive*, maybe. Plus, she had a vagina. That's two strikes."

Loshak thanked him and hung up, feeling that same old frustration well in his gut. So many unanswered questions.

Movement by the doorway to the kitchen caught his eye. Spinks was standing off to the side, peeking in at an angle at something hidden from Loshak behind the wall. The reporter sniffed and turned away, heading for the front door.

He stopped by Loshak.

"Kitchen looks like somebody spilled a swimming pool full of blood, but she was strangled. That's the Cliff's Notes for you."

"Strangled? Manually strangled?"

Loshak's brow creased. First their killer switched up

from men to a woman, now he was switching his technique. It wasn't unheard of, but it wasn't like the methodical, mission-driven killing they'd seen so far. Transitioning from two execution-style gunshots to the head was cold and impersonal. Strangulation on the other hand, well... you almost couldn't get more personal, as far as methods of killing went.

"Hate to say it, but we might need to look at the possibility that this is unrelated to our other four," Loshak said, shaking his head. "A copycat who saw the body staging in the papers and made it look alike to cover his tracks."

"Sounds like the techs have already nixed that theory," Spinks said. "They just pulled a bullet from an overhead cabinet. I heard the short kid in there say, 'looks like another nine.' Am I mistaken, or is that what our other vics were shot with?"

"Yeah, it was."

But that still didn't prove anything, Loshak thought. Lots of people carried nine-millimeter handguns. Ballistics would have to study the slug to make sure it had come from the same gun as the others.

Loshak pressed his lips together and exhaled through his nose. This case felt more and more unknowable. A fire hose of information and yet zero conclusions. Game theory came back to him, games of incomplete information like poker. He had no idea what cards their killer was holding. For all he knew, the guy was playing Monopoly while they sat Five Card Stud.

"Hey, there's the special agent," Pressler said, stepping out of the kitchen and waving them over.

The skin under the portly detective's eyes had gone fully bruised now, and a strip of white tape ran from one side of his nose to the other. Despite this, he had a huge grin on his face. In fact, he looked like he was about to burst at the seams.

"Get over here, boys. We got some news."

Loshak shot a glance at Spinks, but the reporter was already moving. They joined Pressler and a pair of crime scene techs who'd been working the kitchen.

"Tell them what you told me," the big detective said, elbowing a smaller kid who looked more like he belonged in a college chem lab than a crime scene. Before the kid could speak, Pressler added, "About the blood. Tell them."

The kid nodded and pushed up his thick-framed hipster glasses.

"Well, we won't know for sure until we test it, but the spatter indicates quite a struggle."

He glanced over his shoulder into the kitchen, then back at them, blinking behind the lenses.

"I think we've got the blood of two subjects here."

Loshak felt his feet moving before he consciously decided to squeeze past them. The kid in the hipster glasses was still talking and Spinks was asking questions, but he couldn't hear either of them anymore.

The blood stood out against the white cabinets as if it were glowing. Loshak raised his gloved hands and framed the arcs, following them. Sprayed across the cabinets there. Smeared on the wall there. Blood on their vic, looking black against the death-gray flesh of her cheeks, but no wounds were visible on the corpse beyond superficial scratches.

Bullet in the cabinet. Death by strangulation.

Mitzi Davis fought back. She disarmed him, attacked him, forced him to use his hands instead of the gun. Somewhere in the struggle, she broke his skin, something serious, a laceration severe enough to cause all this.

Holy hell. They had it. They had the killer's blood.

DN-fucking-A. The holy grail of forensic evidence.

Loshak had to remind himself to breathe.

CHAPTER 50

Loshak's palms tingled. Overstimulated. The vibration pulsed up into his arms, a dull version of it spreading outward from there. But the pin pricks stabbed hardest in that thin skin on the insides of his hands like fat needles piercing him.

He paced the crime scene now, gritting his teeth, trying to think straight. His thoughts jumbled themselves and untangled over and over again. The adrenaline rush made it hard to concentrate, hard to breathe, hard to exist at all. It felt like he should explode instead, add a fresh coat of red to that blood spatter decorating the kitchen.

Clarity fought through the noise in his head, coming to him in maddening little bursts, but it was getting better as time wore on. He couldn't force the noise out, but he could let it go little by little until it was gone.

Breathe. Focus.

Breathe. Focus.

The DNA was going to be huge. That thought kept running through Loshak's mind as he walked the rest of the house. DNA meant there was some hope that this case would eventually be solved. They had something concrete to link the killer to Mitzi Davis' house. Based on the blood the techs had found in her mouth, there would be tissue between her teeth, too. They could link him directly to her fighting for her life. It was the neatest bow a prosecuting attorney could possibly hope to tie a case up in.

So, why did he feel so ill at ease? He couldn't shake the certainty that something here was incomplete. They had the best evidence a case ever got, and yet he felt like they knew even less now that before.

They still didn't know the why, still lacked that puzzle piece that would make the picture of what was happening here come clear. They had no idea what was linking all five victims. They had no idea where or who he would strike next. They had his blood, but they didn't have him.

No, he shouldn't think that way. This was progress. One step at a time, they were getting closer.

He strode past the kitchen for the hundredth time, eyes catching the dark red splatters and smears in his peripheral vision. There were three doors at the end of the hall. The two on the left and right were open to reveal a laundry room and bathroom, respectively. The one straight ahead led out to the garage. Loshak spun around and headed back in the other direction, but he'd only gone a few paces before he froze.

Laundry room.

He whirled back around and stuck his head into the space, inhaling a big whiff through his nostrils.

Dryer sheets. The only smell he detected was that floral dryer sheet odor — probably a fragrance called Spring Rain or Moonlight Breeze or something like that. Whatever it was called, it made his nose itch.

He stepped back into the hall, feeling silly for even thinking to check the laundry room. What had he been thinking? That Mitzi Davis also buried children in her crawlspace?

Still, nothing ventured nothing gained. It had been

worth a shot.

"Could you grab that door, agent?"

Loshak snapped out of the brooding to find one of the body retrieval teams from the morgue pushing a gurney toward him. The tiny lumps made by Mitzi Davis' body inside the black bag barely looked big enough to be a child, let alone an adult woman who'd opened up a gusher on her killer.

The morgue tech nodded behind Loshak. The door. He opened it and stepped out into the finished garage, holding the door as they lowered the gurney through it and down the single concrete step.

Through the open garage door, Loshak could see the law enforcement vehicles beginning to disperse. The CSI techs would hang around for a while longer, photographing, gathering, loading trace evidence into little baggies. But that first thrust of frenzied bustle was thinning out at last.

He didn't see Spinks, but he knew the reporter was somewhere following Pressler around, trying to absorb any bit of information they could use when they started the interviews with the victim's family. If she had family. No one had come up with any names or contact information yet.

With the gurney and the morgue techs gone, Loshak let the door swing closed. It slammed shut. House must not be level for it to gain that much momentum without any help from him.

He could find Spinks and let the reporter know he was headed back to the hotel. Grab a bite to eat since they'd had to abandon their breakfast plans. Maybe he'd even squeeze in a quick nap. God knew he could use the sleep after all the tossing and turning he'd done the night before.

But instead of tracking Spinks down, Loshak milled around the garage. Mitzi Davis drove an Audi, latest model. Blue. He catalogued the details out of habit, even though he doubted they would ever come in handy. Poked around the metal shelves full of boxes along the far wall. She had a half-empty bag of rock salt and a can of high-performance oil with less than a quarter left in the bottom. Oil pan, funnel, and a box of Shop Rags nearby.

Stacked washer-dryer combo in the corner with a stepladder leaned against the wall beside it.

He froze, shoulders still squared at the washing machine.

Something here. Something wasn't right here.

His eyes squinted into slits as he took a step forward, remembering the laundry room inside.

Why have a washer and dryer out here when there was already a set in the house?

He opened the doors to each, found them empty. Spinning the dial to ten minutes on the dryer, he pressed the "Start Cycle" button. Nothing happened.

Well, that settled that. This must have been an old unit. The ones inside did look a heck of a lot newer. And fancier. Black stainless steel and LED display and all that. No stack, either, which he figured must be easier for someone as short as their vic to reach into.

He shuffled backward, wanting to leave it at that, but something about all of it still bugged him. The house was spotless. It didn't jive with the idea of the Davis woman letting an old junker appliance hang out in her garage.

Then again, the unit was a monster. It would be a real pain in the ass to get rid of. Especially if this area didn't offer a regular community bulk trash pick-up. And wasn't the garage usually where the random odds and ends wound up, even for neat freaks?

Loshak took another turn around the space. Overall, it had a lot more personality than the house did. He eyeballed the enormous Christmas wreath hanging from a hook, patiently waiting for its season to come around again. A collapsible garden hose on one of those rolling holders. A pail full of sponges and shammies and a bottle of wax. She must've really babied that Audi.

It wasn't until he'd stepped back through the door leading inside that he realized what had really bothered him about the washer and dryer in the garage. It was the wall they were stacked against.

He paused there on the threshold, stuck in the liminal space between the house and the garage. Cocked his head.

Something wasn't adding up with this floor plan.

Inside, he thrust his head into the bathroom positioned across the hall from the laundry room. Just a toilet and sink, no shower. He stretched out his arms to make sure his messed-up eye wasn't playing tricks on him. It wasn't. The bathroom was less than seven feet across.

Loshak went back out into the garage.

His heart took off like a rocket. He ran to the wall behind the washer and dryer, feeling along the sheetrock, fingers scrabbling over the high gloss paint.

It was so new he could still smell it.

And there were scrape marks in front of the washer and dryer stack. Places where the feet had gouged arching lines into the concrete more than once. Ragged grooves.

He grabbed the back of the washer and pulled, keeping one hand on the dryer to make sure it wouldn't topple over. Pain flared up in his wrist again, the parting gift from that farmboy bouncer. Still, Mitzi Davis had been half his size, and she'd been able to move these. She'd done it at least half a dozen times, if he counted out each individual scratch.

With a screech, the appliances scraped away from the wall.

There. A panel. He fingered the seams, tracing it from one side to the other. No handle. His fingers were too big to jam into the crack, but he grabbed a screwdriver from the shelves and pried at it until it swung open toward him.

When the light hit their eyes, Loshak's heart stuttered. There in the darkness, sitting on a pair of twin mattresses. He couldn't discern any identifying features; the gloom in that little space was too dense. But he couldn't look away from their eyes. The light from outside made their eyes sparkle.

Two girls and a boy.

Loshak wanted to say something, but he couldn't get his throat to work.

Kids.

It made sense now. The case finally made sense.

Human trafficking.

CHAPTER 51

Spinks and Loshak sat in the rental outside the Davis house, watching the DFS agent drive away in an unmarked car. Loshak didn't make a move to turn the key, and Spinks didn't suggest they get going. They both just sat. Staring. Even after the little gray Saab turned off and disappeared from view.

Straight ahead of the car, a uniform was standing guard over the yellow line of police tape. He looked young. Too young to be wearing LEO khakis. Loshak stared as the kid twisted his arm up behind his back and scratched one protruding shoulder blade. Bored. No one had told him that car was carrying three tiny children scared out of their mind. His job wasn't to know the awful details of what they'd found, it was just to lift up the tape when an authorized vehicle came through.

Loshak scrubbed his hands over his face. His wrist throbbed dully, the tendons and ligaments still angry about that washing machine/dryer combo.

In the passenger seat, Spinks lifted up his hands.

"I know this is sexist," the reporter started, "But I'm just going to say it. I didn't think a woman would be trafficking kids."

Loshak nodded slowly.

"You find it more and more nowadays. Not because it's happening more and more. We're just starting to get a better picture of what's been going on under our noses this

268

whole time."

The words came out in a flat, matter-of-fact recitation, like a poorly rehearsed presentation on human trafficking.

Spinks punched the dash.

"Kids, man."

Loshak couldn't quite lash out yet. Numbers ran through his head, the rest of that PowerPoint. One slide showed America as the number one consumer of human trafficking victims around the world. Another was a list of reports of young mothers stolen with their kids in arm, the babies used to keep the women compliant until they could be ripped away from each other down the line. Accessories sold separately. Less than one percent of the abducted were ever recovered.

Where were they all going? What was happening to them?

The largest consumer. It was fitting, this word "consume." America was consuming these kids, these young women. They were never found again, swallowed by a society that catered to any sick desire if the price was right, that served up the meek to the highest bidder.

He hadn't realized until then that the pressure was building inside, like a closed Tupperware container in the microwave. He felt it all bouncing around, awful, sickening, unforgivable, and knew his container's lid was about to pop off. How could anyone sit in silence while this was going on? It was too big, too awful to contain. If he didn't do something now — scream, curse, hit the dash like Spinks had — he was going to explode.

Three quick raps on the passenger side window made him jump. He almost ducked and covered. In his keyed-up state, the knocking had sounded like gunshots.

Pressler stood outside, a dark frown etched on his face. Loshak relaxed. The sudden noise seemed to have cut invisible strings cinching his shoulders up to his neck, almost as if Pressler had taken care of the inevitable outburst for him. Popped it like a paper bag full of air.

Spinks cracked the door.

"DFS found a short-term foster home for the kids with some folks who speak Spanish," Pressler said. "They should be able to calm them down and explain what the hell's going on."

Spinks huffed humorlessly.

"Good fucking luck. I don't even understand what's going on, and I haven't been trapped in a hole in the wall for God knows how long. None of this makes any goddamn sense. How can anybody… any human being…"

The reporter shook his head, lapsing into angry silence.

"Right there with ya," Pressler rumbled. "Anyway, just thought I'd let y'all know."

As the big detective moved back and started easing the car's door shut again, all the tension returned to Loshak's muscles with a snap.

"It's not a coincidence," he blurted out. The other two men froze as Loshak launched into his rant, the car door not quite shut. "The bodies under Griffin's crawlspace? All kids. Kids hidden in Davis' house. Davis and Griffin dead. This wasn't some planets aligning bullshit. The pieces are finally starting to fit together. These targets were intentional. Connected."

Loshak paused, not sure exactly how the pieces lined up, but he knew there was no way this is all just happened

270

accidentally.

"We just have to figure out how Mike Dent and the other vic, the councilman, fit into this… this… conspiracy. I'm confident now that they were part of it."

Loshak's sentence trailed off, his intuition already leaping to the next set of questions.

Was the serial killer involved with the trafficking? Taking out his competition? Killing people who double-crossed him?

Or could this be a vigilante? Loshak could see that. Someone whose wife or kid disappeared, never to be found again, hunting down Griffin and Davis in revenge.

"We still need more information."

His eyes went from the reporter to the portly detective standing in the wedge of the open car door.

"We need to talk to the kids," Loshak said. "As soon as possible."

CHAPTER 52

A grim silence settled over the conference room the next day. Several members of the task force flipped through the handout with the updates on the case, but most were glaring straight at Loshak, waiting for answers. The news that there were three living kids involved now, along with the thirteen dead ones, wasn't doing morale any favors.

"I guess first of all, we need to address what human trafficking is for any of you who don't have a background in it," Loshak said. "I know one of the departments around Kansas City had a bust not that long ago, three young women being held in hotel rooms and forced to have sex with up to a dozen men a day. Was anyone here involved in that?"

Two hands went up near the front corner of the room. A burly detective and a tall woman with red hair. Loshak thought he remembered them being introduced as part of the Independence PD.

"Could you fill us in?" he asked.

"They were teenagers. Two were lured in online," the burly detective said. "The third was kidnapped from a Wal-mart parking lot after her shift. The Wal-mart girl was told all sorts of lies about law enforcement, how the guys had us in their pockets, and we would just bring her back if she tried to run away. Told her they were tapping the phone so she wouldn't try to call home. Had her so screwed up she didn't know who to trust. She was so scared that she ran

272

from us like she wasn't one of the victims. These guys who'd kidnapped her were using her to draw the other two girls in. She pretended to be a model with a phony modeling agency, got in touch with these other two on social media, and eventually got them to come out to meet her at the motel for a trial photography session."

"How did the bust come down?" Loshak asked.

The female detective took over.

"A unit stopped a DUI in the motel parking lot and spotted one of the girls heading into a room. Recognized her from a missing persons report that ran on the news the week before. We did surveillance, caught eleven guys going into one room, six in another, and eight in the third, all in one day, so we set up the bust. We got one guy, but we're still working on nailing down the other. More likely than not, he's already living large in some non-extradition country."

Loshak nodded and pawed at the stubble he hadn't bothered to shave off this morning.

"We're just now starting to get a real scope of the human trafficking business. The majority of the cases we've seen so far are isolated cells like the case you're talking about. One or two guys or a guy and a gal getting access to a local child — or using their own — and exploiting them. You see young kids sold by their parents into sex work, or runaways picked up by trustworthy-looking older women and held captive much like those three girls were, forced to service men so their kidnapper can turn a profit. We saw that in the case of Marcus and Robin Thompson, husband and wife team, who picked up a girl on the side of the road and spent the next six weeks selling her at truck stops and motels and making child pornography with her."

More cases flashed through his mind, more than he could count. He had to fight to stay focused on his words.

"In some cases, the young women are hooked on drugs so they can be controlled more easily. And with the industry around the globe making well over a hundred billion a year, the pimps can afford to invest a little on one more way to assure their slaves are never going to make it far if they run."

He gestured at a crime scene photo from the Griffin house that someone had tacked to the wall. Between the exposed floorboards, more than a dozen holes in the wet earth gaped like open mouths. Screaming for vengeance.

"But with thirteen bodies under Neil Griffin's crawlspace and three kids in the DFS system, we're talking something larger scale here than a married couple or few isolated cases. One of the largest documented cases in the US involved thirty women and girls who were brought across the border from Mexico and used as traveling prostitutes. They were dragged all around the southern US, shipped from farm to farm and raped up to fifty times a day for months or even years. Something that widespread can't go on without anyone noticing. Because we're not talking just pedophiles paying to rape these victims. Studies show that more often it's your average Joe buying in. Opportunists. Some of them don't realize they're paying to have sex with a minor until they show up, but they go ahead because they're already there. Others just don't care how old they are or whether they're being held against their will or not."

Disgust played across the faces in the room like waves

of a shiver rolling through a muscle.

"Why the hell don't they tell somebody?" Chief Tavares growled.

"The johns, you mean?"

The chief gave a curt nod, still scowling.

"One," Loshak said, "because they're breaking the law, and they don't want to be prosecuted. Two, because they figure it's none of their business, and they can't make a difference anyway."

He braced himself to deliver the piece that was going to take this case from bad to worse in a flash.

"But what I'm telling you is that even with all that, you can't escape somebody eventually finding out about an operation this big. With as many kids as we found under Griffin's house, you can bet at least twice that were getting through to other buyers."

Loshak jabbed a finger against the top of the podium.

"Start getting enough moving pieces together, and little bits and pieces get out. Eventually somebody puts the puzzle together. The only way you keep something like this quiet is if you've got a massive conspiracy on your hands, law enforcement included."

That went over about as well as expected. Exclamations and gruff denials went off around the crowd. Then the suspicion set in. Loshak could read it as it crossed their faces, shades coming down behind their eyes as they started to run through everybody on their force, every public official they'd ever met. He watched for any signs of defensiveness or guilt.

Because statistics said that at least three of them had visited one of these trafficking victims in the last year.

But if the guilt was there, it was well-hidden. Loshak returned to his spot along the wall with Spinks. Rainie and Pressler were on either side of the reporter, the big detective especially furious-looking with his squashed, taped-up nose and black eyes.

Chief Tavares returned to the podium, bleak and hunched over, as if these last twenty minutes had been one punch in the gut after another. He gestured to a plump woman in the front row.

"Mrs. Aarons is from DFS. She has an update for us on the children recovered from the Davis house."

The matronly woman took the chief's place at the podium. She swallowed, flustered, and began.

"None of the children speak English, but their temporary foster parents are bilingual, and they've managed to get a bit of information out of the kids. We know they're nine, thirteen, and fifteen years old. They're healthy, eating well, but they're confused and overwhelmed."

She blinked rapidly. Loshak was certain she'd seen some shit in her day, but this was more than your average pile of hot hooey, as Pressler would say.

"Naturally. Any of us would be, in their shoes. At this point we believe they were abducted about two to three weeks ago. The timeline isn't that clear since it sounds like they spent that time in the bed of a truck and stuffed in a couple of hiding spots. None of them are really sure how many days have passed during all of that."

Loshak made a note in the margin of his papers. At the far outside, that put the kids' abduction at two days before Mike Dent's murder.

"So far as we know," Mrs. Aaron said, "none of them were physically or sexually abused. They're with a doctor today to confirm. We're also working with Mission Hills to set up a time for a formal interview with a child advocate and a professional interpreter."

Beside him, Loshak saw Rainie perk up sharply. Her eyes glinted, and he thought he could see that ten-year plan stretching out in front of her again.

By the time he looked back at the podium, the chief was back up. Tavares leaned on it, both hands gripping the sides.

"Basically, we figure the Davis house was probably a distribution stop. What I mean is that these kids were essentially still in transit, making Mitzi Davis sort of like middle management. A Wal-mart distribution center for kids. She got them from whoever abducted them, and her next step was to sell them to a local buyer or ship them somewhere else in the country. At this point, we don't know yet whether she was in some way responsible for actually bringing them across the border. We've still got a lot of digging to do, obviously."

Rainie's hand went up.

"Is it possible the recent murders led to them being stashed at Davis' longer than usual? Like the operation was scared to move for the time being? That would support the vigilante angle."

Loshak nodded, seeing other heads around the room bobbing. She might be on to something there, but she might also be bending facts to fit the narrative she'd already decided was the most likely.

"It's definitely something to look into," Tavares said.

"Last order of business. Canvassing turned up a possible witness. An elderly neighbor lady. She said she saw a stranger in the area sometime the night before, between nine and ten. Puts this at right around Davis' time of death. Body language suggested they were in pain."

He flipped open the handout.

"Quote 'Not limping exactly, but they looked poorly. Wincing, I guess you might say. Like they couldn't straighten up.' So that fits with our evidence of a struggle at the scene. She also says the person was very tall and frail," he said, glancing back down at the paper. "*Delicate* is the word she used. When asked whether it was male or female, she couldn't be certain. So, it's possible that we could be looking for a woman."

CHAPTER 53

The task force meeting hadn't been adjourned yet. Chief Tavares was answering questions, handing out assignments. Loshak was still leaned up against the wall. Seeing, but not really hearing.

Serial killer A, a girl. It wasn't impossible. Improbable, but… Female serial killers tended toward more passive murders — poisons, smothering, that kind of thing — than violent crimes, but there were outliers. Aileen Wuornos. Juana Barraza. Kathryn Porter.

Loshak's swollen eye flared up, itching like crazy. He reached up to scrub at it, then caught himself just before the pads of his fingers touched the lid. Whorls and loops dominated his vision.

Whether it turned out to be a female serial killer or not, they had to look at everyone. Their suspect pool had just doubled.

A hundred thousand more pieces to a puzzle that just kept getting more and more intricate.

All of a sudden, the weight of the bodies in the crawlspace and the sparkling eyes of the kids in Mitzi Davis' garage crashed down on Loshak. Crushing. Oppressive.

He started to move before he realized he was going to, slipping past Spinks and Pressler and letting himself out into the hall. He crossed the desk pool, out into the lobby. Molly B, the girl at the desk who could pass for sixteen, who looked not at all unlike all those human trafficking victims, said something to him, but all he heard was a distant buzzing.

Loshak shouldered the door open and jogged down the steps. A wave of dizziness hit him, and he lurched between a shrub and an ash can to grab the pebbled stone wall.

Heart attack, maybe? He definitely didn't eat well enough to be surprised. He didn't feel any pain, though.

A breeze brushed across his cheeks, cool for such a hot day, and he realized he was holding his breath. God knew how long he'd been doing that. He let it out slowly and inhaled a long replacement.

The dizziness passed. The crushing weight receded, but not by much. Because he was standing in a country that consumed its own goddamn children and came back for seconds. Its appetite for flesh was so insatiable that it had to steal more from other countries. Forget serial killers. Serial killers were one in close to ten million. People profiting off human trafficking and people paying to rape the victims were closer to one in a hundred. How the hell did anybody fight back against opposition that huge?

Little by little, he started to feel the world shift back into focus. He stood up. Swallowed the soapy, chemical taste of bile in his throat.

A girl? No. Loshak didn't think that was right. It wasn't impossible, obviously, but in his gut, it didn't fit.

Still, the neighbor had seen something, and he had to make sense of that evidence without trying to fit it into any prescribed notion he was leaning toward.

The height. That was the issue he had with the female angle.

Say it was a young male. A teenager, tall, thin. Maybe just out of his latest growth spurt. It could be someone connected to one of the trafficking victims. Maybe even a victim himself.

Loshak nodded. A victim would fit the evidence so far.

The door Loshak had just come out swung open.

"Smoke break?" Rainie asked, a wry smile on her face.

Loshak shook his head.

"Not for me," he said, trying to sound nonchalant. "Just grabbing a little fresh air and sunshine."

The detective did a little jog-step down the concrete stairs.

"Want some news?" she asked.

"Is it good or bad?"

The way the case was going, it was most likely more information they would have no idea what to do with.

Rainie bobbled her head from side to side.

"Unknown."

"Lay it on me."

"The guys from IPD got back to me," she said. "Mike Dent's conceal and carry permit was for a nine mil, same caliber used in the first three murders and the same caliber as the techs dug out of Mitzi Davis' cabinet."

"Interesting," he muttered, half to himself.

Rainie said the rest for him: "Could be a coincidence. Lots of people carry nines."

"True."

But he was getting that tension in his shoulders again, the certainty that this wasn't a coincidence.

"We should ask the widow Dent if we can take a look at her husband's gun."

"Way ahead of you," Rainie said. "She can't find it."

Loshak's eyebrows jumped. He wasn't expecting something like this to go right. He didn't want to get his hopes up, but Rainie had already seen his surprise.

"Right?" she said. "So, if our killer somehow took the gun and surprised Dent…"

"You're jumping to conclusions," Loshak said.

"I'm making a logical guess. If we can get our hands on that gun, we could match it to our murders—"

"Or show that it wasn't the weapon used," Loshak interjected.

"—and tie whoever has possession of it to the crime scenes. We just need to find that gun."

"Let's not get ahead of ourselves," he said. "We can spin a million versions of this, but at the end of the day, the evidence is going to tell its own story."

"Well yeah, for sure," Rainie said, but it wasn't more than a token agreement.

He could see her painting the picture in her head: finding the guy with the gun, coming out the hero and solving the crime, going down as the big fish in the small pond. All part of her Chief of Police plan.

"Anyway, just thought you might like to know. Also, I called in to our Chief down at Mission Hills, and I got the interview."

"The interview?" Loshak asked.

"With the kids they pulled out of the Davis house. I mean, they were obviously going to get a woman to do it because it's kids, but I'll ride that sexism all the way to the top," she said with a conspiratorial wink. "Plus, I've got decent Spanish. If you wanted to observe, it's at four-thirty at the advocate's office. I'll text you the address."

Loshak nodded.

"I'll be there."

Rainie grinned that carefree kid's grin, and all thoughts of her ambition disappeared from Loshak's mind.

"Afterward, we could grab some food. I'd love to grill you about what it's *really* like to be a Feeb. You know, in case I decide to make adjustments to my ten-year plan."

"Sure," Loshak said and then remembered all of Spinks' teasing. If he went off alone with Rainie again, he'd never hear the end of it. "You mind if Spinks joins us?"

Rainie shrugged.

"Of course not. Wouldn't want him to feel left out."

CHAPTER 54

The observation room in the child advocate's office was higher tech than the one at Prairie Village, located on the opposite end of a long hallway from the interview room. Just a few chairs, a table, and a flatscreen on a rolling cart with a live feed into the interview room.

Onscreen, the interview room was decorated in bright colors and decked out with toys, books, construction paper, scissors and glue, a box of arts and crafts supplies — basically anything a kid could ever hope to distract themselves with. Except video games and movies. Nothing with a screen, because the amount of observable information you can glean from a kid plummets if they pop in a DVD and stare blankly at it for the next hour and a half.

There were also no two-way mirrors in the room to make kids feel like they were being watched. Just a hidden camera. Based on the angle, Loshak assumed the camera was concealed in a picture or piece of art on the wall, something about eye-height to an adult.

The door opened, and Rainie and the child advocate ushered in two teenage girls and a younger boy.

The mood in the observation room focused, sharpened in a way that reminded Loshak of a laser light show condensing down to a single point. Spinks and Pressler sat forward in the chairs, eyes locked on the screen.

Pressler was a last-minute addition to the group. The

portly detective had invited himself along when he heard
that Rainie was doing the interview. Loshak had seen a
flicker of frustration in Rainie's eyes, but she had only
smiled and agreed Pressler should join the observation
party in the spirit of inter-jurisdictional cooperation.

The advocate, a grandmotherly woman with heavy-
looking green hoops in her ears, said something in Spanish
to the children. Loshak was nowhere near fluent in
Spanish, but he did remember that "*juegos*" was either
"game" or "toy" and "*confortable*" meant "comfortable."
He suspected she was telling the kids they could make
themselves at home and play with whatever they liked.

The oldest, a lanky girl with her black hair pulled back
in a pink hair tie, gave the woman a jerky nod, then went to
sit at the small table. Loshak checked his notes. She would
be Concepción, the fifteen-year-old. The other girl was
shorter, with baby fat still in her cheeks. Benita, thirteen.
The boy, a nine-year-old named Angel, hung onto his
sister Benita's hand, but he was staring awfully hard at a
bright green table in the corner with a Lego top and a
netful of Lego pieces hanging down in the middle. He said
something, but Benita shook her head and went to sit with
Concepción. Clearly not wanting to let go of his sister's
hand, Angel allowed himself to be dragged along. But his
eyes stayed on that Lego table.

Rainie picked up on the direction of the youngest kid's
thoughts. She grabbed the Lego table and pulled it over to
where Angel and his sisters sat, positioning it where the
boy wouldn't have to leave his sister's side or even let go of
her hand if he didn't want to.

"Here you go, bro," she said, the advocate interpreting

as she went. "They're here for us to play with while we talk."

Then Rainie sat down cross-legged on the opposite side of the Lego table and fished a handful of blocks out of the net.

Loshak smiled. It was the perfect move. It would give the little guy something to do with his hands and build some good will between him and Rainie.

"So, where are you guys from?" Rainie asked, starting work on a Lego stairway.

The advocate relayed her question in Spanish.

Both the younger children looked to Concepción.

The fifteen-year-old folded her long arms over her chest and answered, "Ciudad Obgregón."

Loshak recognized the name from DEA and special cases reports as a major exporter of drugs and humans.

"Did you go to school there?" Rainie asked.

While the advocate interpreted, Pressler turned to Loshak.

"I thought Wilson said she could speak Mexican."

Loshak nodded.

"She doesn't want the kids to know yet. They might say something to each other that they don't want her to hear."

They'd missed the answers to the school question. On the screen, Rainie was laughing at something the boy had said.

"I never liked homework much, either," the detective said. "But look at the bright side, you only have like ten more years before you don't have to do it anymore."

That got a smile from Angel, but the older girls remained stony. Loshak could almost read their thoughts in those bleak expressions. Who cared about school? Who even knew if they would ever see a school again? They were lost in a foreign country that had already stolen them away from their parents and locked them away in a dark room. Whatever else might happen, it wasn't likely to be good.

Rainie went through a long list of friendly questions, covering whether Angel had friends near his house, what they liked to play, and what his favorite food was. The girls listened, but stayed out of the conversation.

Until Angel brought up his mom's *coyotas* and started crying. Benita hugged his flushed face to her side.

"Your mom sounds like a really good cook," Rainie said gently. Then she glanced from Angel to the older girls. "Does she know where you guys are?"

Again Concepción was the one who answered.

"She's dead. Our father is, too. The men who helped us cross the river shot them and took their money."

Loshak tensed up. If Rainie said something that hinted the kids or their parents had done something illegal by coming into the country, they might close off again, afraid of getting in trouble.

Instead, she shifted all the blame onto the men.

"That's very bad what those men did." Rainie leaned toward them and folded her arms on the Lego table, her staircase forgotten. It had served its purpose. "And it's my job to catch bad men and put them in jail to punish them for what they did. Were these men the ones who brought you here?"

Benita shook her head, then raised her eyes to her older sister as if she were scared she might have done something wrong.

Through the advocate, Concepción said, "They brought us to another man who gave us Lunchables."

"He put us in the back of his truck and closed the lid," Benita added. "But first he said if we were good in there, we could have another one later, but if we were bad, he would kill us."

"Do you remember what he looked like?" Rainie asked.

"Like you," Angel said.

"Which part of me?" she asked. "My hair?"

Angel shook his head, and Concepción said, "Your skin color. He was white."

"Do you remember anything else about him?"

Concepción shrugged.

"He was tall."

"How about his truck?" Rainie asked. "Can you remember what it was like?"

"It was big. Loud."

"It stinks bad," Angel said.

"That was the gas," Benita said, the advocate interpreting for her. "The lid on the back of the truck was black and it locked."

"I think the truck was red," Concepción said, her brows scrunched up in concentration. "Or purple."

Spinks shot into motion, yanking the Dick Tracy notebook from his pocket and flipping through it so fast and hard he ripped the edges of a few of the pages. He stopped suddenly, jabbing a finger against the paper.

"A red truck!"

He reached out and pummeled Loshak's arm with his fist.

"There was a red truck on Dent's street when we first

got there. The day we talked to Mrs. Dent. It was parked right on the street outside her house."

"That doesn't mean anything," Loshak said automatically.

But Spinks wasn't deterred. His eyes glittered manically as he settled back into his chair.

"I bet you anything it was Dent's," he said.

"I damn sure intend to find out," Pressler said, shoving out his chair and heading for the door. "I'm calling the widow Dent right now."

In the interview room, the kids were telling Rainie about the woman whose house the man brought them to.

"She said if we made a sound, she would separate us, and we would never see each other again." Benita hugged her little brother even tighter.

"She brought us food and took us to the bathroom," Angel said. "We had to wait until she came to take us because we couldn't get out. Then she didn't get us for a long time, and Conchi said I had to hold it."

He looked down at his hands, eyes glittering with tears.

"But then I couldn't, and I wet my pants, so Conchi said we would go in the corner if we couldn't hold it anymore."

"That was right before the other man opened the door," Concepción hurried to explain, her cheeks flushing a little.

The door to the interview room banged open, admitting a grinning Pressler. He stopped and threw his arms open wide, making Loshak think of a car salesman who had just unloaded a Jag on somebody.

"Boom. Widow Dent confirms that her husband drove a maroon Dodge with a lockable hardtop Tonneau cover," he said.

Spinks did a fist pump, and Loshak felt his heart speed up.

"We can get a warrant for the truck."

"If we get there before somebody sets it on fire," Spinks said.

CHAPTER 55

A little before noon, when he figures Maria and the kids will be on the way back from the library, Dylan heads out.

A pang of regret washes over him the second he shoves through the front door. Sharp pain accompanies the threshold. Stabs an ice pick in his heart.

But the hurt fades to something dull as he pounds down the steps. It's mostly gone as he veers onto the asphalt.

The walk lulls him into something of a trance. Time passing without thought. Without detail. His consciousness sucks up into his head, seems to curl up there and do nothing, like a reptile sunning itself on a rock.

After fifteen minutes of this dreamless sleep-walk, he finds himself milling around with the creeps at the bus station. Waiting. Ticket all ready to go in his jacket pocket.

Time slows here. The bustle of people at the gas station across the way seems to pull him out of his daze. His eyes following the meandering paths of those coming and going.

At last, he boards a Greyhound leaving town and settles in the single seat by the back door, leaning his forehead against the glass. The vibration of the engine thrums through the cool glass, almost massaging the front of his skull. Something pleasant about it. On the other hand, the bus smells like stale Pringles and some kind of soup. Possibly a minestrone, he thinks. Nothing pleasant in that odor. But whatever. It takes the good and the bad to fully capture the facts of life, doesn't it? So be it.

Soon the bus presses forward, and the momentum helps him retreat from reality again. The pulse of the road fills his head. Takes him away.

The next name on the list lives way out in the boonies. According to his phone, he would have a thirty-minute walk minimum from the closest stop.

The bus hisses and whines as they inch through the city. The concrete towers thin out, slowly giving way to fill his window with trees and green. They pick up speed. Everything evens out.

Time speeds up. His mind coiling in The Nowhere again, thinking nothing.

The next thing he knows, they reach his stop. His and a whole mess of swing-shift workers wearing coveralls and packing lunchboxes. They all spill out of the aluminum tube together.

The workers head for a shuttle across the parking lot. Dylan moves for the highway. It is going to be a trip in this sun. And here he thought it was going to rain today. Must've missed them and blown over.

There's barely any traffic here, way out in the middle of nowhere. And it's empty. Flat. It's weird to get away from all the bustle and concrete and people for once. He can hear frogs hollering from the scummy water and cattails in the ditch. Won't be too long before the little amphibians would go into hibernation. And all those cicadas he could hear singing would die off. Winter is on its way.

But summer is here now, fall creeping in. He breathes it in, loving the hot, green smell of the air.

Something nice about being out there in nature.

Refreshing. Like being back home. It feels good to know that these little slices of nature are still alive out there no matter how much smoke the factories around their house belch and spew.

When he draws within view of the target's house, Dylan realizes that he hadn't made any arrangements for getting home. Hasn't bought a bus ticket or even checked the schedule. It never crossed his mind, because he knew he wouldn't need one.

You don't come back from your last ride.

CHAPTER 56

Pressler spent the rest of the interview talking to the Independence police and getting a warrant underway. By the time Rainie told the kids bye and led them back out to their short-term foster parents, Pressler was making arrangements to join up with the impound team.

The door to the observation room swung open, and Rainie breezed in.

"Well, guys, what do we think?" she asked.

"I think we're about to hit it out of the park on this maroon truck thing," Pressler said.

"Maybe," Loshak said, not willing to give the guy the win yet.

While he wanted the maroon truck lead to prove fruitful for the sake of building the case against Dent, something about Pressler had started to rub him the wrong way, and he didn't want to give him any credit until it was earned.

"The girl said it was red, not maroon."

Pressler snorted.

"She said it might be purple, too. Kids know like three colors tops. Anyway, we'll find out one way or the other," he said, tapping the phone in his pocket. "I'm on the way out to help the IPD impound team serve a warrant for one Mr. Michael Dent's maroon truck with locking Tonneau cover."

Rainie's brows scrunched together, but she smoothed

them out so fast that Loshak was pretty sure no one but him had seen it.

"Great idea," she said. "We can ride together to save the gas. You want to drive or do you want me to?"

Pressler looked gobsmacked. Loshak had to pretend to cough into his elbow to hide his smile. He watched the portly detective realize that he couldn't turn Rainie down, not when she'd just let him tag along on her interview.

"We're taking my truck." Pressler's voice was a degree away from a growl. "Come on, get the lead out."

Rainie shot Loshak a grin.

"Guess I'll have to interrogate you about life in the FBI another time," she said, then followed the big detective out.

When the door had closed behind them, Spinks favored Loshak with a knowing look and waggled his eyebrows.

"Oh yeah. She's got it bad for the Shak."

Loshak rolled his eyes.

"Yeah, I doubt that."

His stomach growled, and he checked his watch. It was a quarter to six, and he and Spinks didn't have anything else scheduled until the next day's task force meeting. He hadn't felt much like eating over lunch, but now he was starving. Better to spend all that free time obsessing over the case files on a full stomach.

"I saw a food truck on the drive over. I think it was called Catfish Heaven."

"Where all good fishies go." Spinks gestured toward the exit. "Let's do it."

Thirty minutes later, they had steaming hot plates of cornmeal fried catfish — buffalo, fresh caught, no farmed fish here, according to the owner of the truck — coleslaw, and homemade chips dusted with seasoning salt. It was too bright and hot out to eat on the plastic tables set up outside the truck, so Loshak and Spinks retreated to the rental's air conditioning.

"I was skeptical when he said fresh-caught, but I think these are worth the potential worms," Spinks said, popping a catfish nugget into his mouth.

He began the usual ritual of meticulously wiping his still-spotless fingers and mouth on his napkin.

Loshak already had a speck of tartar sauce on his tie, and he hadn't even taken a bite yet. He scraped it off with his thumbnail.

"Wait. What about worms?" he asked.

"Wild caught fish," Spinks said. "Like, all of them have parasites. Most are harmless to humans, but it's still gross to think about. You get farmed fish, you're paying for the parasite-killing pellets they feed their stock. That's why I think it's so funny that all these fancy restaurants are pushing fresh-caught, never-frozen stuff. The freezing kills the worms, but I guess then you're still eating the dead wormies."

Spinks downed another nugget and wiped his mouth, apparently unbothered by this idea.

"In fact, I had this buddy who dropped eighty bucks for a fancy seafood dinner for him and his girlfriend. They bring home their leftovers, open the box next morning—" Spinks wiggled his fingers at Loshak. "There were like five worms coming out of it. He sent me the picture, but I think it might have been on my old phone."

Loshak stared down at his plate with a lot less enthusiasm than he'd felt a second ago.

"Oh, don't worry about these puppies," Spinks said. "Oil fryers burn at about 350 degrees. That's plenty for killing parasites. But most expensive restaurants don't bring the temperature up past 120 because it makes for a more tender fillet."

"What a lovely topic for dinner conversation. Definitely not grossing me out for life," Loshak said.

He took a bite of nice, safe coleslaw. Shook his head.

"And all these restaurants are pushing their wild catches of the day."

"I know, right?" Spinks chuckled and shook his head. "Crazy what a little branding can do."

They ate in silence for a few minutes. Loshak finally stopped imagining worms chewing their way into his muscle tissue and tried a catfish nugget. Tender, flaky meat in a crispy, slightly spicy breading. Almost delicious enough to forget Spinks' friend's wriggling leftovers.

He swallowed the bite in his mouth and forced his brain to shift focus.

"If we can tie Dent's truck to the kids somehow, it's going to go a long way toward connecting all of our misfit victims to the conspiracy. We might have to dig to find how the councilman was involved, but I think at that point, we could reasonably assume he was connected."

He took a sip of sweet tea from the enormous Styrofoam cup, then set it back in the console's cupholder.

"But Dent's picking up the kids could fit. According to his wife and fellow coaches, he spent most of the year on the road."

Spinks was watching him sidelong now, a half-smile on his face. It made Loshak feel like the little green notebook was about to resurface, but the reporter just kept watching him talk it out and cleaning up with his napkin.

"It's the perfect cover," Spinks agreed.

Something lit up in Loshak's brain. Something Flickinger had said when he'd found the pistol safe.

"So, say Dent wasn't really mugged while he was on the road. Say one of his kidnapping victims fought, left some bruises. He feeds his wife a story and buys a gun so it won't happen again."

"Definitely possible," Spinks said. "I wouldn't tell my wife I'd been beaten up by a kid I was trafficking, either. A strict *ixnay* on the *affickingtray*, you might say."

"Dent brings them into the state, turns them over to Davis, she turns them over to… Griffin?"

Loshak scratched at his eye, immediately pissing it off again. He kept talking, working through it.

"Except Griffin looks like he was the last stop for a lot of them." He frowned. "But he couldn't have been the only one. Thirteen kids in five years — that would've cut into profits too fast to make it sustainable. Maybe Davis sends them to the councilman. Or I don't know, maybe from her they go straight to Trufant's underground arson club where they meet guys like Griffin and Carter Dupont."

"Which is why our killer took Dupont out first?" Spinks suggested. "Why wait a year before going to town on the rest of them?"

Loshak grimaced, his bad eye squinting involuntarily.

"Dupont's doesn't look like the rest of the crime scenes." But what he meant was it didn't *feel* like the rest of them. "Maybe Dupont felt sick about what he was doing. Or maybe he finds out what's going on in the basement

298

club, but realizes he'll never stop it because the guys are too powerful. He feels ashamed, eats a gun, and nobody but Trufant connects the deaths."

A grin crept across Spinks' face.

"What?" Loshak glanced down to make sure he hadn't dropped anything else on himself without noticing.

"I'm glad you're back to spit-balling theories, partner," Spinks said. "We missed you over here in the real world while you were hiding behind the We Need All the Evidence banner."

Loshak snorted.

"We still don't have enough to prove or disprove any of this."

"Well, while we're hypothesizing, what if Dupont didn't kill himself at all? What if he was murdered, and they staged it to look like a suicide?"

"You back on the Illuminati?" Loshak said, shaking his head.

"Hey, you said it yourself during the task force meeting."

"Said what?"

"You called it a conspiracy. Exact word you used."

Spinks' phone chimed. He wiped his hands again before getting it out.

"Text from Pressler," he said. "The fire marshal filed his report on The Wooden Nickel fire."

"That was fast."

"Yeah. And guess what he ruled it?"

Another bite of coleslaw dripped white juice onto Loshak's tie. Might be better if he just took the damn thing off and went tieless today.

"Not arson," he answered.

Spinks pointed the phone at him.

"Give the man a cookie. They blamed it on a grease fire in the kitchen."

"I wasn't expecting to hear back on that for at least a week or two," Loshak said, loosening his tie and slipping it off.

Spinks was nodding along with him.

"You know who pays off fire marshals to declare their evidence-destroying fires accidental without a full investigation?"

"Here we go," Loshak said.

Spinks held his hands up defensively and put on an innocent face.

"Hey, I was going to say local rich dudes, but whatever tinfoil hat theory floats your boat, cap'n."

Loshak set his plate on the console and got out his phone.

"We need to talk to Trufant," Loshak said.

CHAPTER 57

When Trufant answered the phone, he heard some kind of New Age music in the background and possibly the burble of a fountain.

"Agent Loshak. As delighted as I am to hear from you, I'm afraid you've caught me in the middle of an appointment with my esthetician."

"I just had a few quick questions for you," Loshak said, not sure what an esthetician was.

"Yes, well… I'm not sure how well I'll be able to answer when Grace goes to rip out this next patch of chest hair."

"When she—" Loshak made a wiping motion with his hand, as if that would make the mental image go away. "Never mind. I don't want to know."

"You mean you've never been waxed before?" Trufant said, and Loshak could hear the maniacal grin on his face. "You should try it. There's nothing like a chest so smooth and hairless it looks like it's made from plastic. Makes me feel like a full-sized Ken doll."

"I think I'll pass."

Trufant sighed.

"Suit yourself. Look, I'll come to you when I finish up here. How does that sound?"

"Fine," Loshak said and hung up.

After maneuvering the car over to a shadier parking spot, he and Spinks settled in to wait.

"So that's the kind of thing you're jotting in that little

301

notebook of yours?" Loshak asked.

He couldn't hold it back any longer. After the revelation that Spinks had written down the color of Mike Dent's truck, Loshak's curiosity in the little green book had reawakened.

"Say what?"

Loshak gestured at the other cars parked around them in the lot.

"The color of random vehicles we pass by on the street? You're keeping track of that?"

Spinks shrugged.

"I like to take note of my surroundings. Helps take me back to the moment when I sit down to write. Plus, I can use those little details when I'm writing later to set the scene, you know? So as we're walking up to the Dent house, I observe. The way the window trim looks freshly painted, what kind of trees are planted in the yard, the color of a truck parked out front. Doesn't mean that'll all make it into the book."

Loshak wasn't sure if he felt better or worse about the notebook after that explanation. What things was Spinks observing about him in there? Would he keep track of the fact that there'd been a smear of tartar sauce on Loshak's tie while they had this conversation?

His thoughts were interrupted by the sound of Spinks cracking his door.

"Where are you going?"

Spinks had already climbed out and stooped to thrust his head back inside the car.

"Trufant just pulled in. And I," he patted his belly, "am ready for a second helping of nuggets."

Despite Spinks singing the praises of the catfish while they stood in line, Trufant refused to order anything from the truck.

"Eating catfish out of a truck is for hicks named Bubba. Do you see me wearing a ratty ballcap and bib overalls and calling them my over-hauls? You do not."

Loshak ordered another sweet tea, hoping the guy running the truck hadn't overheard Trufant's remarks. The tea was too sweet for someone who had grown up drinking tea hot and sugarless, but he didn't want to sit at the plastic tables without ordering something. It seemed too much like taking advantage of the guy's hospitality.

They sat down at the table farthest from the serving window to talk while they waited for Spinks' order.

"Who owned the club?" Loshak asked.

Trufant shrugged.

"Some untraceable shell corporation, I would imagine. Even if you knew what you were looking for, you'd never find out who the insurance money is really going to."

Loshak nodded. He'd expected as much. He planned to use his contacts within the Bureau, but he'd seen this song and dance play out before. Likely all they would find were dead ends, Swiss bank accounts, and strings of anonymous numbers.

He tried another angle.

"Who would want it burned down?"

"Anybody rich and important enough to be a member is worth burning the whole club to the ground for. Rebuilding is a minor inconvenience when you've got more money than God."

Trufant touched a spot on the table, his finger sticking

to it slightly as he pulled it away.

"It could've been one of them; it could've been all of them."

"What do you think the odds are of talking to a few members one-on-one?" Spinks asked. "You could kind of feel around and see if anybody spilled anything about Griffin."

Trufant laughed.

"No, my dear sweet Jevon, I would say our ship for nosing around the old boys' club has sailed. Anyone who knows anything about Griffin will be clenched tighter than a sphincter now."

Spinks' order came up in the window, and he left to retrieve it. He came back with extra napkins.

"Could we haul them in for questioning?" the reporter asked as he sat back down. "Maybe one of them will crack."

"You'll never get within a hundred feet of them," Trufant said. "All you'll ever see is their lawyers. I would have done the same when that buffoon from Prairie Village PD brought me in, but the notion of chatting with Special Agent Loshak was just too good an opportunity to pass up."

Spinks downed a piece of catfish and frowned.

"So, what's our next move?"

"I'm going to give The Wooden Nickel's details to a friend at the Bureau and see what they can turn up," Loshak said, spinning the Styrofoam cup of sweet tea with his fingers. "And we wait for CSI to come back with something on Dent's truck. In the meantime, we go through our dead councilman's records with a fine-toothed comb looking for some connection to all of this."

CHAPTER 58

Loshak and Spinks had almost made it back to the hotel when Rainie called.

"Crime scene techs are hauling the Dent truck back to the lab as we speak," she said. "I've got to get back to the station and type up my report, but I figured if you wanted to head on over now, I could meet you there later."

"Sounds good. Can you give me an address?"

"Sure thing. I'll text it to you. See you then."

As he set his phone back in the cupholder, Loshak analyzed the tone of Rainie's voice while she'd suggested meeting him later. He knew what Spinks would say about it, but he couldn't shake the thought of her long-term plan. Having him there while the techs worked over the truck was a good way to make sure she had a hand in as many parts of this investigation as possible, even when she wasn't around.

Loshak showed his badge at the lab, but security said Detective Wilson had called ahead and put them on the admittance list. They were led through the halls to the garage on the ground floor. They passed an old sedan that looked as if it had been dredged up from the bottom of a quarry, a classic Fairlaine refurbished to a bright shine, and a pickup with both doors off. A few techs were working on those vehicles with black lights, evidence tags, and tweezers, but most of the activity was centered on the far end of the garage. Techs swarmed around a maroon Dodge

Ram like worker bees at a hive, taking pictures and rolling video.

Loshak and Spinks stood back and watched while every detail of the truck was photographed, videoed, and recorded on a pre-workup log sheet. Everything that came out would have to be accounted for when the investigation was finished.

"That could be red," Spinks said, squinting at the truck. "If you were scared and getting pushed around, it could be red."

With Pressler gone, Loshak didn't mind agreeing.

"It does run more toward the red end of maroon than the purple end," he said, nodding.

Under duress, a young, scared girl might have trouble assigning an exact name to a color like that. He couldn't even decide what it was himself, and he qualified for the senior special at most restaurants.

"And it's got a black hard-cover over the bed like Benita said."

The techs moved slowly from the intake assessment to beginning the search. One team dismantled the Tonneau cover for easier access to the bed while another team started cataloguing macro evidence in the cab. As soon as the major pieces of evidence were out of the way, a third team would come in and sweep for trace evidence like hairs, fibers, blood, and semen.

While they were at it, Loshak had to visit the restroom at the far end of the garage to offload some of his sweet tea.

When he came back, one of the techs was pulling a rag out from under the seat. It looked like a grease rag made from an old t-shirt nobody wanted anymore. Electric blue, dirty, torn. The tech bagged it and leaned back into the cab.

Then came out with another grease rag. Except this one was clean, and Loshak could clearly see that it was a shirt. One way too small for Dent and his four teenage children. It looked just the right size for Angel, the youngest of the kids from the Davis house. The front showed a duck in shades, Spanish writing across the duck's belly. The kind of weird thing companies put on little boys' shirts so moms and grandmas would buy them.

The shirt went into a bag. Out next came a sandal. A pair of shorts. Finally a little plastic shopping bag with more clothes in it. One of which looked like a school uniform.

Loshak strode over to the tech before she could bag this last piece, his phone in hand.

"Can I get a picture of that crest?" he asked.

The tech held it out obligingly while Loshak snapped the photo.

"Thanks." He studied the picture as he went back to Spinks' side. He held out the screen. "What do you think that translates to?"

Spinks squinted at it.

"Unless I'm screwing up some false cognates, that says School of St. Mary, the Blessed Virgin."

"Did you hear what school the kids said they went to back in Obgregón?"

Spinks screwed up his mouth and looked to the side trying to remember, then shook his head.

"Why don't you just text Rainie? She probably has it written down."

"Yeah, probably," Loshak said, not wanting to let on to

his reluctance to play the younger detective's on-the-scene eyes and ears. He didn't really have a choice, though. He sent off the photo with his questions.

Three minutes later, his phone rang.

"That's their school!" Rainie's voice vibrated with excitement. "That's the school the kids went to. You found Angel's uniform."

CHAPTER 59

Margaret Smith was on the tail end of her shift at the 911 dispatch center. Ten minutes left to go. She was tired, hungry, and desperately in need of a warm-up for her coffee. But as she was pushing back her ergonomic rolling chair with plans to nuke her half-full mug in the break room, another call came in.

The dispatch program on her monitor identified it as coming from a cell phone, like almost every other call these days.

"911, what county are you in?" she asked.

"There's someone sneaking around my property," a man's voice said. Harsh, scared, breathing too hard. "It's him."

"Slow down, sir," Margaret said in a calm but firm voice. "Give me your address so I can send a unit out to you."

"He's going to kill me. Like the football coach and all the others. I know it. He's out there right now."

"I can't help you unless you give me your address, sir," she said.

Finally, it seemed to get through to him. He gave her an address in Platte County.

"Please hurry! He's going to kill me."

"I'm sending someone right now," Margaret said. "Stay on the line with me until they arrive."

"Just tell them to hurry."

"Sir, can you see the man right now?"

"Hell yeah I can, I'm looking right at him on my security cam feeds."

"What does he look like?"

"He's walking the perimeter of my house," the man hissed. "Oh Jesus, he's looking for a way in. I know he is."

"Can you describe him for me?"

"Tall. Skinny. Light hair, like between blond and brown. Oh Jesus God, hurry up!"

The phone jostled, and she heard running feet in the background. When the caller spoke again, his hushed whispering raised and lowered in time with the footfalls.

"Tell your men I'm in the panic room at the center of the house. And I think he has a gun."

Margaret sat forward, weight shifting the edge of her chair, the wheels rolling a few inches with the momentum. She swallowed and reminded herself to remain calm, to sound as if she were in control.

"Can you see the weapon, sir?"

A door in slammed on the other end of the line and Margaret could hear electronic beeping.

"That's what he used every other time," the caller said. "That's how he killed them."

"Every other time? Who did he kill?"

"I told you, the football coach and Mitzi Davis. Councilman um… whatever the fuck his name is. He's the serial killer that's been all over the news, damn it, that one."

This time she relaxed for real. The dispatch center had been getting about a dozen paranoid calls a day related to the serial killer since the news had started reporting on him. Someone paranoid enough to have a panic room in their house fit right in with the rest of the false alarm pullers.

"Why do you think this man is related to the serial killer, sir?"

"I knew one of the victims," he said, his breath slowly calming now that he was locked away. "Mitzi Davis. Now he's coming for me."

"How did you know Miss Davis?" Margaret asked. "Were you friends?"

"Yeah. Well, uh, more like business associates, I guess."

Margaret took a sip of her lukewarm coffee.

"What kind of business were you two in together?"

"Oh God, oh jeez, where did he go? I can't see him anymore! He's in a blind spot somewhere where the security system can't pick him up. Oh shit, could he have found the cameras?"

The man's breathing ratcheted up again. His voice dropped back down, lower than when he'd been whispering, and she wondered whether he even realized he was speaking out loud.

"Oh God, I think I'm going to wet myself. I've never been this scared before. Where did he go? One of these useless, piece of shit cameras should have him."

"Listen to me, sir, help is on the way," Margaret said. "Try to stay calm, and remember that you're in a safe room. If you can, get—"

Breaking glass crashed through the line, making Margaret jump. Coffee sloshed over the side of her cup and onto her fingers.

The man screamed.

CHAPTER 60

Dylan runs.

He keeps his head down. Squares his vision on the ground below.

The floor of the woods slides by underfoot. Endlessly rushing past.

Crumpled leaves paint the land in shades of brown and orange. Black swatches of wet earth lying exposed here and there.

He scans for branches, rocks, dipped places in the earth. Ready always to sidestep or hurdle. Anything to keep moving. Keep going. Keep running.

And daylight streams through the leaves above. Harsh sun that seems to move whenever the wind stirs the branches. Little spotlights crawling over the ground.

Searching for him.

Finding him.

He isn't the shadow anymore. He hasn't been a shadow at all today.

He, Dylan, had walked right into that fucker's house and blown a hole in the window of his fancy safe room. Not the shadow. Him.

It was the feeling of inevitability that made him do it. No rage, no fury, just that pull of fate like a fishhook behind his belly button.

He'd known what was going to happen as soon as he saw the security cameras all over the place, knew that one way or another, he was finished.

The cops have his face now.

They will find him eventually. A when, not an if. A bullet probably the same size as the ones in his stolen gun will punch a hole through his head, splatter blood and brain and bone everywhere before he can tell anyone that he knows their dirty secret.

His fate turns into a ticking clock, already winding down, winding down, winding down to zero.

Still he runs. He can't say why. Maybe it's instinct. Some basic survival coding wired into all mammals. Something that turns all humans back into unthinking prey when they're being hunted, whether they know the end of the game or think they can outrun it.

Dylan knows the end. He won't fool himself into thinking he is going to survive this. It's way too late for that fantasy. But he runs anyway.

What else can he do?

CHAPTER 61

Loshak's phone rang again as he and Spinks were leaving the forensics lab. It was Chief Tavares.

"A little bit ago, two units out in Platte Woods responded to a 911 caller claiming the serial killer was trying to break into his house. They got there before the caller was hurt and chased somebody off the property."

Loshak wanted to ask what about the call made the dispatcher think it was legit, but Tavares didn't slow down long enough for him to get the question in.

"Now this might be the real deal or it might not, but I'm pulling in everybody on the task force, every uniform in Platte County, and all the K9 units I can get Parks to lend me," the chief said. "Whoever this guy is, he's on foot. There's about eight thousand acres of woodland, lake, and summer residences around there he could be hiding in."

Spinks had stopped walking beside Loshak, staring with brows high.

"Tell me where to meet up with the team," Loshak said.

"Nope," Tavares said. "You're going straight to talk to our caller. I'm sending you his address. We've finally got a survivor on our hands, and I want you to lead the interrogation."

"You sure that's a priority? If we can find the killer before he gets away or kills someone else trying to escape—"

"I've got enough manpower to comb Platte County,

314

Agent Loshak, and I'm going to have choppers in the air and dogs on the ground. What I don't have in surplus is profilers who can get information out of this guy about the trafficking ring. If our killer's still at large when you're finished talking to the 911 caller, then you can join the search."

"I'll be there," Loshak agreed.

When he hung up, Spinks threw his hands up in the air.

"What?! We've got a live trafficker *and* the killer?"

"We've got somebody connected to the case," Loshak said. "It's our job to figure out exactly how he's connected."

CHAPTER 62

Running.

Running.

If he runs, he lives. If he stops, he dies. That simple.

So he runs.

His pulse pounds in his ears, the beat matching that of the big drum slamming away in his chest. Beat and swish. Beat and swish.

The steady rhythm of it seems to block out all other sound. It pulls him up into his head to leave the outside world at a strange distance.

It feels physically like he is somewhere else. Mostly removed from the real world even if his body still runs there. Like his mindscape exists on another plane than the one his body traverses.

And his thoughts seem to go clear in this place. All of existence turns to something simple.

He ducks under a low branch. Face pressing down into the shade. Ferns brushing his cheeks and forehead for a second like feathers.

And then he's upright again. Back in the waning daylight. Running.

Those first pains of exertion have passed. His lungs. His side. His joints. Endorphins rush into his skull to take all that hurt away.

It's almost spiritual when it first hits. Euphoria seeps into his bloodstream, and all negativity flees. The evil vanquished. Defeated for this little piece of time. Obliterated.

There is no hell. There is only heaven. And it is right here, all around him. Inside him.

He thinks he could run forever so long as he paces himself. Keeps his breath.

The churning of his legs seems the most natural thing now. The movement grows infectious, irresistible, takes on a strange significance. Right here and right now have become the only things he knows are real, and his motion within them seem to turn spiritual. Each step forward an act of prayer, perhaps.

Leaves smear him. Branches grab for his shirt. Poke out their tips like turtle heads to try to snap at his limbs. But they cannot slow him.

The terrain pulls him, and he obliges. He follows the downward slope of the land until it bottoms out into something of a ravine.

There's an opening there in the brush. A little gap like the curtains of leaves lie parted just here. A beaten spot in the ground to match.

The path slits a muddy gash into the green. Narrow. A game trail.

He veers onto it. Finds the going easier.

The leaves stand aside. The turtle heads retract into their shells.

His shoes suck a little with each step. The mud grabs them. Wants to hold on.

He hates that he's leaving such a clear trail of footprints — a dotted line along the earth that leads straight to him — but taking the trail is faster than picking his way through the thick stuff. He'll roll with it for now and change it up later.

He thinks of Maria as he runs. Thinks of the kids. Thinks of what he's given up, what he's risked. Not only for himself. For them.

It was selfish. He sees it now. He wanted to protect them, yes. But he wanted vengeance just as badly.

Wanted catharsis. To feel the violence in the flesh of his hands and arms. The squeeze of the trigger. The little jerk of the gun as the bullet tore through skin and skull and brain. Wanted to feel it in his breath, in the beat of his heart, in the clench of his jaw. Taste it on his tongue.

He'd developed an appetite for revenge. A lust for it. Impulses of desire so forceful that they clouded his vision, warped his thinking patterns, blackened his spirit.

But vengeance offers no satisfaction. No comfort. Just one moment of sick joy and a gaping emptiness after, an aching need for more to fill that hole.

More violence.

More death.

This appetite will never be sated. Never be contented.

It will never be stilled until he stops feeding it. Until he starves the fucking beast. Casts it out from his mind. Kills it.

The path narrows further, the greenery once more cinching tight around him.

He contorts himself. Twists his shoulders to try to squeeze through the little gap.

It works, but it's slower going than before. He'll need to leave the trail soon. The prospect makes him nervous somehow. Elicits a fresh pang of doubt, of fear.

He licks his lips. Reminds himself.

If he runs, he lives. If he runs, he lives.

So fucking run.

He pushes himself a little harder. Better to press for speed while he's still on the path.

A sound interrupts the monopoly his pulse has maintained over his ears. Something loud. Mechanical. Unnaturally rhythmic.

He thinks he's imagining it at first. But no. It's getting louder. Getting closer.

A helicopter.

CHAPTER 63

Loshak spotted the helicopter from the car, watched it circling a stretch of woodland to the northeast. The singsong voice of the GPS system told him to take the next left, and his gaze bounced back to the road.

There was a full-fledged manhunt on for the killer, and Tavares had called in every possible favor. Along with the chopper, there were over half a dozen K9 teams scouring the forest.

"I've got to admit, I'm having a real bad case of fo-mo," Spinks said from the passenger seat.

As Loshak veered left, Spinks swiveled around in his seat to keep his eyes on the helicopter.

"The what-mo?"

"Fo-mo," Spinks said, then spelled it out. "F-O-M-O. Fear of missing out."

The reporter angled his face toward Loshak and shook his head.

"I guess it's not even fear, technically. I *know* I'm missing out."

Gripping the steering wheel, Loshak nodded. He felt amped. Almost tingly with anticipation. He'd been wondering for most of the ride if they'd caught the guy yet, kept expecting his phone to ring at any second. He imagined Pressler's booming voice over the line, *We got 'im, boys! Trussed up like a Christmas goose!*

But the search teams had their mission, and Loshak had

his. He had to talk to their newest victim and find out what he knew.

And if they could get him to talk, it might finally start to explain how everyone fit into this whole thing. Who was bringing the kids in. Who else was part of the trafficking ring. And who was at the top.

He might even know the killer.

Loshak inhaled deeply through his nose, trying to settle his mind. He needed a plan.

"We have to tread lightly here. With this guy, Chapin, I mean." Loshak ran his fingers over his scalp. "We don't want to go stomping in with our accusations of human trafficking and spook him."

"But he already admitted to knowing Mitzi Davis on the 911 call," Spinks said.

"That was in the heat of the moment. He might not even remember doing it. Now that the immediate threat has passed, he'll go back into self-preservation mode. Wrap himself back up in layers of denial."

Loshak stretched his neck on one side and then the other.

"The good news is that he already let something slip once. He was spooked. Beyond that, even. Terrified. Maybe he's still a little off-balance. If we play it right, maybe we can get him talking again."

CHAPTER 64

The buzzing, *whumph*ing sound of the chopper is like the bass turned up way too loud in a car down the block. There are trees everywhere, and the horizon has the sun about halfway swallowed up, but he can't count on the dark or the foliage to shield him from the searchlight.

He stumbles in his panic, going down in years' worth of dead leaves.

An image flashes through his mind, a shining fall day when he was five or six, raking leaves with his dad, jumping in the piles. It clashes with the noise from the helicopter. Jarring.

And he sees it now.

Bright light throws shadows through the trees like long-bodied monsters sprinting after him. The chopper will be on top of him in no time.

Almost before he thinks about it, he is sprawling on his back, scooping armfuls of crackling brown onto his legs, then stomach, and finally covering his head.

His arms wiggle in under the leaves at his side, two snakes writhing to get under. He closes his eyes. Prays that the motion won't cause a leaf avalanche that would uncover any other part of him.

The chopper blades are so loud that it has to be right overhead. The ground almost seems to shake along with the thrum of the propeller.

The searchlight illuminates the backs of the leaves

covering his face, making a curtain of veined silhouettes.

Dylan realizes he's holding his breath. Maybe breathing wouldn't create a big enough motion to attract their attention, but he's not taking any chances. He won't move again until the helicopter is long gone.

A tingle assails the top of his head. Feels like a bug is crawling through his hair. Lots of legs. Like a millipede.

His hand twitches, but he catches himself before he moves. Later. Later he can scratch his scalp off and smash anything that comes squirming out.

Finally, the searchlight moves away. Disappears. The sound recedes. Moves on.

He is left behind in a grave of leaves, listening to the rotors whirring away up there. They're still too close to break cover.

His lungs hitch, desperate for air. He takes a single breath, then holds it again.

It seems so dark without the searchlight on the leaves. Pitch black. Wet from the other night's rain. The dirt beneath him feels cold and damp, and he can already sense that it's stealing his body heat, chilling the flesh everywhere it touches.

It feels like being back in the crawlspace.

The claustrophobia hits a second after he thinks this. He's got to get out, get away from this death trap. If he doesn't, this is where he'll die.

The chopper still sounds so close, but he can't stay here.

He breaks the surface of the leaves with a gasp like someone coming up from a deep dive and lurches to his feet. His back and butt are cold and wet from the ground. His hair still feels like something is crawling in it.

323

He can see the helicopter's light through the trees, heading what he thinks is south.

Dylan turns north and takes off running again, the sound of the chopper growing smaller with every step.

He knows it will be back. Sooner than later, most likely.

But the sun flees the day now. Darkness falling, falling. Everything going gray. Losing its color.

A gift and a curse, the dark. What hides him will also make travel harder, make running dangerous.

He wonders when this will end. How this will end.

He knows the gist, of course. They will kill him. It's only a matter of time before they catch him, and he knows too much for them to let him live.

But how will they do it? Will they shoot him in the back? Or will they want to bring him in alive? Wait until they've flashed the pictures of him in handcuffs — **SERIAL KILLER APPREHENDED**, the headlines will read — then stage a suicide once he's locked in a cell, like they did with Jaro?

He wonders these things, and he runs.

Exhaustion creeps in little by little.

That small ache in the ankle spreads to the knee.

That heat flushing the face flickers hot and cold from the sheen of sweat there.

That little spark in the lungs catches and smolders, until at last it rages. A strange wet flame in the chest. Those two shrunken flaps of moist flesh hovering in his ribcage feel like they're about to cave in. Dank and heavy while they burn.

He wants to quit. Wants to stop. Wants to lie down on the ground and die.

But he can't.

A blade jabs him in the liver with every other step or so, somehow out of time with the patter of his footsteps. The opposing rhythms are jarring.

Just keep going.

He moves in the thick stuff now. No path to funnel him forward. No low ground to make things easy.

Here the ground itself becomes another obstacle. Sloping up and then sucking down into craters. Potholes that want only to snap an ankle.

Reality goes in and out of focus. All that shrubbery blurring. Distorting. Green blobs everywhere.

And his stomach grumbles. He's hungry. Thirsty. Overheated. Running out of energy. Lightheaded. A little dazed.

He knows he's in danger. But he can't stop. Can't stop. Stopping is dying.

Run or fucking die.

So he runs.

Great rivulets of sweat gush down his face now. It almost feels like sheets of moisture sliding over his features. He wipes at it some with his sleeve, but he can't keep up.

Droplets catch in the corners of his eyes. That bright sting bites there. Makes him squint.

He's swiping at his brow when his foot catches on deadfall. Trips him.

Gravity gives up its hold on him, and he lifts off the ground. Lays out flat in the air.

Floating.

Floating.

Falling.

He bites his tongue when he slams down. The weight of the world crashing back to reality. Thumping him into the dirt in a belly flop. The sheer force crumpling him. Knocking the wind from his lungs.

Makes him feel so small.

Everywhere hurts. He can't breathe.

He wants to quit. Wants to lie here until the chopper comes back. Until the dogs come to tear the flesh from his face.

Let it go.

Instead he fights to get to his feet. Arms and legs thrashing through ferns. Head woozy.

He's wobbly on his feet. Chest still stuck. Trying to draw wind, but it can't. Feels like everything inside his ribcage is imploding, caving in, sucking up into a vortex with a sound like one of those pneumatic tubes at the bank drive-thru inhaling a cylinder with someone's paycheck in it.

And still he shambles forward. Staggers. Slower now. Choppy steps. Uneven. Buckling a little at the waist, but moving. Moving.

How will this end? Badly, he thinks.

And when? Soon.

When he sees it, he stops in his tracks.

A cabin juts from the top of the hill.

CHAPTER 65

Anders Chapin was a middle-aged man with a failing comb-over and the big, brown eyes of a basset hound. He sat at a reclaimed wood table that could easily seat twenty people, wet eyes flitting briefly from Loshak to Spinks, then returning to search the windows for threats.

Loshak took the seat across from Chapin, still a good three feet away. *Cavernous* was the word that kept coming to mind. As in, this dining room is cavernous. He wondered whether his voice would echo. No way to check without breaking the silence he was intentionally drawing out.

All the various markers of money were present — vaulted ceilings inside, landscaped lawn surrounded by acres of woods outside. You'd never know you were just off a high-traffic street.

From across the table, Chapin laughed nervously.

"I feel a little silly, especially with all this," he gestured to where a crime scene tech was dusting a door for prints. "I realize now it was probably just a burglar."

"A burglar?" Loshak repeated. "You seemed pretty convinced that it was the KC serial killer when you called 911."

Chapin reached up and wiped at the corners of his mouth.

"Yes, well… My imagination can be a bit overactive, I guess you could say." A sheepish expression flitted over his features. "I realize now that intruder probably thought no one was home, and then fled when he realized someone was."

"This burglar… Did he take anything?" Loshak asked, glancing around.

"No. I don't think so." Chapin licked his lips. "But like I said, I think I startled him into running off."

Loshak drummed his fingers on the wood surface of the table and leaned back in his seat.

"Is that why he shot into the panic room, you think? Because you startled him?"

Chapin touched his mouth again.

"I… don't know. I guess… it could be."

"Maybe he wanted your watch," Spinks said, pointing at the Cartier timepiece on Chapin's wrist. "That could be why he shot into your panic room."

Loshak watched Chapin blink in confusion at the reporter's dry tone and figured this was the moment to blindside him.

"How did you know Mitzi Davis?"

Chapin looked startled and brushed his fingers against his mouth again.

"Who?"

"Mitzi Davis. You mentioned her in the 911 call."

Eyelids fluttering, Chapin quirked his head to one side.

"Oh right. She was one of the victims, wasn't she? I must have seen her name on the news."

"You said you knew her."

"I did?" Chapin's gaze went from Loshak to Spinks and then back to Loshak. "When?"

"You told the 911 dispatcher that you knew Mitzi

Davis."

"I mean, I imagine I said a lot of things. I barely remember even making the call, I was in such a panic. I'm sure what I meant was that I knew *of* her. From the news. Like I said."

Loshak opened the manila folder he'd brought along. One at a time, he set out the pictures of the bodies under Griffin's house. The wet, shallow graves. The desiccated skin and bones. That swollen foot.

Chapin's upper lip quivered, and Loshak thought he actually heard the man's teeth chatter. Finally, he watched Chapin's shoulders sag.

The man leaned forward and rested his head in his hands, and Loshak knew they had him.

CHAPTER 66

Dylan's fingers scrabble at the soil. Digging. Loosening the black dirt and moss from around the tool he needs.

The rock. It's about the size of a bowling ball with a jagged point at the top.

He gives it a little shove with the heel of his hand, and it wiggles in its socket like a loose tooth. Ready to come out and play.

He pulls the stone from the ground. Stares for just a second at the cratered place where it had been lodged.

A black hole. Wet dirt.

And now he stands. Adjusts the heft of the thing in his hands so the point will hit first. Heavy.

Two steps later, he thrusts it with both hands. Arms trembling as they heave it.

The stone punches through the big bay window at the front of the cabin. Plunging through like a cannonball and disappearing into the shade inside.

Big shards of glass topple. Shatter on the deck at his feet. Tinkling and glittering.

It's fucking loud. Shrill. Percussive. Unbelievable.

He holds his breath and listens for a beat. His heart still thundering in his chest.

No one is home. He hopes.

He'd knocked on all the doors before he dug out the rock.

No answer. Nothing. Then or now.

He bats a few remaining bits of glass out of the way and climbs through the empty window frame.

His hands and knees find a little built-in bench inside. This is good. Makes it so he's not dropping so far from the height of the window to some floor he can't really see. Less awkward.

He squats in a living room. Scans it left to right. Head swiveling.

Matching black leather furniture. Couch. Love seat. Recliner. Flat screen. Upper-middle-class vacation home with details that he has no time to examine just now.

No one is here. Not this room, anyway.

The cabin smells musty inside. Like it's been empty for a long while. A layer of dust coats most everything he can see.

He licks his lips. Needs to be sure.

He yells.

"Hello?"

His voice sounds raspy. Loud. Raw. Something about the sound is so stimulating that the hair on his arms pricks up right away.

"Anyone there?"

Now he holds his breath. Listens over the pounding of his heartbeat in his ears.

Nothing.

It's empty.

He needs to be quick.

He shuffles straight to the kitchen. To the fridge. Opens it.

Not much. Various condiments. A jar of olives that looks not of this century.

A can of Sunny D in the back catches his eye.

He grips it. Cracks it. Drinks.

Cold. Disgustingly sweet, but delicious in this moment. So bright and acidic that it tingles on his tongue. He remembers a joke he heard once about a man being chased by a tiger. The guy ran right off a cliff, but grabbed a branch growing from the rockface on his way down. There was a peach on the branch, so with the last of his strength, the guy picked and ate it. Tiger above, jagged rocks below. And hanging there, the guy thinks the peach is the best thing he's ever eaten.

Dylan chugs most of the Sunny D down. Decides to save a little. Savor it. After all, this is his peach.

It's not until he retracts the can from his lips that he realizes how dry his throat was, that he still can't catch his breath.

Even now, his breathing remains accelerated. Little gasps sucking in and out of him that he can't seem to slow, can't seem to calm.

He digs through the cupboards. Finds some Cherry Pop Tarts. Frosted.

He rips the foil off. Wolfs them down. Little crumbly bits of pastry tumble down the front of him, leaving powdery bits on his t-shirt.

When the four Pop Tarts are gone, he chases them down his gullet with a handful of Rold Gold pretzels. Stale as fuck yet heavenly nonetheless. The salt stings his wet lips a little.

Rifling through the drawers turns up mostly junk, but he finds a couple of packets of saltines from Wendy's. Shoves them in his pocket for later.

Another handful of pretzels goes in, and then the last of the Sunny D to help wash the dry stuff down.

The food is so good, but he can't enjoy it. He can only gorge himself. Cram it down as fast as possible. Needs it inside his belly. Needs the calories.

All the while he eats, the impulse to leave nags him. He can't dally here. Can't afford to stand still for this long.

They're coming for him. Closing in.

And right in the middle of checking the freezer, the impulse for flight wins out. His feet carry him toward the door.

He needs to leave here. Now.

CHAPTER 67

"Look, I didn't know," Chapin said, voice wavering. "I heard rumors, but I didn't know."

Chapin's hands formed a shield over his mouth, as if that might make his words less damning. Less reprehensible.

"Didn't know what?" Loshak kept his expression harsh and unreadable. "That Griffin was killing kids by the dozen?"

"That wasn't supposed to be how it went!"

Chapin's shout actually did echo a little. He flinched, startled by his own vehemence, then sort of shrank into himself.

"It was supposed to be business, you know. Just business. Griffin wasn't supposed to hurt them, but… He got out of control. He wasn't supposed to be… disposing… of them."

Loshak glanced down at the pictures, then back up at Chapin. The guy looked one hard blink away from tears.

"Sounds to me like you did know, Mr. Chapin, and you didn't do anything to stop him. That makes you complicit in multiple homicides. Child murders. Telling your fellow inmates that you're in for killing kids doesn't usually go over well in prison."

Chapin's throat worked convulsively, as if he were trying to swallow but couldn't get enough saliva to do it.

"Look, I want to help you out, but you've got to help me

first," Loshak said. "Is there anything you can tell us about the operation? The more you tell us, the more it seems like you're on our side when this goes to court."

Chapin shuddered.

"I'll tell you everything, just don't let him get me."

"Who?"

"The killer. He was here. He knows who I am."

Loshak nodded, trying not to show his disappointment. He'd been hoping for that one-in-a-billion shot that Chapin knew their killer by name.

"Have you ever seen him before?"

Giving a little shudder, Chapin shook his head.

"How do you think he found you?"

Chapin had a faraway look in his eyes now. His voice had grown small. Distant. Almost like he was thinking out loud.

"Mitzi must've told him about me. Or maybe he found me in her phone. I don't know," Chapin said. His Adam's apple bobbed some more. "It was only a matter of time before he came for me. I've been hiding out since I heard about Mitzi. Loaded the panic room full of essentials for when he came, just in case I needed to survive a few days."

He scowled and sat up a little straighter.

"I didn't realize the damn contractor stiffed me on the bulletproof glass. What a fucking joke. I guess I'd threaten to sue, but…"

"Not if you're in prison," Loshak said, bringing Chapin back to the present.

The man blinked a few times, deflated again.

"You really think I'm scared of prison? You think I'd be talking to you at all if I thought that was the worst possible outcome? If I could trust anyone around here? My lawyer could be… My best bet is to talk to you. Cooperate. Make a deal. With the feds, maybe I have a chance… maybe…"

Loshak fought back a smirk at the notion of a human trafficker lamenting the fact that he couldn't trust anyone. What a shame.

That distant look had come over Chapin's features again, however. Loshak spoke quietly, his voice steady, not wanting to disrupt whatever trance the man had seemingly fallen into.

"Tell me how this operation worked. Where did you fit in?"

"I picked the packages up from Mitzi or Griffin and took them to the next drop. Usually up here to another courier. Once to a buyer in town when Mitzi's in-city courier couldn't make it."

Loshak filed away Chapin's use of the word *packages*. Not children. Not human beings. Packages. Chapin had to distance himself from what he was doing in order to sleep at night in the house that human trafficking had almost certainly bought him. The installation of the panic room was interesting. Had Chapin thought that he would eventually be found out and have to hide from authorities or had he been worried about an attack by someone in the same business? Or was he just naturally paranoid?

"How many?"

"Fifteen, maybe twenty. No more than that."

"Over how long?" Loshak asked.

"I only got involved three years ago."

Only, Loshak thought. He'd *only* be trafficking kids for three years.

"You said you made one of the deliveries to somewhere 'in town.' Does that mean Kansas City?"

Chapin's bulbous head bobbed up and down. Loshak stared across the table at him, studying his face for any reaction his next question might elicit.

"To a bar called The Wooden Nickel?"

Frowning, Chapin shook his head.

"No, it was to some vacant lot out back of a gas station. A guy in a Suburban picked up the package that time," he said, wringing his hands. "I can't remember the plates, but I think it was black."

Loshak was disappointed but didn't show it. If Chapin had implicated The Wooden Nickel directly, it might have been enough to launch a full-scale investigation into the club's members.

"Could you identify the guy who picked them up?"

Chapin leaned forward, hands flat on the table now.

"What about, like, a lesser charge or immunity? You have to help me, and… you know, put in a good word. I'm a whistleblower, you know? Don't they get a deal? If I get immunity, I'll describe everybody I ever saw working for them. I know names for at least two other couriers."

Loshak nodded slowly. People got this idea of "immunity" as a Get Out of Jail Free Card from Law & Order and courtroom dramas like it. The word itself didn't mean anything, though too often the deals criminals cut in exchange for information seemed like magic tickets out of the consequences.

"I'll see what I can do. As a show that you're willing to cooperate, tell me where Mitzi and Griffin got the kids."

"That football coach," Chapin said. "He got a lot of kids

from down south, mainly Mexican teenagers. I think they had a deal with some guys down there on the border. But sometimes he picked up American kids, too. And sometimes Griffin would find kids through this charity he ran for runaways and homeless orphans. As far as I knew, he would be the one who was supposed to be making the deliveries to The Wooden Nickel."

That would go a long way toward explaining Trufant's mystery of how new money like Griffin had been allowed to join the exclusive club for the local super-rich.

"Who was running this operation?" Loshak asked. "There must have been someone at the top, calling the shots."

Chapin flapped his elbows in a bird-like shrug.

"I don't know. I was just, you know… a pawn."

Loshak had to bite back a contemptuous smirk. How many "packages" had Chapin delivered over the years? Tens? Hundreds? And yet he saw himself as merely a cog in a machine, as if it hadn't been a choice. That was rich.

"Did you know Councilman Long?"

Loshak slid the councilman's crime scene photo across the table. The exit wound stood out raw and red against the dead man's corpse-white skin.

Chapin blanched and scrubbed his hand over his mouth. He swallowed audibly.

"I saw on the news that he was dead, but I never met him in real life."

"Do you know how he was involved in all this?"

Chapin shook his head.

"Mitzi never told me."

"I want the names of the two couriers you mentioned

before." Loshak tossed a notepad and pen down in front of Chapin. "And the names of anyone else you know or suspect were involved."

Hand shaking, Chapin reached for the pen.

"This killer, the one that came after you," Loshak said, unable to stop himself from making one last desperate stab. "Chief Tavares said he's reviewing the tapes from your security system. You saw the guy. Do you have any ideas or suspicions about who he might be?"

"I think…" Chapin paused in his writing and closed his eyes. "I think he might be the price of our sins."

CHAPTER 68

Dylan crashes through the wall of green at the edge of the woods before he sees it.

A road.

There aren't any streetlights out here, so he ran right onto the asphalt before he realized it was there.

He turns and starts jogging along the shoulder. If he sees something coming, he can run off into the tree line. He'll make better time here, instead of tripping and stumbling his way through the woods like he has been for the last... what has it been? An hour? It feels like longer, but he doubts it's even been that long.

It isn't a big highway. Just a winding, two-lane road with dense forest on either side.

He wishes he knew what time it was, had some sense of how long he's been running, but he'd ditched his phone as soon as he realized they had his face on camera. If they put a name to the face, they could track his phone. He saw something like that on TV once, he thinks, one of those CSI shows with the dramatic lighting and CGI re-enactments of bullets ripping through brain tissue.

He suspects it's ten or eleven, but it could just as easily be as early as nine or as late as two in the morning. Each possibility seems plausible.

How long ago was the chopper? He gropes after the memory of it, the searchlight creeping over the leaves, the violent whump of the blades. He doesn't know. He can remember it, but it seems distant now. The experience already seeping away from him, the details losing clarity and context.

Part of him feels like he's been running for days on end. His thighs and calves burn, and his right knee twinges with every step. His lungs feel like punching bags. Even his neck aches, though that's probably the endless tension cramping the muscles there. He keeps having to stop himself from grinding his teeth, an old habit he picked up just after his mom died. It always comes back when he's really scared.

Headlights flash around a curve up ahead. A pale blaze that seems to open up a piece of the darkness.

Dylan sprints off into the tree line and ducks down in the thicket. Watches them come around the corner.

A little sports car appears. Dark. Sleek. Low to the ground. Not a cop.

He relaxes a fraction.

Then the little car slams on its breaks, squealing its wheels a little. Its taillights throw hellish red light onto the street and trees behind it.

Not five yards from Dylan — and less from the car — a yearling buck, just out of velvet, stands still as a tree, rooted to the middle of the road and probably scared to death.

The sports car honks at it. Throaty bleats piercing the night. Startled, the buck spins around and leaps back the way it had come, its white tail flagging, hooves clicking on the asphalt.

The little sports car's engine revs. The driver puts it back in gear.

It's a stick, Dylan thinks. Then, *I can drive a stick.*

He sticks the gun in the front of his pants where he can

reach it easily and blouses his shirt to hide it. Jogging a little, trying not to look like he's been on the run for the last however many hours, he runs out onto the road, waving his arms back and forth in the international distress signal.

The sports car pulls forward, its headlamps drenching him in light. The taillights flicker again. It's slowing down. He hears a power window rolling down.

Dylan moves to the driver's side, letting the car pull up alongside him as he fishes a hand for his gun.

The man's face angles toward him, an older guy, fluffy white hair lit up blue by the radio lights. The eyes go wide as the man sees the gun.

"Shit!" the man yells, cranking the wheel.

The sports car revs again and jumps as the man tries to floor it to get away. For a second, Dylan thinks it's going to die.

His muscles tense, ready to rip the old man out of the little car. Club him upside the head with the butt of the gun. Race off into the night.

But then the engine catches, and the wheels spin. The back flounders a little, then straightens out, and the car is gone, disappearing around the next curve in the little road.

Frustrated, exhausted, and embarrassingly close to tears, Dylan screams. He points the pistol at the little piece of shit car and pulls the trigger. Four or five times. He loses count. Eventually the slide locks back, empty.

"Fuck!"

He throws the gun down. Watches it skid down the asphalt a few feet.

Somehow unsatisfied to find it still in his field of vision, he chases it down. Kicks it to the far side of the road, its metal zinging across the blacktop.

And a new sound. Barking. Not some house dog's warning bark, either.

This was the consistent barking of a working dog on a track. He'd heard it often enough when he was a kid, back when his dad still had time for coon hunting and wanted to hang out with him.

The search party has sicced dogs on him.

And they're close.

Dylan follows the gun across the road and slides down a grassy incline into the woods. He can see the glint of water at the bottom of this hill. A river. Maybe he can lose them there.

CHAPTER 69

"Think he'll get a deal?" Spinks asked as they descended the front steps of Chapin's home toward the Prairie Village's Mobile Command Unit.

"I think odds are good that someone will offer him one, whether it's the feds or the district attorney," Loshak said. "A string of arrests looks a lot better in the paper than one does."

The back doors of the MCU were open wide, letting in and out police personnel. Yellow light poured from inside. Loshak grabbed onto the rail bolted to the door — it was slanted like those metal bars in elderly people's bathtubs — and climbed the stairs into the semi-trailer.

A bank of computers was lined up along the short wall at the farthest end. Two uniforms and a woman in an EMT jacket wore headsets and took calls that were being routed to the MCU from various departments with any snippet of information or possible sighting of their killer.

Tavares, the Platte County Sheriff, and the head of the K9 teams paced the inside of the trailer, alternating between listening to walkie talkies and snapping orders into them.

When Tavares saw Loshak coming, he said, "Hold that thought," into his walkie.

The little man propped a fist on each hip and squared himself toward the agent, a maneuver that made him appear larger than he really was.

"You get anything usable?"

"Plenty that'll hold up in a court, but nothing that will help us identify this guy," Loshak said, gesturing to a grainy black-and-white still from one of Chapin's security cameras.

Someone had printed out a whole stack of them, presumably to distribute among the search teams so they knew who they were looking for. Loshak studied the blurry face, wondering again how the killer fit into all of this.

Tavares pointed the antenna of his walkie-talkie at the computer bank.

"Well, we might have a lead on him. Caller on Locust Road, about three miles from here, was attacked by a carjacker. He described him as a tall, skinny, white boy who looked like he'd been rolling around in the mud. Sound like our guy?"

"Could be," Loshak said. "The profiles tend to get pretty similar for all serial killer types when it comes to an escape scenario. They'll do anything they can to get away. Kill, lie, hide, run. Whatever it takes."

"Sounds about right. The vic said he thought the carjacker was trying to shoot him through the back window. You still ready to do some legwork, Agent?"

"Sure, tell us where you need us."

Tavares' eyes jumped to Spinks as if he hadn't noticed the reporter before.

"There won't be any 'us,'" he snapped. "I'm not sending a reporter on a manhunt, no matter what government agency he's got a permission slip from."

"No disrespect, Chief," Spinks said, "But I have been on manhunts before. I was part of the stake-out team that helped Agent Loshak take down Edward Zakarian in Miami."

Tavares waved a hand at him.

"Argue 'til you run yourself down, Mr. Spinks, but it's not happening."

Spinks scowled, but before he could protest, Tavares turned to Loshak and started talking again.

"I've got Pressler and a rep from the Mission Hills PD at the point last sighted. Grab a vest and join up with them there. Got a gun on you? 'Cause it sounds like you're going to need it."

CHAPTER 70

Loshak followed the directions on his GPS down several winding, tree-lined roads until he found an unmarked car with its cherry flashing away on the hood.

Pressler's wide silhouette was even bulkier with the added padding of the Kevlar vest. Loshak parked his vehicle nose-to-nose with the unmarked car and flipped on his hazards. As he did, a smaller form climbed up the embankment beside Pressler. All Loshak had to see was the bouncy ponytail to know who it was.

Fingers in everything, he thought. If she didn't come out of this the charge-leading hero, it wouldn't be for lack of trying.

As Rainie crossed in front of the headlights, Loshak realized she was holding an evidence bag with something inside. She wiggled her fingers at him in a wave, then pointed to the rear of the unmarked car.

Loshak grabbed the flashlight he'd taken from the MCU and climbed out, rounding their vehicle. They were both hunched over the trunk, studying the bag in the light from Rainie's phone.

She grinned that ten-year-old's smile when she saw him.

"This, Agent Loshak, is a Glock, nine-millimeter. I just sent off a pic of the serial numbers to IPD for confirmation that it's Mike Dent's missing nine. How much you want to bet this is it?"

Beside her, Pressler was beaming and fidgeting like a toddler that had to pee.

"You know it is," the portly detective said. "Just you wait. We've got him now. Fingerprints are going to show this boy all over it!"

Rainie looked practically giddy.

"It's possible," Loshak agreed. "You're thinking the killer dropped it when the carjacking failed?"

"Maybe," she said. "The embankment's kind of steep here, though. Drops down to a little creek. It's possible he lost it running and didn't think he had time to stop and search for it."

"So, what's the plan?" he asked. "Tavares said a team was on the way here?"

Rainie glanced away while she stuck the bagged gun in the trunk and slammed the lid.

"They are," she said. "But—"

"But who the hell's waiting around." Pressler turned toward the embankment, pointing a little handheld flashlight that looked like it clipped to the barrel of a gun. "See down there? That disturbed mess a' leaves and mud cutting down to the crick? It's fresh. That call came through less than ten minutes ago."

"I figure we can catch up to him before the K9 unit gets here," Rainie said. "Last I heard the closest one was ten minutes out, anyway."

"Alright, let's go," Loshak said.

From the edge of the road, it was a good twenty feet to the bottom of the embankment. They half-climbed, half-slid down. Loshak's shoes skidded on loose rock and dead leaves. He had to grab for trees and underbrush to keep from going into free fall, but he made it without major injury.

The little stream Pressler had called a crick had cut a path into the rock there. Loshak could clearly see a shoe print in the sandy mud and a spot where a bit of the bank had been smashed away by someone in passing.

Pressler followed the stream one way, swiping his flashlight over the rocks and deadfalls in the water, searching for any sign the killer had gone north, while Rainie and Loshak followed the stream south doing the same.

They'd gone about a hundred yards when Rainie's phone rang.

"Wilson," she answered. "Yeah? What do you mean it wasn't?"

She stopped walking, and Loshak stopped beside her. Even with the flashlight beam pointed away, there was enough ambient light for him to see her face scrunch up in anger.

"OK. Yeah, thanks."

She stuck the phone back in her pocket. Took a long breath and let it out.

"The fucking gun isn't Dent's. This one was reported stolen last month," Rainie said as she massaged her temples. "Somebody else must've dumped it out here."

"You're jumping to conclusions," Loshak said. "You decided the killer's gun must have belonged to Dent, so now you're accepting the opposite as true. That it can't be the killer's because it didn't belong to Dent."

"Well, then where the hell is Dent's gun?" Rainie snapped. Then she sighed. "I'm sorry. You're right. It might still be our killer's gun. Anybody can buy a stolen gun in KC if they know where to look. But that still leaves us with one missing nine."

"It will turn up or it won't," Loshak said. "Not every loose end in investigations like this get tied up. The gun's not what's going to make or break this case. We've got DNA under Mitzi Davis' fingernails and in her teeth and blood from her kitchen to tie our killer to the scene."

"That ties him to one murder out of five. That murder was different enough that if he claims he was just copycatting the pose based on newspapers, the defense won't even have to say, 'reasonable doubt.' Everybody will already be thinking it."

Up the creek, Pressler gave a shout.

"Got something up here!"

"Comin'!" Rainie yelled back, then started following the stream north again.

A thread of anger ran along the edge of her voice, and Loshak noticed she'd dropped her 'g.' Reverting to a formative accent was something people usually did at times of high emotion or intoxication.

Loshak caught up to her.

"We'll find this guy, and the evidence will put him away."

"Yeah." She nodded, not looking at him. "We'll get him."

But the "we" part sounded strained, as if she'd almost said "I." And she had her free hand on the butt of her service revolver.

CHAPTER 71

"Right there and there," Pressler said, pointing his flashlight at a scuffed-up clump of moss on a rock, then following the trajectory upstream to a muddy hole shaped like a shoe. "He musta gone up to the shin on that one."

"Good eye, Pressler," Rainie said and patted the portly detective on his meaty shoulder. "Alright, let's get moving."

Loshak glanced up the embankment toward the flashing red light of the car.

"Hang on. Someone should stay up here to point the K9 team in the right direction."

Rainie scowled. "If you say that the girl should stay behind—"

"I wasn't going to," Loshak said, raising his hands. "But I do think someone needs to do it. Save them time letting the dogs sniff up and down the stream."

"Fine, but let's not stand around arguin' about it while our guy extends his lead," Rainie said, that edge back in her voice. She turned to her larger counterpart. "Pressler, you stayin' behind, too?"

"No way, good buddy-gal, let's motate."

Apparently Loshak had drawn the short straw by default. He watched them start to pick their way upstream, flashlights trained on the water.

Before they got more than a few yards away, Pressler turned back to Loshak.

"If you get back on Locust and head out to T, take a left

and come around on double-O 'til you get to a bridge. Unless I'm crazy, that's the other end of this crickhere. You can meet up with us after you talk to the dog team."

Loshak nodded.

"Thanks."

Pressler gave him a little salute with his flashlight, then hustled to catch up to Rainie.

Getting back up the embankment to the cars was a lot harder than getting down. Loshak had to claw at the dirt and pull himself up using trees. He ended up going down on one knee and ripping a hole in his suit pants, but eventually he made it to the top and pulled himself up onto blessedly flat asphalt.

He leaned his butt against the passenger side of the rental while he caught his breath. Down below, he could just barely see Rainie or Pressler's flashlight. A little farther and they'd be hidden in the trees.

Rainie with her hand on her gun.

Saying, *We'll get him,* when what she meant was, *I'll get him.*

She wouldn't shoot their killer, Loshak told himself. Not unless he pulled a gun first. And they had what was most likely his gun in an evidence baggie right up here.

But he'd been in the game long enough to know that sometimes acute lead poisoning started to look like the only possible way to bring a killer to justice. Every now and then, when a sure thing started to slip through a cop's fingers…

I'll get him.

Loshak pulled out his phone and dialed 911 as he headed around to the driver's side. He gave the dispatcher his name and credentials, then asked to be put through to Tavares at the MCU. While he waited for the transfer, Loshak got the car turned around and headed toward T. Hopefully Pressler was right about which creek went under that bridge.

"Tavares." The gruff voice on the other end of the line startled Loshak out of his thoughts.

"Chief, this is Agent Loshak. I've got directions for the K9 team en route to the last sighted point."

"Go ahead."

"When they get to Pressler's car, they need to head down the embankment and follow the stream north. Rai— uh, Detective Wilson and Pressler are following what they believe to be our killer's trail in that direction."

Loshak rounded a curve, then pushed down on the accelerator. The rental's engine growled as its speedometer climbed.

"I'm driving to meet them at the other end of this path, see if I can't cut our guy off before he gets through."

CHAPTER 72

Thorns and brambles tear at Dylan's face and bare arms and rip holes in his jeans and shirt. A whole thicket of blackberry bushes. He bleeds and hurts from the poisoned thorns, grunting and snorting as he tries to force his way through. Tears streak down the edges of his face, snot running down the middle, but he's too exhausted and in too much pain to feel any kind of embarrassment.

He hurts so bad he keeps seeing bright flashes whenever he closes his eyes.

And the now all the running begins to catch up with him. He's tired, and his side hurts, and his lungs burn, and he just wants to fucking die already.

He isn't thinking about fate or predator and prey or evading search parties or helicopters or dogs or anything. All rational thought has been driven from his mind by fatigue and frustration. He has more in common now with a sleepy toddler throwing a tantrum than the cold, logical shadow who metes out justice to human traffickers.

The shoestring on his left foot gets caught under his right foot. He stumbles, crashes into the arms of a younger bush. Small thorns prick and stab and scratch all the exposed flesh they can find.

He screams, almost more of a ragged sob, thrashes around in a frenzy. Eventually, he rips away from the branches and falls to the ground, whimpering and shaking.

He scrunches together, pulling in his arms and legs,

desperate for even the small amount of comfort the fetal position offers.

A ball. He curls into a ball and lies still.

And the voice in his head lays out a case for quitting.

It's over now. You know it is. So why fight it? Why torture yourself for another few hours? What for?

It's so fucking easy to just be done. You don't even have to do anything.

He breathes. Chest rising and falling. The ground once again sapping the heat from him.

A beam of white light from behind him throws the thorn bushes into sharp relief.

"Get your hands where I can see them!"

CHAPTER 73

Loshak slowed as he came around a curve on OO, the two-lane county highway that supposedly led to the bridge. He'd been on this road for three miles and hadn't seen a bridge yet. It was possible Pressler had been mistaken about the stream. There might not even be a bridge on this road.

None of it looked familiar to Loshak. That was for sure.

His headlights slid over the trees and undergrowth lining the road, then a yellow sign with a black leaping deer. The old joke bubbled to the surface of his brain — *How do they get them to cross at the signs?*

Then a flicker of motion in the brush caught his eye. A bush twitching. He stepped on the break instinctively, ready to put it to the floor if a deer ran out in front of him.

It wasn't a deer, though. Something was flailing around out there. He saw black fabric, faded like old material washed too many times. Pale, whitish parts. Then he saw denim.

That was a person. Thin, frail-looking. Tall.

Loshak pulled the car over and put on his hazards. His heart hammered as he jumped out, but the hand that unsnapped his holster and drew his Glock was steady. He braced the flashlight he'd taken from the MCU on the barrel, aiming it into the trees.

Less than two yards in, the trees were tangled with matted, knotted thorn bushes. As he crept toward them,

356

his breathing sounded unnaturally harsh in his ears. There was another sound, too.

Was that crying?

The body he'd seen snarled in the bushes came free with the ripping sound of cloth being torn, then slammed to the ground. Loshak finally caught sight of the head, hair sweat-matted and full of leaves and twigs, and followed it down to a throat angled with the razor-sharp Adam's apple of a teenager.

The boy's shoulders shook, and he turned on his side and hugged his arms around his stomach and pulled his knees up. He was crying.

Edward Zakarian, the coked-up serial killer who'd murdered men, women, and children across Miami flashed through Loshak's mind, sniveling and begging for his life in a shed not twenty minutes after murdering a little boy.

"Get your hands where I can see them!" Loshak shouted. Adrenaline made the order come out a gravelly roar, a surprise to the agent — his own voice turned hateful in this moment.

The boy's head lifted, but he didn't move his hands.

Rainie was right, it was someone else's gun, Loshak thought. *He's still armed.*

He leveled his Glock at the boy.

"Get them up!"

Nothing. The boy just stared at him.

Or he had more than one weapon all along. He's going to pull it as soon as I say:

"Last warning!" Loshak bellowed, slipping his finger inside the trigger guard. "Get your hands where I can see them or I shoot."

The boy moved. For a second, Loshak saw a gun. Clear as day, a matte black pistol in the boy's right hand.

Loshak's forearm flexed, his finger squeezing the trigger.

But there was no pistol. Only a pair of dirt-caked, bleeding, empty hands.

Loshak let go, the trigger springing back out.

The heat was on him then, flushing his head with feverish blood.

Sweat streaked out of his hair, wetting his temples, and more trickled down the back of his neck and pooled in the folds of his armpits.

Cold flashed across the surface of his skin, the air now downright frigid compared to the fire inside.

"Lie flat on your stomach and put your arms behind your back."

He was breathing too hard, had to keep taking breaths between words.

Slowly, the boy complied with Loshak's orders. Loshak fought his way into the thorns, almost catching one right in the bad eye, then he knelt and cuffed the kid. The kid's arms and wrists were like twigs, one of those skinny teenager types, so wiry that they seemed frail close up. Sinewy.

He helped the boy to his feet, then guided him back out so the brambles wouldn't tear him up any worse. Loshak could feel the boy shaking as he grabbed the sweat-soaked back of his head and helped him duck into the back seat of the car.

Only when the door was safely shut did Loshak return his gun to his holster. He leaned against the car for just a second, arms and legs tingling.

A wave of dizziness washed over him. He let his breath out in a rush, and his chest shuddered when he sucked in the next big gust. His hands moved to push himself upright, but he hesitated. He had to take a second, standing out in the night air, filling and emptying his lungs a few times.

Finally he could see straight enough to walk back around to the driver's side and get in.

CHAPTER 74

Jittery breathing and the occasional sniffle from the back seat were the only sounds in the car. Loshak drove slowly, looking for a driveway or pull-off to get turned around and headed to a station.

"Are—" The boy swallowed. "—you going to kill me?"

Jesus, he wasn't even old enough to get through a full sentence without this voice cracking.

Loshak had met and read about plenty of kids who committed their first murder at a younger age, but he didn't think he would ever get used to seeing it in real life.

"You're being detained on suspicion of attempted homicide," Loshak said. "No one's going to hurt you."

The boy let out a bitter laugh. "Right."

Loshak's gaze went to the rearview mirror. In the green light from the dash, he could see the kid had torn himself up pretty good in those thorns. He was frowning out the window, his jaw working.

A half-overgrown gravel patch came up on his right. He stepped on the brake, turning in, headlights falling on a rotting wood gate hung with poison ivy.

The jagged breathing in the backseat went completely silent. But as Loshak reversed out of the spot and turned the car back in the right direction, the kid let out a huge breath. Almost a sigh of relief.

Poor kid must've thought that was the end of the line for him. Some anonymous poison-ivy lined parking spot

360

out in the middle of nowhere.

"What's your name?" Loshak asked, barely stopping himself before he added *son*. No teenager had been fooled by the fatherly act since about 1952.

The boy didn't answer.

"You live around here?" Loshak checked the rearview again, searching for a tell in the kid's expression.

The angle of the kid's chin said he wasn't going to answer that, either.

"Do your mom and dad know where you are?"

No reaction.

"Where's your family?"

A flicker then. Loshak couldn't study it closely enough to know what it meant because he had to make sure he was still on the road, but there had definitely been a flicker of emotion.

"I killed them all, you know," the boy said finally. "The councilman. The football coach. Even the woman."

Loshak kept his expression blank. The speedometer climbed now that they were headed in the right direction.

"You don't believe me," the kid said.

Loshak did, but he wanted proof.

"It's tempting for some people to take credit for stuff like this. They see it running as the lead story on the news night after night, and they think, maybe this is it. Their chance at fifteen minutes of fame."

The boy shook his head.

"You're arresting me because you know I did it. You saw me on that guy's security cameras."

"That doesn't prove you killed the other four."

"You guys've got my blood," the boy said, his tone flat.

Resolved. "You know it was me."

"They were human traffickers," Loshak said. "But you knew that."

The boy shrugged.

Loshak ventured a guess. Vigilante victim made the most sense, now that he saw how young the kid was.

"Who picked you up? Was it Griffin or Dent?"

"Doesn't matter," the kid said, eyes still staring blankly out the window.

The rental pulled up to the intersection with T. If Loshak turned right, he would be headed back to the MCU. Tavares would be waiting. Rainie and Pressler might get back before the kid was shipped off to one of the stations. Probably Prairie Village, since they were leading the case.

He checked both directions, then turned left.

And while he was at it, might as well swing for the fences.

"Because I think it was Griffin," Loshak said.

He caught another ripple of emotion as it crossed the boy's face.

"What happened?"

"All I remember is waking up," the boy said. "I don't remember any faces. I don't remember anything."

"You don't remember anything, but—"

A shrill scream came from Loshak's pocket. He pulled out his phone. It was Spinks.

"Hey, listen." The reporter's voice was low, and he sounded strange, as if he were cupping his hand around his mouth. "Our rich survivor guy is dead. The one we interviewed earlier? Chapin."

"What?" Loshak's mouth went dry.

"Just listen a minute, man," Spinks hissed. "Tavares said he pulled a gun out of a breadbox or something and shot himself."

Loshak swallowed hard, and Spinks' whispering took on a hysterical edge.

"Did Chapin seem like he was contemplating suicide to you? Because he didn't seem like that to me."

Loshak loosened his death grip on the steering wheel after a painful protest from his bum wrist.

"Partner?" Spinks pleaded. "Did you hear me?"

"Yeah. Yeah, I heard. Uh, it's possible," Loshak said, floundering for an explanation. "Maybe it hit him that he was definitely going to prison. Maybe he faced up to what he'd done and couldn't live with himself. Did he have a family? Some people can't live with their family finding out what they've done."

"Maybe somebody heard you say you got plenty from him that will hold up in court. Maybe he made himself a liability the same way Dupont must have," Spinks said. "There's a crime scene unit here now, but I notice nobody's testing all these fine officers of the law for gunpowder residue to see if they gave our buddy Chapin a helping hand."

"Call a cab back to the hotel," Loshak said. "Get out of there as nonchalantly as you can manage. I'll be there in a little while."

"Where are you?"

Loshak glanced in the rearview mirror to find the kid hanging on his every word.

"Nowhere," he told Spinks.

He hung up and dropped the phone into the cupholder.

"You think I'm a local cop," Loshak said. "That's why you wanted to know if I was going to kill you."

The boy's silence answered for him.

"I'm not from around here. I can put you under federal protection. If you tell me what you know, the locals won't be able to touch you."

The boy shook his head.

"Take me in, and you'll never prove any of it. I'll disappear. The evidence will disappear. Anybody who can tell you anything will disappear. Up in smoke."

Loshak pictured the flames licking upward from The Wooden Nickel.

The pit of his stomach was sinking. It felt like everything was draining out of him, swirling down into a void he could never get it back from.

"Tell me how the councilman was connected," he said.

"Won't do any good," the boy said. "He'd already destroyed all his evidence before I got to him."

"Tell me, and I'll let you go."

The boy's head snapped around to meet Loshak's eyes in the mirror. In that moment, he looked incredibly young and innocent. Not a killer. Just a child. A child who wanted to believe him.

"He bought… someone…" the boy said. "But she got away. He had all their names, in case the bastards ever tried to blackmail him."

"That's how you tracked them down," Loshak said. "Could you get her to go into federal protection with you? If she knew who all was involved, we could make a case against them. Bring them all down and stop this from happening to anyone else."

The child in the mirror was gone. He was back to the wary teenager who'd seen way too much of the injustices of the world. He shook his head.

"She's an illegal. They'll just say she's lying and deport her and kill her on the way back to… where she's from."

Loshak chewed his lip. The hell of it was, he knew the kid was right. Somebody had the balls to shoot Chapin with Spinks standing right outside. There was no way he and Spinks would make it through a crowded KCI terminal and onto a plane with an illegal girl and a serial killer whose photo they'd be flashing across every news outlet in the tri-state area.

He remembered the bloodbath in Detroit. Knew the lengths these elaborate organizations would go to protect themselves. Knew that corruption like this could reach the highest levels of society's power structures. Knew that sometimes the system did not work.

The kind of people who dealt in human trafficking had no scruples. Were not interested in a fair fight. Did not play by the rules.

Maybe that meant Loshak couldn't play by the rules, either.

"You said…" the boy started, then hesitated.

Loshak could hear the dry click in his throat as he swallowed.

"You said if I told you, you'd let me go," he finished.

"They're going to be looking everywhere for you," Loshak said. "What are you going to do?"

The boy thought about it.

"Run."

"Where to?"

He didn't answer.

Loshak nodded. He drove on, thinking back on their conversation so far. The different subjects which had triggered the kid's emotions. He was protecting someone. Or multiple someones.

"How many are in your family?"

No answer.

"More than five?"

The boy glared out the window. "You said."

"Use your brain, kid. You can't run on foot."

The boy squinted at him, confused.

"This car only holds five," Loshak said.

Loshak called a cab from a gas station inside city limits. Then he called and renewed the rental for another week.

CHAPTER 75

Dylan drives the speed limit, his shoulders bunched with tension the whole way. He wears his seatbelt, doesn't run any yellow lights, puts on his turn signal way before he comes to a turn, and stops for a full five seconds at stop signs instead of the required three.

If they don't use the seatbelts, if a couple of the kids sit on the floor in the back and Kegan squeezes down by Maria's feet in the front, if he drives super carefully… All the ifs keep running through his head. He tries to block out the ones that end with him in a jail cell, hanging from a noose made of bedsheets.

When he pulls up in front of the abandoned house, a streetlight that had burnt out three months before flickers back on. It scares him. Make his heart race.

But it's only a light.

Dylan slips out of the car, easing the door shut, and goes inside to wake up his family.

CHAPTER 76

"Crap, man." Spinks shook his head and leaned back in the cushioned seat at the gate.

Outside the wall of windows in front of them, planes taxied and took off.

Loshak nodded. "Yeah."

The five a.m. back to JFK was running behind. If this delay stretched out much longer, he didn't think they would make their connection to Virginia. He'd wanted to wait until they were out of Missouri to fill Spinks in, but the reporter hadn't been able to wait, and they were alone anyway, except for a businesswoman in a wrinkled suit asleep on the couch by the boarding counter.

"What did you tell Tavares?" Spinks asked.

"That I got turned around on the way to find Pressler and Rainie."

"Do you think he bought it?"

"I'm not a local. There's no reason I'd be able to keep those driving directions straight while we were on a manhunt for a serial killer."

Spinks blew out a long breath, his eyes wide. Then he seemed to think of something.

"Did you talk to Rainie?"

"It would've been suspicious if I didn't," Loshak said. "I apologized for screwing up the directions. She said it could've happened to anybody and that she didn't think Pressler had them right in the first place."

After a second, Spinks chuckled.

"You've got to hand it to her. She's going to make a great Chief of Police, finding somebody besides herself to lay the blame on."

Loshak smiled. "Yeah, I guess she will if she keeps that up."

Spinks gazed off into the planes swimming through the early dawn light outside the window.

"I hope he makes it," the reporter said. "Away. To wherever he's going."

Loshak nodded. He hoped so, too.

EPILOGUE

Loshak was frowning down at his phone when he heard the tinkle of ice cubes. Jan came through the door with a glass of iced tea in each hand and quirked her head at him.

"Something wrong?"

He accepted the tea she handed across the table to him, thanked her, and took a sip. Beads of condensation ran down the glass, wetting his fingers.

"It's nothing," he said. "Just a loose end from the case I was working on."

A loose end that someone snipped, he thought to himself.

Spinks was back in Miami, ostensibly incommunicado working on the book while Loshak visited Jan in New Mexico, but the reporter had emailed him a link to the news story that morning. The headline on the Kansas City Star's website read, **MAN IMPLICATED IN CHILD SEX RING COMMITS SUICIDE IN JAIL**.

Loshak recognized the name of the man as one of the couriers Chapin had given him only minutes before he allegedly shot himself. And now that man had met the same fate. Had these men really taken their own lives? Or had they been silenced because of what they knew and what they might tell? Under normal circumstances, Loshak wasn't sure he'd care. But he knew they hadn't got them all. Someone was still out there, trimming the loose ends.

"I hope you're not still beating yourself up about that

kid getting away," Jan said, stirring her tea with a metal straw. "I know it's probably the wrong way to look at it all, but those people he killed… well, they had it coming."

He hadn't told Jan the truth about letting the kid go free, and he never would. Spinks was the only person who knew, and he planned to keep things that way. It wasn't an issue of trust; Jan was rock solid when it came to loyalty. But Loshak refused to put her in a position where she might have to lie for him.

Some things a man had to hold onto to keep his family safe, he thought. Some things were for no one to know.

He took a long drink, felt the icy liquid slide down the back of his throat and into his gut.

No matter how well he did his job, how hard he tried to make things right, the darkness in the world never seemed to thin.

As he gazed out at the Santa Fe sunset, Loshak tried to remember what he'd told Darger so many times. That they can never really make things right. They were the clean-up crew, there to pick up the fresh mess. They sorted through the dead, tried to give them some kind of justice, but they could never bring any of them back.

And if they were lucky, they might get a break now and then — might crawl out of the shadows and find a little place in the sun to relax for a while — before they moved on to the next disaster.

THANK YOU

Thanks so much for reading *What Lies Beneath*. Want another Loshak novel? Leave a review on Amazon and let us know.

MORE LOSHAK

But wait! How will you find out about more Loshak?

It's a sad fact that Amazon won't magically beam news of upcoming Loshak books into your head. (I wish.) Don't miss out! Choose one of the options below to keep up with Loshak, Jan, and Spinks:

1) You can join our Facebook Fan group. Then you'll hear all about our new and upcoming releases. Join at: **http://facebook.com/groups/mcbainvargus**

2) You can follow us on Amazon. Just go to one of our author pages and click on the FOLLOW button under our pictures. That way Amazon will send you an email whenever we publish something new.

3) You can join the E.M. Smith mailing list. In fact, we'll give you a free copy of the next book in the Loshak series (a short) if you partake in this one. Just visit: **http://ltvargus.com/emfreebook**

See where it all started for Loshak in the *Violet Darger* series...

Her body is broken. Wrapped in plastic. Dumped on the side of the road. She is the first. There will be more.

The serial killer thriller that "refuses to let go until you've read the last sentence."

The most recent body was discovered in the grease dumpster behind a Burger King. Dismembered. Shoved into two garbage bags and lowered into the murky oil.

Now rookie agent **Violet Darger** gets the most important assignment of her career. She travels to the Midwest to face a killer unlike anything she's seen. Aggressive. Territorial. Deranged and driven.

Another mutilated corpse was found next to a roller rink. A third in the gutter in a residential neighborhood.

These bold displays of violence shock the rural community and rattle local law enforcement.

Who could carry out such brutality? And why?

Unfortunately for Agent Darger, there's little physical evidence to work with, and the only witnesses prove to be unreliable. The case seems hopeless.

If she fails, more will die. He will kill again and again.

The victims harbor dark secrets. The clues twist and writhe and refuse to keep still. And the killer watches the investigation on the nightly news, gleeful to relive the violence, knowing that he can't be stopped.

Get your copy now: **http://mybook.to/DeadEndGirl**

ABOUT THE AUTHORS

E.M. Smith came by his redneck roots honestly, his barbwire tattoo dishonestly, and his sobriety slowly. Recovery isn't a sprint, according to his friends, it's a marathon. That's probably why he turned into such a fitness geek when he quit drinking.

L.T. Vargus grew up in Hell, Michigan, which is a lot smaller, quieter, and less fiery than one might imagine. When not glued to her computer, she can be found sewing, fantasizing about food, and rotting her brain in front of the TV.

If you want to wax poetic about pizza or cats, you can contact L.T. (the L is for Lex) at ltvargus9@gmail.com or on Twitter @ltvargus.

Tim McBain writes because life is short, and he wants to make something awesome before he dies. Additionally, he likes to move it, move it.

You can connect with Tim via email at tim@timmcbain.com.

Made in the USA
Middletown, DE
19 June 2023